The Education of Joey G.

Gus Kearney

The Education *of* Joey G.

Gladstone Manor Publishing

Printed in the United States of America
First Edition

Despite diligent efforts, the Publisher has been unable to locate the
photographer or copyright holder of the following images:
Cover: young boy dancing
Interior: boys in a field, page 15

The characters in *The Education of Joey G.* are purely fictional and not
based on any real people living or dead.

Library of Congress Control Number: 1-23793058

ISBN 978-0-578-16524-0 softcover

Book design by Elizabeth DiPalma Design +

Gladstone Manor Publishing
Sonoma, California

To Karla, for believing in me.

Contents

"Growing up is losing some illusions,
in order to acquire others."
– Virginia Woolf

"...surviving hard winters makes a tree grow stronger,
the growth rings inside it tighter."
– Hiruki Murakami *Yesterday*

Part 1

Gladstone Manor

Joey picked up a white dandelion and blew the fluff into the air. He watched it scatter, got a stick and began wandering through the field. Once last year, his kindergarten teacher, Mrs. Watson, brought a big bag of milkweed pods to school. She took the class out to the baseball field and released them into the wind. He tried and tried to capture one but it always flew right out of his hand. His mother said that dandelions were weeds and too ugly to be flowers. However, he liked their bright yellow color and the way they stood up straight like soldiers.

Looking down, Joey saw a bright orange-and-black caterpillar crawling across a leaf. He picked it up and watched carefully as it moved across his thumb. Then he put his index finger underneath the caterpillar and studied the way it humped its way across the rest of his fingers. Margaret said that caterpillars turned into butterflies, but Chris Atkins said she was full of it. Margaret started to cry and ran off the playground. Chris said everyone was full of it. Margaret always told the truth, as far as

Joey knew, but it was hard for him to imagine how a slow, bumbling insect could turn into something as beautiful as a butterfly.

He put his right hand beside his left and watched the caterpillar move to his other hand, full of purpose. Squashing it would be messy; he'd have to wipe the dead body across his jersey, which would make his mother mad. So he put it back on the ground, because after all, he told himself, someday that caterpillar will become a butterfly! Hahahahaha.

There was a clump of hollyhocks up ahead, pink, purple and red, moving slowly back and forth, like dancers in the breeze. Big yellowjackets flitted in and out of the flowers. If he had an empty peanut butter jar, he could capture a few, but he didn't. Unlike bees, yellow jackets were big trouble. It didn't hurt that much to get stung by a bee. But when yellowjackets got mad, they came right after you and stung hard.

Billy Dunlap, on a dare from Mitchy Burns, opened a jar full of yellowjackets and let them fly into his mouth. Billy smiled as he spit them out with no problems. But one that had flown away came back and stung him right on the cheek. He grabbed his face, yowled and fell to the ground. All the guys started to laugh. Joey did too. He felt very relieved to see Billy get up with just a jawbreaker-sized lump on his face. Mitchy said it was stupid to give in to a dare, especially when the other person won't do it first.

Mitchy did that a lot, cause a problem, then act like it wasn't his fault. Joey stayed with Billy after the other guys left. They sat on a boulder while Joey watched his friend cry and cry. They walked down the hill to Darby Creek and put some wet mud on the bump. A train went across the trestle, shaking the ground underneath. Archie Delemont dared him to play chicken with a train last week. Joey refused and Archie called him yellow. As he walked home, the older boy walked right behind him, calling Joey sissy, baby, dumbass and jerk. Joey answered *sticks and stones will break my bones, but names will never hurt me* before running home. Archie was stupid. He didn't even play with kids his own age.

Picking up the stick, Joey started waving it around like he was conducting an orchestra. Yellowjackets started to buzz furiously. Joey walked closer to the flowers. Three bees flew toward his face. He turned around and ran as far as he could, yelling at the top of his lungs, holding the stick up in the air like a sword. When he felt safe, Joey turned around and stared at empty air. Feeling triumphant, he stood on a little mound of dirt and pounded his chest, bellowing like Tarzan.

Madison Avenue was a row of red brick homes with railroad tracks right behind them. The houses were newer and prettier than Joey's. Most had black shutters on the front windows. He loved hearing the trains go *woo-woo* during the night. He'd think to himself that all the passengers were ghosts, sitting in their seats reading invisible newspapers, the conductor collecting invisible tickets. His teacher, Miss Kilgore, who had long red hair that she usually bunched up on the top of her head, said he had a wonderful imagination, when he told her a story about a magic dwarf who could look at things and make them disappear. When she gave him this compliment, Joey put his hand on her shoulder and his head against her arm.

Joey walked down Madison to the Gladstone station. His friend, Stevie Oates, lived at the end of the street. He knocked on the door and Mrs. Oates answered, wearing a checkered apron on top of a white blouse and black shorts. After asking if his friend could come out to play, she turned her head toward the back of the house and said in a very loud voice, "No, Joey. Stevie cannot come out to play. He might not get out of the house until he's 60 years old!" Joey wondered what his friend had done to make his mom so mad. Maybe he got caught playing with his own poop. Or maybe he broke a piece of good china. He broke a dish once and had to stay inside for two weeks.

Going into the middle of the train tracks, Joey picked up three rocks and laid them on the rails. Tommy Skeedow said that if you did this, the train would jump off the tracks and cause a big accident. Joey and his friends put rocks on the tracks all the time; the only thing that happened was that the rocks got so squashed they became part of the track. Noreen put pennies on the tracks a few times; they almost disappeared into the metal. This made no sense to Joey. You could buy a tootsie roll, a stick of licorice and a lot of other candy for a penny.

It might have been exciting to be the cause of a train wreck, Joey thought, *but very scary too*. If the train cars started flying off the tracks, he'd have to run away as fast as he could. A twelve-year-old girl, Lisa Fredericks, got killed a few months ago, playing too close to the train. Joey got a sick feeling in his stomach when he heard about it. Yet, even though his mom warned him and warned him to stay away from the tracks, he wouldn't.

The trestle was about a hundred yards south of the station. Joey and all the other younger kids in the neighborhood were forbidden from ever going there. The big danger was to be on the trestle when a train came. But the oncoming ones always blew their whistles very loudly, which made it easy to get off the tracks in time.

The railroad bridge was about fifty feet above the ground, and if someone did fall off the side, they were a dead duck. Once he and Stevie squatted down beside the trestle when a train went by. The ground shook so hard, he thought he was going to be thrown into the air like a kite. It felt like a monster had grabbed the earth and shook it. Joey's body began to tremble, just like the train. It was a big relief to watch the train go away, down the tracks toward Philadelphia. He pretended he wasn't scared afterward and thought Tommy did the same.

Walking to the middle of the trestle, Joey looked down through the tracks at the slow glide of Darby Creek. He could do a dozen somersaults if he went off the side. It would be the greatest dive in history. But almost no one would see him hit the water, if he was lucky enough to miss Scottdale Road. And if he did fall into the creek, it was probably not shallow enough to break his fall.

Joey began to hop along the tracks, making sure his foot didn't get caught between the railroad ties. It was Saturday afternoon. Where was everybody?

On the other side of the train tracks was a dirt road that led to Shrigley Park. Joey had walked it many times. But lately, he had been avoiding the road because Andy Slater told him a lynx wildcat lived right near there and showed him the animal tracks to prove it. Andy's older brother heard him talking about the lynx and started laughing. Joey felt his friend was full of it, as he so often was. Andy probably had an old wildcat paw he dug into the ground just to scare him to death.

Once, he locked Joey into a closet. It was full of old clothes and the smell of mothballs. At first, he thought it was just a joke and that when Andy opened the door, Joey was going to give him a big smack in the arm for his troubles. But time dragged on and on, and the door stayed locked. He sat down on the floor, choked with the smell of camphor. It became obvious Andy didn't care about him, and that spiders were going to come out of the walls and bite him to death. Joey began pounding and kicking the door. Andy's mother opened it and let out a gasp. She screamed for her son as Joey ran down the steps and out the front door. Andy was in BIG trouble.

Shrigley was a scary park because it had a very high cliff. Joey had heard stories about older kids climbing to the top before losing their grips and falling onto the ground, breaking their backs. Nobody dared anyone to climb the cliff. It was pretty, though, covered in brush, with a spring running down the side. Joey followed the road down until it ended at a green field. There was a small swing set and a little slide right by some picnic tables, but mostly it was just grass.

A young man and woman were in front of the tables throwing a stick to their yellow dog. Joey hoped they would not start hugging and kissing. It felt icky when big kids started doing that. He sat down on a swing and began to rock back and forth. If his friends saw him doing that, he would be called a baby. Some black birds flew above him. Twisting the swing into a big metal knot, Joey enjoyed getting dizzy as he let it unravel. There was another clump of dandelions in the grass right in front of the parking lot, but he decided not to pick any.

You had to be careful walking along Scottdale Road because there was no sidewalk. Two curves were particularly dangerous; a person had to walk into the road to get around them. Joey approached the first curve, his stick dragging on the ground behind him. He stopped and turned around. The coast seemed to be clear. But just as soon as he stepped onto the road, two cars arrived quickly before whizzing by him. Joey jumped back and took a deep breath.

He walked back to the edge of the curve, hiked up his dungarees and ran onto the road. No cars were coming. Relieved, he went around the curve, got back on the roadbed and started to walk again. One more curve and he was safe. Joey sat down on the ground and watched a half-dozen cars go by. It might be a good idea to wait until a hundred went by, he thought. He was one of the few people in his class who could count that high.

Counting got boring, so he stopped at eighteen. Listening carefully again and hearing nothing, he was sure the coast was clear. He ran onto the road and a bright red convertible came up right behind him. A blonde-haired man jammed on the brakes, stopping a few inches from Joey's back. The driver started pounding his dashboard and began to yell. A black car came behind the convertible and screeched its brakes also. Joey began running, not looking back. As he sped away from the cars, the words "goddam kid" and "shit" echoed in the air.

Feeling like he was going to throw up, Joey put his hand against a birch tree and bent over. No vomit came out of his mouth, but he still felt weak. He sat down on a big rock and watched Darby Creek drift along. The creek was stinky today, like it was sometimes. As he calmed down, Joey thought about how good it would be to be a fish and never have to deal with roads and cars.

Time passed. Clouds were gliding slowly across the sky. Joey thought they looked like camels. He thought about Willie the Worm, who wasn't really a worm but a puppet. And Clarabelle the Clown, who honked a bicycle horn instead of talking. Joey figured that Clarabelle probably knew how to talk, but got paid a lot of money for acting like he didn't. Howdy Doody was also a puppet. Buffalo Bob, who was a real man, seemed to really love Howdy even though the little cowboy was made out of wood.

Joey walked down to Baltimore Pike, a very busy road. On the other side of the street were some old, ruined houses. Every parent in the Gladstone Manor neighborhood forbade their children from entering them. Many of the windows were broken. There was trash all over the yards. Bums lived inside them from time to time. The floors were very old and older kids said if you stepped on the wrong spot, you could fall right through.

Joey heard some of the big boys bragging that they had gone inside. He couldn't tell if they were full of it or not. Chippy Taylor said he went inside once and saw a ghost in a long gray robe walking from room to room. Joey wasn't sure he believed in ghosts. He almost never believed Chippy.

Cars were traveling pretty fast down Baltimore Pike. Joey started walking up the hill to Saul's Drugstore. The old houses seemed to be beckoning him. He stopped and sat down in the grass. If he crossed Baltimore Pike and went inside the beat-up homes, he could become a big shot. Of course, people might not believe him. They would laugh and say he was full of it. The whole world seemed to be full of it sometimes. Stevie might believe him because they were best friends.

He could finish walking up the hill, cross at the light and get an ice cream cone. Dinner would almost be ready when he got home. Spaghetti and meatballs, his favorite. The houses were just a bunch of old buildings, what the heck. If he was careful, he wouldn't get hurt. Turning around, he sped down the hill and waited for the light at the intersection to turn green.

When he got to the houses, Joey crouched down behind a bush. One of the neighbors might drive by and tell his parents he was there. He closed his nostrils with his thumb and forefinger. There was a terrible smell of poop in the air. He couldn't tell if it was animal poop or human poop, or both mixed together. *People smelt worse than animals*, he thought, *but they were both pretty bad*. There was broken glass all over the ground; when he stepped on a piece; it made a loud crunching sound.

The lonely, worn-down house scared Joey and made him want to get out as soon as possible. There might be something interesting in these old wrecked homes, though. Something he could brag about seeing. Maybe if he could find a ghost, he could talk to it. Maybe there was an old map, like in *Treasure Island*.

There were three houses, two white ones on the ends and a brown one in the middle. Cars continued to zoom by, one after the other. The sun was not as hot as it was earlier in the day. Still crouching down, Joey skulked to the back of the brown house, where the back door was wide open. He crept up the rickety stairs and walked inside.

The floor was filled with empty beer bottles and metal cans that said S-t-e-r-n-o. Joey did not know that word and could not sound it out in his head. He picked up a bent can. It smelled like vinegar and pee. Ugh. There were pieces of burnt wood all over the floor. When his family drove past these houses last week, his father said that someone should light a fire and burn the damn things down. Joey would get in trouble if he said damn, but his Dad said it all the time and nothing happened to him.

As he began to make his way through the kitchen, a big brown rat came through a door. He looked at Joey and kept walking, disappearing into a hole in the wall. What if there were more rats? What if there were a hundred rats? What if they were a lot bigger than the one he had just seen? He dared himself to go into one more room.

It was a pretty big room and smelled like vomit. An old red chair stood in the middle of the floor with white stuff coming out of it. Even though Joey was feeling suddenly tired, the chair looked like it would cover him with bugs if he sat in it. Someone with a piece of charcoal had scrawled I LOVE BEER, DON'T PISS ON THE FLOOR and KATIE FUCKS FOR FREE on one of the walls. Joey could read all the words and knew what most of them meant. He thought "piss" meant the same thing as "pee" but he had never heard the word "fuck" before. The word rhymed with "duck" and "luck." When he said it out loud it sounded nasty, but he didn't know why.

It seemed like Katie doing fuck for free was a bad thing. That was a head-scratcher, Joey thought, an expression his father used when something was hard to figure out. Maybe if he asked his Dad what fuck meant, he could understand this puzzle. Then he remembered that he was not supposed to be in the old houses. If he was going to find out about fuck, it would have to be from one of the older boys, maybe Andy's big brother. He didn't like not finding the answer to something he was curious about.

A strong breeze rattled the weather-beaten house and made Joey shiver. He picked up a big rock from the floor and threw it through a windowpane. The sound of the breaking glass sent a thrill up and down his spine. He thought for a moment about busting up more stuff. But it was starting to get a little bit dark, time to get out of this place. Picking up his trusty stick, Joey hopped down the back stairs, moved quickly through the trash and broken glass and sped up the hill.

Saul's Drugstore was in a shopping area that included a small grocery store, a furniture repair shop and a real estate/insurance office. There were apartments on top of each of the shops. Saul and his family lived on the top of the drugstore. Joey did not know who lived in the other ones.

A long marble soda fountain ran about half the length of the store. An area for making medicine was in the back. The rest of the shop was filled with shelves selling grown-up things like tissues, Ex-Lax, aspirin, Epsom salts and rubbing alcohol. Joey knew that tissues were for blowing your nose, but he didn't know the uses of the other things. There was a long glass counter right inside the front door for ladies' stuff like lipstick and nail polish. There were three mirrors on top so that the women could see how they looked when they put them on.

Saul, whose last name was Rosenbloom, always looked the same. He wore a white shirt, white pants and a black bow tie right under his chin. He had a mustache and was almost bald. His huge belly hung over his waist, making it impossible to see his belt. Usually he had a cigarette in his mouth with a really long ash on the end. Joey's mom always worried that the ash might fall into a milk shake or sundae, but it never did.

He was a nice man who didn't smile very often. His dad said once that Saul was a nice guy for achoo. This confounded Joey, who asked his Dad how a person could be like a sneeze? He added sound effects to make his point. His father thought this was very funny. His mom made a face and returned to reading the paper. When Joey pushed for an answer, his father hugged him and continued to laugh. It was nice to be hugged, since his Dad didn't do that very often, but he still had no answer.

One great thing about Saul's was that they served Breyer's ice cream. It was much better than Sealtest, in Joey's opinion, which only had three flavors, vanilla, chocolate and strawberry, and didn't taste that good. He took a dime out of his pocket, put it on the gray-and-white marble counter and ordered an orange ice and coffee double-dip cone. This was the first time he'd ever had a double dip. Saul, cigarette dangling from his mouth, got two giant scoops, put them on a cone and handed it to Joey. There was so much ice cream on the cone, it was hard for him to hang onto. Joey wasn't even allowed to hold his own cone until he was four. He had dropped two cones on the ground before getting the hang of it. The cone must be held with two hands and licked from the bottom to the top, so the ice cream wouldn't drip all over everything. The orange ice on the top got very lopsided and looked like it was going to fall onto the counter. Saul watched Joey struggle. He took the cone away and scooped the ice cream into a small bowl, putting the empty cone on a napkin.

Mrs. Reuss came in, a neighbor from up the street. She was an old lady and very nice. A lot of times, she and Mr. Reuss let Joey, Tommy and Stevie watch their television set, as none of their families had bought one yet. Smelling of perfume, Mrs. Reuss complimented Joey for acting like a "young adult." He wasn't sure what that was exactly. Adults were older people and not young at all. As he bit into the orange ice, he had a thought that made him stop enjoying the treat. What if Mrs. Reuss told his mother what a young adult he was, sitting at the counter at Saul's and eating ice cream. She'd ask him where he had gotten the money.

The truth was that he had taken a dime out of her purse. Joey had been taking coins from his mother for some time. Other than giving him a quarter for the Saturday matinee at the Lansdowne Theater, he didn't get much money from his parents. Whatever he wanted it for, they usually said he didn't need it. He'd wait until no one could see him, reach into her purse and take a quarter, dime, nickel or penny. He always felt nasty and bad when he did this. Maybe he should ask for an allowance, like the older kids got.

Finishing, Joey wiped ice cream from his face and hands with a napkin. He said goodbye to Saul and his wife. The sky had gotten even darker. The wind was blowing the branches on the trees that lined Mansfield Road. When he got to his house near the end of the block, Joey opened the front door and walked in. His mother, who was setting the table in the dining room, saw him and asked what he had been doing since lunch. He looked at her with a blank expression and said, "Oh, nothing much."

Part 2

The Jungle

The rats are big as dogs," Tim Martin said gleefully. "They bite people's noses off and chew on them and when they're done, they start on the ears."

"Yeah, and you know what I heard?" Jack Mill, a wide-shouldered boy with muscular arms and legs, a blonde crewcut and glasses, added. "This kid from Clifton Heights went inside, never came out the other end."

Joey Garden knew a dare when he heard one. And he knew these guys were ladling out bullshit by the ton. But rats did hang around the two fifty- foot storm drains that went downhill from the cul-de-sac into the Jungle; he had seen them. As for the Clifton Heights story, he was sure it wasn't true, but maybe some Lansdowne guys did capture and harass some Clifties. Relations between the youth of the neighboring towns were not exactly rosy. There was a rumor that a huge fight was looming; the tensions had been building for years.

The reason he was the last of his gang to crawl the drain was that he hated being closed in. He had visions of being grabbed by his friends and shoved into the tunnel, being forced to endure the thing he hated most and being humiliated at the same time. He had seen this happen; Martin made a number of guys do it and when they finished, still called them yellow-bellied sapsuckers, pussies or worse.

Joey smiled. "You guys think I'm a chicken, but I'm not; I just don't like getting all dirty. My mom told me not to come home for lunch if my clothes were all messed up. She said that she was only going to wash one jersey and one pair of dungarees for the whole rest of the week."

"Move your ass, Joey." Martin said, hopping from one leg to another. A husky boy with a wiry build, his body never seemed to be still.

"Shut up and start crawling," Mill added.

"Another thing you don't know is that I screwed up my knee. I fell from a tree last week and it's still swollen. "

"What a chicken shit!" Tim Martin said, drawing his thin lips into a sneer. "If there's a fight with the Clifties, you'll be totally useless. They'll run right over your sorry ass."

Joey took a big breath and sighed. He was caught and knew it. Taking off his Phillies cap, he folded it and put it in his back pocket. "You guys go in first," he said. "I'll follow you."

"No, *you* go first, Joey," Martin threatened, running a hand through his slicked-back pompadour. "We'll be right behind you to help." Both he and Mill laughed and stared defiantly at their friend.

"Your mother's nylons." Joey said.

"That's *it*, Garden, move!" Martin commanded.

Joey touched his index finger to his tongue, held it up as if checking for wind, then said, “Tutti Fruitti All Rootie,” and plunged into the narrow drain hole. He wanted to turn around right away, but Mill’s head was already bumping against the soles of his sneakers. The scent of the wet, dusty concrete made him feel nauseous and its rough, grainy texture felt as scratchy as a dead man’s whiskers. His two friends egging him on, Joey continued forward on his hands and knees. He felt like he was inside a dinosaur’s belly. It would have been a relief to be attacked by a rat. In the middle of the journey, he thought he saw one, big and fat with ugly, yellow teeth sharpened like daggers; he was about to yell “Rat!” when the vision evaporated.

After a few minutes, a wafer of yellow light appeared about twenty feet ahead. Joey started to move more quickly, not caring how badly his palms and knees were being scratched. Seconds later, he was in the Jungle, a wooded area about a half a mile wide and twice as long. He stood by the creek, raising his arms in the air, yelling like Tarzan.

Mill appeared, then Martin; they walked slowly over to their jubilant friend.

“Let’s go back and do it over!” Joey chirped. “Hell, that wasn’t so bad after all.”

“Way to go, Joey,” Martin said, putting his arm across his buddy’s shoulder. “It only took you two years. Maybe you can help against the Clifties after all.”

The three boys started to walk, picking up stones and throwing them at trees. The trio sat down on some rocks. Joey pulled out a pack of Kents and passed it to the other two boys. Tim Martin took out a Zippo lighter and quickly lit three cigarettes.

"I've been dying for a cig," Joey said, lying back on his rock and blowing smoke toward the brilliant summer sky.

"You don't even inhale, Garden," Mill said with disdain. "If you really knew how to smoke, you'd be dangerous."

Joey bolted upright, puffed out his chest, took a huge drag and immediately had a coughing fit. The other boys laughed. It went on a bit longer than it should have; Joey fell to the ground and began to roll around, his face red and his body contorted. Tim and Jack each grabbed one of Joey's arms and held him up as his body went limp.

Looking at his suffering friend, Mill knelt down and said, "Joey, come on, wake up. It was only one drag."

Martin added, "Man, maybe we should go call the cops. He really looks sick."

At that, Joey bounded to his feet, extending his middle finger and waving it in front of his buddy's faces. "Assholes," he shouted, "the world's biggest shitheads!"

"You'll get yours, Joey," Martin said, returning to his smoke.

"Yeah, just wait," Mill echoed. "It will come when you least expect it."

Joey smirked and leaned back on his rock, looking upward again, "Do you ever think that the sky is just like this big curtain and there's all kinds of stuff going on behind it, stuff we can't even imagine? Like big machines miles high with all these gears and things. Angels with a dozen heads. Animals that look like tails with tails that look like animals."

"What a nut," Martin said. "I wonder why I even listen to you at all?"

"Heaven is behind the sky," Mill said. "Everybody knows that."

"No, Jack," Joey answered, "heaven is an infinity away. We can't even figure out where it is, it's so far."

Tim Martin said, "If you gorps[1] want to sit here and talk, let's talk about tits. Has anyone noticed how Carole Mussny's shirts have started to bulge? Two weeks ago, an ironing board; this week she's Queen of the Grapefruits."

"Falsies," Joey said, "definitely falsies."

"Yeah," Mill agreed. "Sometimes they grow real fast, but not that fast."

"Looks good though, even if they're fake," Joey added. "Most of the girls are starting to wear bras now even if they don't have to."

"Barbara Turley's needed one since fourth grade. I'd give up half a year's allowance to just to see them," Martin moaned.

"Great deal," Mill agreed.

Joey nodded and laughed. The bushes directly behind them stirred. Two boys appeared with dead muskrats dangling from each of their hands.

"Yo, Mike! Catch dinner?" Joey said, addressing the shorter one, Mike Dilfer, a squat, barrel-chested kid with an Elvis haircut, a fellow member of the sixth grade at Ardmore Avenue Elementary.

"Yeah, for your mother," Mike said in a gravelly voice. "Bastards from Clifton Heights got into four of our traps, took the bodies and left the heads. Louie will get their asses."

The other boy, Joe Musgrave, lankier than Mike and quieter, said, "Sears Roebuck is paying $5 a hide. They're taking money out of our pockets."

---

[1] A "gorp" in Lansdowne, Pennsylvania, circa 1956,was a boy who farted in the bathtub and bit the bubbles as they came to the surface and/or someone who went around sniffing girls' bicycle seats.

"Clifties are sewer rats," Tim said, "and we're going to call the exterminator."

"They built a fort above the Big Field, even have some dirty pictures tacked up," Mike said, "like they were planning to stay."

"I hear it will all be taken care of in a couple of hours, guys." Martin announced.

Clifton Heights, quite different from Lansdowne, was a blue-collar town. Most of the adults there worked in the textile mill and lived in row houses. Clifties scared the hell out of Joey; he had gotten captured by two of them a few weeks ago, something he hadn't told anyone. They had punched his arms until they were black and blue, then gave him a pink belly, dismissing him with the threat that if they saw him again, he would be tied up and fed to their dogs.

"We're going to go home and skin these things," Mike said, "I'll bring the guts to school in a hoagie roll for your lunch, Joey."

"Your grandmother."

After the two trappers departed, Martin pulled out his lighter and clicked it open and shut half a dozen times. "The nerve of those goddam Clifties coming onto *Lansdowne* land and actually building a fort. We should go and wreck the damn thing."

"Let's hang around here for a while longer," Joey said, getting the cigarettes out again. "We can play mumbledy peg. Then we can go find the fort."

The three boys lit new cigs, walked over to an old beech filled with woodpecker holes and began flicking their penknives through various twists and flips, occasionally sticking them into the side of the tree. The leaves on some bushes began to quiver and another sixth-grader, a towheaded boy with his hair falling into his eyes, came out, holding hands with two girls, a blonde and a brunette: Tina Livingston and Sandy Browner.

"Jimmy Eakins, " Martin said, "my hero. You want to drop one of them with us?"

"Fat chance, Tim," Tina said, "just keep playing your little boy games."

"I'll show you how little my boy is."

"Dream on, twerp. Let's get out of here, Jim." Tina said.

Moments after the three disappeared, Joey said. "Bras, both of them definitely wearing bras. Bras bras bras."

"It's a wonderful world," Martin added.

"Girls have different bodies than boys." Joey said. "Do you think their souls look different too?"

Exasperated, Mill said, "The way you look on earth is how you look in heaven, just without any flesh."

"So if you weigh five hundred pounds like that guy in the circus or you have both of your legs cut off, you'd be just the same in heaven?"

"Of course, it doesn't really matter because in heaven, you don't weigh anything."

"It'd matter to me."

"Bag it, you two," Martin said, "it's Saturday, not Sunday."

Mumbledypeg quickly lost its appeal. The three boys stood with blank expressions on their faces, not sure of their next move. Two more of their friends, Ted Maxville and Tom Meyer, both wearing white tee shirts, dungarees and white hi-top Converse All-Stars, came up behind them, jumping from rock to rock in the creek. Both boys had brown eyes and brown crewcuts. Their short, thin bodies moved with a fluid grace. When Maxville spoke, he put his hands in his pockets and looked at the ground. Meyer had a birthmark right below his right eye, which he was always rubbing with the bottom of his palm, as if trying to eradicate it.

"Hey guys, come here," Maxville said, gesturing with his hand. "We found some stuff down by Scottdale Road."

"What is it, Max?" Joey said.

"You'll see."

The five boys scurried down the creek, not caring if their sneakers got wet. Five minutes later, Maxville and Meyer turned toward the woods and a small clearing amidst some oaks and sycamores. Pointing to a circle of stones, Meyer said, "Look at this, will you?"

Inside the stones was a smoldering fire; beside it were two empty Dinty Moore Beef Stew cans, an empty bottle of Old Crow, and another half-filled with Thunderbird wine.

"Clifties again," Martin said, "bastards!"

"No, I don't think so," Joey said, picking up a stick and dragging it through the dirt. "Those guys don't have the money to buy stuff like this and even if they did, they'd never leave it out to be taken."

Tom Meyer agreed, "Yeah, it seems like stuff somebody would bring who's never been here before. A grown-up."

Everyone nodded. No one could remember seeing a person over twenty in the Jungle.

"Could be the guy escaped from the jail in Media," Jack Mill said, "a murderer who stopped and moved on."

"Might be a homo sex fiend," Martin said, "and I don't think he's gone, with half a bottle of wine left."

"Maybe he's staying here and robbing houses," Maxville said. "Wouldn't be that hard."

Joey was the first to see the man, his unshaven face sticking out of a clump of bushes. He was tall and thin, with a long neck. His alert, feral eyes sagged at the corners and his gray-and-black hair was in a very uneven buzz cut that was higher in the back than the front. The boys began moving away when a voice called out, "Hey, gents, what's doin'?"

The man had sat down in the center of an old mattress, wearing army boots with no socks, a stained gray suit, a dirty white shirt open at the collar. A powerful stench of sweat, cheap whiskey and Sterno emanated from him. He was smiling an enigmatic smile, which did not make the boys feel welcome but did not scare them away, either. The group made a tentative semi-circle around the man, and Tim Martin asked, "What's your name, buddy?"

The tramp answered without hesitation. "Franklin Benjamin, son, or at least that's what it was this morning. Hitched and rode freight for two days until I reached this beautiful spot."

The rest of the boys backed away from the hobo, but Joey stayed put. "I bet you've been a lot of places," he said.

"I've squatted and dumped in just about every open field, toilet and privy in this great country of ours: Kissimmee, Florida, in the winter; Concord, New Hampshire, in the fall; San Diego, California, almost any time. Never knew Pennsylvania was so nice until I decided to make camp here. You lads are lucky to have this spot, I tell you."

"And we want to keep it that way," Tim Martin challenged. "This is no place for an old bum."

"Hey, wait a minute, Tim," Joey snapped, "he wasn't bothering anyone. Why don't you just shut the hell up?"

Martin stood there mute, searching for words. The others

looked tense and nervous, their eyes filled with edgy fear.

Joey was very much on his own. "You guys are just like me," he said. "About the only places we've been are the shore and the Pocono Mountains. I hear that in California, Mr. Benjamin, people wear hardly any clothes and if they want some fruit, they just go out and pick it from a tree."

"That's close to right," the man said.

"And that you could put New York City inside the Grand Canyon, it's that big. He can tell us about all that stuff." Joey found no allies among his friends. He turned around to see the gangly hobo pick his nose, looking briefly at the wad of snot before rubbing it across his leg.

The other boys began moving slowly away from the hobo. Tom Meyer yelled, "My uncle owns all of this land, mister, and if you don't leave right now, he's gonna call the cops on you."

"Yeah," they all shouted in unison. When the tramp stood there immobile, they reached down and picked up rocks, holding them in their hands like they were baseballs. Joey was horrified. The bum stared back and grabbed a big stick.

Joey stepped between the hobo and his friends. "Put down the damn rocks," he said, shaking. "If you're going to hit him, you're going to have to hit me first."

Ten torturous seconds went by before the four boys dropped their stones, looking at their friend with disgust and disbelief. Joey's chest was still heaving, but he felt like the moment of danger had passed.

"Stay with the homo," Martin said.

Maxville laughed. As they turned and began to leave, Mill paused long enough to look back and flip him the bird.

Joey spun around to see Franklin Benjamin stuffing the wine bottle into his back pocket and rolling a can of baked beans, the

Sterno heater and some flatware into a torn-up striped sheet.

"Don't go," he said, "they were just bluffing. I can show you a place where no one will ever find you."

Franklin immediately stopped packing.

"Hey, did you really go to all those places?" Joey asked. "I just read about the Petrified Forest, all those logs turned into stone."

"It's in Arizona, son, and it's quite a sight. There's so much beauty out there, it just about knocks you on your butt sometimes." At that, the man knelt on one knee, bent his head, covered his eyes with his hands and began to weep.

Joey gently put his hand on the man's shoulder and asked him what was wrong.

Franklin raised his head. "I been walking this world for forty-two years and not many people stood up for me like you just did. My daddy used to hit me with a chain and throw me into the pig sty. That was real bad, but what was worse was the names he called me: low-life pile of shit, rat's asshole, sack of dog puke. Momma used to sit there nodding her head because if he was whomping on me, that meant he wasn't beating the shit out of her. The thing was, I never did anything real bad. So I ran away from home when I was just about your age, about twelve years old. Leaves some bad marks, I can tell you."

"I'm really sorry, mister," Joey said, shrugging his shoulders. "At least you've traveled a whole lot."

"I want to thank you so much, pal. Do an old tramp one more favor and give him a big hug."

Keeping his arms by his sides, Joey stood there limp and overwhelmed; the hobo's strong arms and stench overpowered him. Franklin began to cry again, this time, great wracking sobs. Joey began to pull away. If anyone saw him being hugged by this bum, he might as well commit suicide. Saying, " You are a truly beautiful person," Franklin just would not release his grip.

Joey kept pushing and kicking. Frustrated, he twisted and turned and then smacked the tip of his sneakers into the bum's shin. Franklin finally loosened his grip on the boy's arm, enough for Joey to pull away and dart up the creek. When he felt that he was far enough away from the hobo, Joey stopped and took a few deep breaths. The goofy part was, that except for the awful smell and not being released from his hugging right away, it felt kind of good. He couldn't remember the last time he'd been hugged.

Maybe the guy was a homo, like Tim Martin said. He'd always thought homos had long foreheads, curly hair, small eyes and big hooked noses. But Franklin looked like a regular old bum, the kind he saw when his father drove through Philadelphia, lying on the sidewalk right before the Ben Franklin bridge that led to the Jersey Shore. And his story was so sad. It didn't sound like bullshit; a man wouldn't cry like that if his story wasn't at least partly true.

Joey's parents never beat him or cursed at him. When he behaved badly, they sent him to his room, but that didn't happen often. He hated it so much, his room became a jail cell. It felt like someone had turned off a spigot and life just kind of stopped moving forward.

Sitting on a boulder, Joey looked up at the sun, a big golden plate in the sky. It was way too early to be going home; his parents would suspect something was wrong and ask a lot of questions. He kept wondering if someone had seen him. How could he ever explain what had gone on? It was going to be bad enough justifying why he had defended the bum in the first place.

Looking down the creek, Joey noticed a small speck of bright green a few boulders away. It had been ages since he had seen a frog; sometimes he thought they had left the Jungle for good. Moving quietly and quickly, he got behind the rock and looked at the small creature, its back covered with orange and yellow speckles. The frog's stomach swelled as it breathed in and out. Crouching down, Joey cupped his hands and lowered them over the unsuspecting creature, who lunged forward, only to find itself trapped.

"Meet your master, little frog," Joey said, curling his hand around the tiny torso and bringing the frog up to his face. "If I want to put your head in my mouth and suck out all your brains, I can. If I want to smash your body into a thousand pieces against one of these rocks, I can. If I want to throw you up into the sky and tell you to fly like a bird, I can do that too."

Pushing his thumb and forefinger around the frog's neck, Joey began to squeeze and watched it wriggle, trying to escape. Loosening his grip, he ran a finger over the tiny amphibian's head and said, "Now, now little froggie, don't be scared."

"Hey, Joey," said a girl's voice said close behind him.

Startled, he looked over his shoulder and saw Sally McKee, a girl from his class, smiling at him. Carrying a paper bag streaked with oil stains, she quickly hopped over the rocks until she was standing right beside him. Joey was happy to see her, although it was unusual to see a girl alone in the Jungle.

Sally was very popular and moved easily between both sexes, which didn't seem to bother anyone. She jumped rope and played jacks, but was often picked ahead of guys for touch football and kickball games. With her short brown curly hair and lively brown eyes, Sally could be categorized as "cute," though nowhere near the heartthrob status of Barbara Turley or Margie Peters. She definitely drew interest from boys, however, when she put on lipstick and wore nylons and a skirt.

"What have you got in your hand, Joseph Garden?" she said, moving onto Joey's rock. "Oh my God, what a cute little frog! It's so green! Here, let me hold it."

Joey handed over the amphibian. "Yeah, took about an hour to catch; it kept hopping from rock to rock. Followed it all the way up from Scottdale Road."

Intrigued, Sally let the frog jump from one of her hands to the other for a few moments, then bent down and released it into the creek.

"Hey," Joey said, "that was *my* frog."

"He needed to be back in the water. I got a hoagie; you want to share?"

"Yeah, I'm starving. From your parents' shop?"

"Nothing but the best, at your request."

Making her way to a small clearing behind a boulder, Sally unwrapped the sandwich. Joey found the familiar aromas of oregano, olive oil, provolone cheese, tomatoes, onions, ham and salami intoxicating. It was all he could do to keep from grabbing the stuffed Italian roll, ripping off a big hunk and stuffing it into his mouth.

"Let's see, Joseph," Sally said, putting her hand over the sandwich like an imaginary knife, "should you get an end piece, half, or bigger than half?"

Joey said nothing; Sally smiled and tore the sandwich in two, giving him the slightly larger piece. "Your eyes were bugging out, " she said, laughing.

At that moment, he was a little in love with Sally. The sun

was glistening on her skin and hair; her eyes were flickering like lightning bugs.

When the sandwiches were eaten, Joey wadded up the wrapper and paper bag and threw them toward some trees.

"Thanks a lot, Sally," he said, "that was really great."

"It's pretty hard for me to finish a whole hoagie by myself, anyway. And...I brought dessert!"

Reaching into the back pocket of her red shorts, Sally produced a Bonomo's Turkish Taffy wrapped in a red-and-white tinfoil wrapper. It was Joey's favorite candy bar.

"Boss," he said, "that's so cool!" He took the candy and smacked it against the boulder, breaking it into small pieces. A Bonomo's could last all day, even with two people sharing. He took a medium-size piece of the delicious vanilla taffy and handed the rest to Sally.

A half-hour passed. They barely spoke, happy just to be eating the candy and watching clouds scud across the sky. To his left, Joey spotted a garter snake slithering through some weeds about three feet from his head. He swung his hand in a lazy arc, landing in the middle of the snake's torso, and grabbed it.

"Look what I got!" Joey said, watching the snake coil around his fingers, opening its mouth and displaying its bright red tongue.

"That is so beautiful," Sally said, petting the snake's head. "You find some great stuff, Joey."

"Come over here by this rock," he said.

Joey reached for a tree branch with his free hand, took some bright green leaves and put them in her hair, behind Sally's ears.

"I, Joey Garden, bestow upon Sally McKee this serpent bracelet and declare her the fairest maiden in all the land." With those words, Joey took the garter snake with the red-and-green markings on its back and watched as it coiled around Sally's small, delicate wrist.

Sally looked up at Joey and smiled. Moving closer, Joey did something he had never done before, aside from a few Spin the Bottle games at birthday parties; he leaned over and kissed a girl. Letting the snake fall to the ground, Sally put her arms around him.

This was the second person in two hours to hug Joey Garden. It felt super good to him, like taking a cool shower after playing basketball. He opened his eyes to see if anyone was looking. Sally still had her eyes closed. He slid his fingers through her mass of curls and she opened her mouth a little bit, sighing. Joey pulled Sally closer, kissing her harder. She dug her fingers into his back. *This is what all the fuss is about with the high school kids*, he thought. *I want more.*

They clasped hands and began walking south toward Darby Creek. Just before they reached a clearing surrounded by a clump of birch trees, Martin, Mill, Maxville and Meyer came up behind them, laughing and talking loudly.

"Oh my God!" Martin yelled, the first to see the pair. "Joey Garden has given up homos and has a new girlfriend, cute little Sally McKee." Martin put his hand behind his head and puckered his lips.

The four boys quickly gathered around the two. Joey dropped Sally's hand and looked at the ground. He needed these guys like he needed another foot.

"What a lovely couple!" Mill said, "probably be married in a few years."

"Yeah," Maxville added, looking down, "they'll have ten kids. Joey'll work at the hoagie shop."

This remark really tickled the group. "Joey the Hoagie King and Sally the Hoagie Queen!" Tom Meyer yelled to more raucous laughter.

"Your mothers can come after hours and clean up," Joey rejoined.

Tim Martin walked up and put his fist right on Joey's nose. "How dare you insult my momma, boy?" he asked in a menacing tone, not letting on whether he was serious or not.

"Go home and get some brains, *Martass*," Sally barked.

There was loud chuckling.

"C'mon, Tim," Mill said, "Louie is waiting for us at the Big Field."

"Yeah, we'll let these little love bugs alone," Martin said, going up to Joey. "While you were away, Garden, Lansdowne and the Clifties officially declared war. It's supposed to start in half an hour."

As the boys disappeared into the woods, Sally grabbed Joey's hand again and said, "Tim Martin gives me a big pain, always bothering girls and not just *saying* things, if you know what I mean. The other day he pinched Jane Healy's butt and chased her all the way home from school trying to kiss her. He's a gorp and a twerp. I don't know why all you guys follow him."

"He's good with his fists and good in sports," Joey answered. "But, you're right, Tim isn't that smart. He puts up a big front and all, but I know it bothers him when he gets bad grades on math and spelling tests. He spits on the papers before throwing them away. I thought we were in for it when you told him to go home and get some brains."

Sally adjusted the leaves in her hair. "Does this mean we're going together?" she asked. "Everybody's gonna know, we might as well."

"Yeah, I guess so, Sally. Hey, can I have some more Turkish Taffy?"

"Sure, take all the rest."

They kissed again. "I think it's stupid to fight the kids from Clifton Heights," she said, emphatically. "They live only a few blocks away, just past the creek, so what's the big deal? Boys just like to start trouble. You should come home with me, Joey."

Joey looked at Sally nervously before reaching down and picking up a stick. "Yeah, well, sometimes you gotta stick up for your town. I think I'll at least go see what's going on."

"Yeah well, I hope you don't get hurt," Sally answered, clearly disappointed. "I told my mom I would be home to help clean the house. She's going to kill me if I'm late."

"Bye."

Taking out another hunk of taffy and sucking on it, Joey sat down, tired and exhilarated. He guessed he would not get ragged on *too* badly about Sally and it would take the guys' minds off the incident with Franklin Benjamin. The rumored war between Lansdowne guys and the Clifties had turned out not to be just a bunch of hot air, as he'd hoped. As for fighting, Joey Garden would never be confused with Rocky Marciano, but he was not a complete waste, either. There were tons of guys he could beat in his class and he might even be able to take Martin, if he caught him off-guard.

But Joey shuddered at the thought of duking it out with those Cliftie guys with their ultra-greasy ducktails, tough words and pitiless eyes. He knew some of them carried switchblades. If he didn't go, he'd have to listen to stories for the next ten years and would have no idea what was true and what wasn't. And he might never know if he had the spine to participate in such a huge, dangerous fight. Dawdling for a few moments, Joey got up and started walking toward the battleground.

The Big Field was the largest open area in the Jungle. The scene of many Capture the Flag, Tag, Hide and Go Seek games and World War II battle simulations. When he reached the clearing, it looked like every Lansdowne boy twelve years and over was there.

Martin and his other friends were standing with their hands in their pockets, looking grim.

"What's up?" he asked.

Martin stepped forward and said, "The Clifties sent a message to Louie to meet in the Big Field at 3:00 and to bring his friends. Can little lover boy handle it?"

"I think so," Joey said. "I've never seen so many Lansdowne guys all in one place."

"Yeah," Tim continued, "we got most of Ardmore Avenue, Gladstone Manor, even a bunch of guys from Tintown; they've been waiting for this for a long time."

Joey nodded, trying to look cool. The instant he'd seen everyone milling around, he wished he were back at the creek.

"Hey, Joey," Tom Meyer said. "We found the Clifties' fort, come look."

Racing up a hill with his four friends, Joey looked at the backs of the houses on Marlyn Avenue. All those people inside, he thought, listening to their radios or watching TV, eating tuna sandwiches and drinking Cokes, having no idea Custer's Last Stand was just about to start in their backyard.

The group walked for about fifty feet, to where a makeshift light brown lean-to stood beside an old, decaying weeping willow. The lean-to was made out of cheap plywood and an old refrigerator box. Inside, the walls were covered with dozens of pictures of naked women, most with large breasts, round nipples the size of baseballs, big clumps of hair between their legs.

"They come up here to whack off," Tim Maxville said, "in *our town.*"

"Yeah, let 'em go do it in their mother's bedrooms," Mill added.

"Some fine-looking livestock," Tim Martin said, running his tongue across his lips. "It's a shame we have to burn the whole thing down."

"Clifties!" a voice yelled. "They're here!"

What Joey saw next turned his blood to ice water. A crowd of about forty boys was standing on top of a small hill just beyond the Big Field. The ones in the foreground were wearing leather jackets and holding baseball bats. There was a smaller group of boys his age, standing behind the older guys. They did not seem to have any weapons, but who knew what was in their pockets? He got in the rear of the Lansdowne mob and began to yell, just like everyone else.

Louie Wheeling, a greasy black curl planted in the middle of his forehead, walked to the middle of the space that separated the warring factions. A huge Cliftie named Tony Adonelli, in a black leather motorcycle jacket studded with rhinestones, came out to meet Louie. The two bent their heads down and began to talk. If they began to fight, the place was going to be like D-Day. No great plan of action occurred to Joey, he just planned to stay on the edge of things and try not to get hurt too badly.

"No weapons," Louie said, returning to the group. "Adonelli said they wouldn't use bats or pull out any knives."

"Do you believe him? " someone asked.

"I think so," Louie answered, looking back at the Clifties worriedly. "We made piles of rocks over by the trees; if they start any rough stuff, run over and get them. The fight will start when I lower my arm. Lansdowne is the best, don't you guys fucking forget it."

Walking to the front of the group, Louie raised his fist in the air, paused for a moment or two and dropped it. The two sides ran toward each other. The lead players began to circle around warily, fists clenched, waiting for the first blow to be thrown. Getting behind Sugar Bear Harris, a lineman on the high school football team, Joey crouched down, expecting the worst, fear spreading from the bottom of his stomach to his neck. Martin and Mill had run to the front, but Tim Maxville and Tom Meyer were standing right beside him, not making any moves. There was a quick movement; fists began to fly. The brawl was on.

Joey saw Tom Meyer being picked up by a Cliftie and thrown to the ground, where he rolled over, clutching his stomach. Joey felt a Cliftie at his back; he swung around and threw a wild punch. As his knuckles landed squarely in the enemy's mouth, he ground his fist into the boy's teeth. Exulting, he watched the older Cliftie bend over, blood dripping from his lips. He had never punched anyone so violently and so well. His skin began to tingle. If his butt got stomped by the Clifties, at least he had made this hit. Joey moved toward the center of the fray, where the older boys were cursing, screaming and stomping each other. Louie was picking himself up off the ground. Sugar Bear was kicking a guy in the thigh. It was impossible to tell if any side was winning. A few minutes later, the enemies went back to their original positions to regroup. Louie lifted his fist; the Lansdowne boys ran to his side.

"They're gonna be back," Louie said, blood gushing from his nose. "Is anyone really hurt bad?"

No one answered. Louie continued, "Do we have any hostages?"

Vinny Novello, a Tintown guy, said, "Yeah, we got one, if you can call him that." He produced a weeping, olive-skinned boy, about ten years old, wearing a Hopalong Cassidy tee shirt and a pair of black bermuda shorts.

"We should let him go, Louie," Buddy Kirkland said, "he's only a little kid." At almost the exact moment he said that, a voice boomed from the Cliftie side, "Send my little brother back or we'll destroy your puny Lansdowne asses."

"You guys agree to keep away from the Jungle for good, and we'll send him right away," Louie yelled back.

Tony Adonelli had moved to the top of a small hill. "I want my brother back now," he said, pointing a menacing finger, "or we're coming back with bats and chains. You got five minutes to decide."

Louie motioned toward the group to huddle around him. "This is it," he said. "We can take care of these bastards once and for all." He looked at the boy's avid faces and told them the plan. "We're really going to need the sixth graders. Tim, Jack, Tim and Tom, run down to the rock piles and bring back as many as you can. Joey, Max told me he saw you really pound a Cliftie, so I'm giving you the most important job: Get Adonelli's little brother up to the fort and don't release him until *I* tell you. Take him back behind the trees, so they can't see what is going on."

Joey walked over to Novello and stared at the pitiful kid, who looked like a little boy who'd lost his mother at the A&P.

"You gotta stop it," Joey said, taking the boy's arm. "Nothing bad's gonna happen to you. It's a sissy thing to cry."

Gulping back tears, the boy made an heroic, unsuccessful effort not to cry.

"Look, what's so damn bad?" Joey went on. "You're the smallest, youngest guy and you got captured. You didn't even get hurt. So, *please*, shut the hell up."

Reaching the fort, Joey tightened his grip and pushed the boy inside.

"What's your name?" he asked.

"Michael Adonelli."

"What grade are you in?"

"Fifth — Clifton Public."

"Maybe this fight will settle things between us," Joey said, sitting down by young Adonelli. "What you gotta realize, Michael, is that the Jungle is on *Lansdowne* land, even though Clifton Heights is close by. You guys got your own places, which we leave alone, but the Clifties are always over here."

"I didn't even want to be here," Michael said, rubbing his hand into his eye, "but my brother said if I didn't come, he would call me a baby for the rest of my life."

Joey could not help but feel sorry for the boy, who he thought just wanted to be home watching the Lone Ranger, playing with his dog, and eating a peanut butter sandwich.

A wild roar rang out; Joey ran to the edge of the hill. The Lansdowne guys and the Clifties were in battle, a seething, intertwined mob. The Clifties were swinging bats as rocks rained down on their heads. A minute passed. No side seemed to have an advantage. Suddenly a Cliftie raised a bat, clubbing Buddy

Kirkland on the arm. His yowling could be heard all the way back to the fort. Joey flinched; he was sure the arm was broken. He went back inside the fort and paced around the tiny structure. What in hell was he supposed to do? If the Clifties won, they would come and massacre him. If Lansdowne triumphed, how long was he supposed to imprison a helpless little kid? Frustration mounting, he kicked at the rear wall, almost knocking it down.

The yelling grew louder and more savage. Joey went to the boy and said quietly, "Michael, I really believe that you got forced into this mess by your brother and that you never meant any harm to Lansdowne guys. I'm going to ask you to do something that may sound crazy, but I really need you to do what I say."

Joey motioned for Michael to stand up and when he did, got right beside him and whispered, "I want you to punch me in the nose."

The young prisoner looked at Joey with confusion. "You've been nice to me," he said.

"It's a way out for both of us."

Michael hesitated for a few moments, then cocked his arm and released it, driving his fist into the center of Joey's nose. Yelling "Ow!" Joey fell to the ground and when he arose, streams of blood were streaming from each nostril. Putting his fingers underneath his nostrils, Joey covered them with blood and wiped them on both of their shirts. "You can tell your brother that you hit me, we wrestled and you escaped. Run off toward Scottdale Road and don't go near the fighting!"

Joey leaned his head back to stop the blood flow. When he checked the battleground again, the Lansdowne crew was in a shambles. Those who had not run off were lying on the ground, nursing various injuries. The Clifties were holding bats over their heads, yelling triumphantly. He watched in horror as Tony Adonelli and a few of his henchmen ran up the hill toward him. If he tried to escape, he was sure to get nabbed. It felt like the soles of his feet had grown roots. He stood there paralyzed.

Quickly surrounded by Clifties, Joey was sure he would be annihilated. "Where's my fuckin' little brother?" the massive Adonelli barked.

"He was a tough little kid," Joey said. "He kept trying to get away and finally punched me in the nose and ran off toward Darby Creek. It happened just a few minutes ago."

Adonelli looked toward Scottdale Road, grabbed Joey's shirt and twisted it. "If Michael is hurt in any way," he said, "we're coming back for you. I don't care how scrawny-looking you are. Don't mess with this fort either; if anything happens to it, you're the one we'll be looking for."

"Yeah, that's right," another Cliftie said. " We caught your little ass a few weeks ago. Give us your name and address and if it's wrong, you'll be chewing bloody Chiclets."

Tony pulled Joey off the ground until the two were face to face. "My name is Jimmy Holland," he muttered, "and I live on 182 Wickham Court over by Lansdowne High."

"That better be right," Adonelli said before tossing Joey unceremoniously to the ground, "or you're going to be one sorry little shithead."

Reaching the battlefield, Joey was met with a horrible scene. Few people were standing; most were on the ground, making a variety of awful noises. Buddy Kirkland, holding his right arm across his chest, was being helped up. Sugarbear, the toughest Lansdowne guy, was bleeding from the head. Louie Wheeling was on the ground in a daze. When he saw Joey, he looked up and asked, "Did you let the kid go?"

"Nah," Joey answered. "Another Cliftie came by and got him away from me. But I didn't make it easy."

Joey's buddies were sitting in back of the older boys. Martin's cheeks were bruised. Mill's eyes had turned black. Maxville had blood on his nose, and Meyer looked ashen. Never had Joey seen his friends messed up; they could have been cast as zombies in a horror movie.

Tim Martin yelled out to no one in particular, "Goddam Cliftie bastards, they won the battle, but Lansdowne's gonna win the war."

Joey sat down. He wanted to tell his friends exactly what'd happened, how senseless and dreadful he had found this skirmish, how he had outsmarted everyone by forcing Michael to hit him. How excited he was to kiss Sally, and how cool it was to be with her. How they didn't really give Franklin Benjamin a chance, that if they knew his story, they might have even liked the bum a little bit, ugly habits and all.

Looking into their dull, defeated eyes, Joey realized that this was not the time or place. Sadly, he wondered if there would *ever* be one. It felt like he was back sitting alone in his bedroom, banished by his parents, door closed, books read, posters on the walls holding no interest and the hours before sleep dry, empty and endless, a long, gray road that went on for infinity.

"We got to get that fort," Martin said, getting up laboriously. "No way those bastards are keeping it. C'mon guys, let my mighty Zippo do its job."

Slowly, the others arose and started to head back up the hill.

"Hey, Tim, don't do that," Joey said, panicked. "Tony Adonelli came by there to get his little brother and he said he was going to beat my ass if it got burnt down. The Clifties won and there's nothing more we can do about it."

"Oh bullshit, Garden," Martin answered, "fuck Adonelli, his brother and his mother."

"Maybe we should back off, Tim," Tom Meyer said, rubbing the birthmark on his cheek. "I think Joey is telling the truth. Enough has happened for one day."

Mill was having none of it. "The Clifties will know that even if they won today, we aren't scared of them. Anyway, they aren't going to come traveling into Lansdowne looking for a skinny little sixth grader."

"Yeah, and half of what Joey says is nuts anyway," Martin added. "We all know what Mrs. Applegate called him, 'A most unusual child.'"

"Fuck you, Tim," Joey said, having had enough. "Burning down that fort will cause me big trouble; you should have heard those guys. And it might start another war, where we could get hurt even worse. It's stupid and dangerous. Don't do it."

"You want a taste, Garden?"

Joey swallowed before saying, "I'm not moving, Tim."

Martin snorted, "I'll deal with this little problem later, guys. Anyone who stays with Joey is a pussy for the rest of their lives."

Maxville hesitated, ran his hand through his crew-cut and joined the other two.

Tom Meyer tugged on the bill of his cap and refused to budge. "I'm with you, Joey," he said.

A few minutes passed; the two boys stood transfixed, watching flames erupt just over the crest of the hill.

"We're pussies forever," Tom Meyer said. "You know he'll never let us live this down."

"Guess so, Tommy," Joey answered, as they both started walking home. "I'll have to fight Tim and figure out a way to avoid the Clifties when they see that their fort is just a big pile of soot."

"Jack was probably right: they'll forget about you after a while."

"I hope so. I gave them a false name and address."

"Man, my ribs are really sore. That Cliftie threw me down like I was nothing."

"Yeah, put some ice on it when you get home, and tell your mom you fell out of a tree."

The boys walked silently for a while. Tommy turned west when they got to Willowbrook Avenue. "See ya, Joey," he said.

Looking back toward the Jungle, as the last sparks of sunlight glinted on the leaves, Joey crept up the hill past the storm drains, the residue of the day settling on him like black, sticky ashes. He shook his head back and forth, beginning to run as hard as he could. Breathless, he reached the top of the hill before seeing the Tudor-style homes lining Mansfield Road, where his house sat at the end of the block. As he gulped the early evening air, the hard pounding of his heart began to subside.

Joey stopped at the biggest tree on the block, an old spruce whose fat, twisted limbs extended over Mr. and Mrs. Ryder's front porch. He must have climbed it a hundred times. This time, instead of shinnying up the trunk, Joey stood there and put his hand on the hard, unyielding bark, moving it up and down, wanting something, but not knowing what. He tried to cry out but couldn't.

Mr. Ryder, sitting on his porch, yelled through the screen door, "What are you doing out there, Joey? You look terrible. Get home and get cleaned up before dinner. Your parents must be worried stiff."

Joey looked at the old man and nodded. His house was only twenty feet away. He could see his mother's head in the kitchen window. She was probably cutting onions for the meat loaf and wishing he was around to help. His father would be in the easy chair in the living room, reading *The Evening Bulletin*, snorting about the sorry state of the world. Joey began to move toward home. There was nowhere else to go.

Part 3

Peaches

The first line of my report card has this information: Third Quarter, Lansdowne High School, April 1958, Joseph Garden — 9th grade. It's always the same for me, straight "A's" stacked like teepees one on top of the other like a totem pole. I usually take great satisfaction in looking at them and anticipating being taken out to a celebration milkshake or sundae at Saul's Drugstore. I always receive "S" (Satisfactory) in Citizenship because it simply isn't cool to be perfect, and if you can't be cool at least some of the time, there's just no point to anything.

I can conjugate Latin verbs: amo amas amat ; count in Spanish: uno dos tres quatro ; explain the Scientific Method; give you the dates for the major battles of the Revolutionary War. I can tell you the major countries of southeastern Africa: Uganda, Kenya, Tanganyika, Mozambique, the Congo and South Africa.

I know that when Romeo had to leave Juliet, he was sent to Mantua and that on his way back to Verona, when he heard his true love was dead, he bribed an apothecary to give him some poison that would kill half an army. When we had a discussion in class about whether or not love was worth dying for, I sided with guys who said, "No way!" Inside, though, a voice was saying to me: *If you're going to die for something, what could be better than love?* I cursed myself for not saying so out loud. Even though I am an honor roll student and a starting guard on the Lansdowne High freshman basketball team, my main claim to fame is being friends with Peaches Davenport, a senior and the hottest-looking girl our town has ever seen, maybe the most beautiful in all of Pennsylvania. What I learned from knowing Peaches won't show up on any report card and, quite frankly, I'm not altogether sure exactly what I did find out. But somehow I feel my experience with her will be a source of truth and inspiration for the rest of my life.

For as far back as I can recall, Peaches has had large, full breasts that she showcases in tight semi-see-through blouses or soft colored sweaters that button up the front. If someone were to ask me to describe her, I would say that she reminded me of Marilyn Monroe or Jayne Mansfield. The same kind of body, of course, but also a way of acting a lot dumber than she really is, like the two movie stars, who have to be at least secretly smart to be making all that money. I've always felt that both Jayne and Marilyn were generous people and not stuck-up at all. If you met them on the street and said hello, they'd probably stop what they were doing and talk to you without acting all moviestar-ish. Maybe that would be just a big act, but who cares?

It's not fake with Peaches; she's really not conceited. She calls me *Joey How Does Your Garden Grow* when she sees me and runs her fingers through my brown crew-cut. Life is heaven in these brief moments, being real close to those sweaters, smelling her perfume, having that soft blonde hair brush against my face — va-va-va-voom!

She lives with her mother, one of the cafeteria ladies, on the top floor of the Windemere Apartments on the corner of Nyack and Wycombe Avenues. You see them walking home from the A&P, cart loaded with bags in front of three giant Pepsi bottles or coming out of the beauty parlor right past the bridge by the train station. Her mother has lost her shape completely and has frizzy brown hair that sticks out at very weird angles from scarves or the food server cap she wears when she's working. From looking at them, it doesn't seem like they're related; in fact, it seems like they're from different planets. But as far as I know, and that isn't very far, they seem to love each other.

Despite looking like a matinee idol, Peaches does not exactly have it easy. Many of the junior and senior guys have a way of turning into apes when she walks by, "Hey Peaches, can I have a few gallons?" Or, "I think your name should be Cantaloupes, not Peaches." Word was that Teddy Crosby just walked right up to her at the Ardmore Avenue Field, put his hands right square on her boobs, and got black and blue nuts for his troubles.

Girls were even worse, spreading rumors about Peaches gangbanging guys or giving blowjobs in the last row of the Lansdowne Theater. I knew none of this was true, because you can bet that whomever she did it with would go right straight to the outdoor basketball court and start bragging his ass off. No one ever did. She only has one good girl friend, Nancy Taylor, who also has a big chest but is not nearly as beautiful as Peaches.

As far as boyfriends are concerned, you see Peaches driving around town with older guys from Secane or Upper Darby in

'50 Fords or '55 Chevys. Usually they have Elvis haircuts, wear black motorcycle jackets and mean expressions on their faces. I'm not sure what she sees in any of them, but why should she mess with Lansdowne guys? Their big mouths gave her nothing but trouble.

I've listened to a great many long and twisted discussions at the basketball court about whether Peaches was "doing it" with these guys or not, and most held to the theory that with such a hot, outstanding body, once she and the guy started to make out, there was no way either of them could keep their pants on. I was a champion of the negative view. "Just because a girl is built like World War III, doesn't necessarily mean she's a skank," was my main arguing point. To prove this, I used the example of Linda Fletcher, a tall skinny girl with stringy hair, who had to leave school last year to have a baby. A hard argument to refute, and no one ever did.

Peaches and I came to be friends last spring when I got a job sweeping the floor and stocking shelves at Sandler's Pharmacy. Even though Old Man Sandler and his brother only paid me $.50 an hour, it was a cool job because everyone hung out there and you were always in on the latest gossip. Peaches would come in after school with Marcy and maybe one other girl. They would order strawberry milkshakes and cheeseburgers and take a very long time to finish them. After they arrived, I would make sure I swept the areas beneath their feet very thoroughly. It became a big joke. I would arrive with my trusty broom and they would laugh and hike up their skirts.

When Mr. Sandler wasn't looking, I would slip Peaches Clark bars and boxes of Jujyfruits, which I knew to be her favorites. Sometimes she would motion to me and we would sit together at the end of the counter and talk the usual teenage stuff, who was the best dancer on Bandstand, the latest Buddy Holly song and who was better looking, Sal Mineo or Tab Hunter? Often, she would lower her voice and tell me about her period cramps and how most guys were bullshitters about love and only wanted one thing. She held my hand and made me promise I would never be like that. I felt very grown-up during these conversations and wished they would never end.

When school began in September, people saw how she treated me and I became a mini-celebrity. Whenever my friends saw me talking to her, they would rush right over and ask me to tell them every word she said. Usually I told the truth, which really wasn't that startling; she was going to the football game, or her mother was restricting her for staying out late. Sometimes, because I felt this stuff was a little bit boring, I made things up, like she was going to have dinner in Philadelphia with a thirty-year-old man. My friends would get real bug-eyed when I dropped these bombshells, and I felt bad about it afterwards. But God gave her that body and made guys go ape shit over big knockers, and what Peaches didn't know wouldn't hurt her.

One day, a few weeks ago, when the wind was blowing real hard and leaves were swirling in every direction, I was on my bike headed for the basketball court. Peaches was walking down Highland Avenue, books clutched to her chest. When I waved and she didn't wave back like she always did, I stopped real quickly and pulled over to the curb. She kept walking and wouldn't acknowledge me at all; I knew something was really wrong. Looking at her face closely, I could see little rivers of tears sliding down her cheeks.

"Peaches, what's wrong?" I asked, letting my bike drop onto the sidewalk.

"Nothing's wrong, Joey. I'm fine."

"You are not; tell me what's bothering you."

She shook her head no and the tears really started pouring. I put my arm across her shoulders; her nose was red and her whole face was flushed. I told her a bunch of goofy stuff like everything was going to be okay, even though I had no idea what she was so upset about. My guess was that she had forgotten her code and had become involved with a Lansdowne guy.

"Let me give you a ride home," I said.

Upset as she was, Peaches couldn't resist a smile. "Joey Garden, do you expect me to get on the handlebars of your bike so the wind can blow my dress up over my head. You must think I'm stupid *and* crazy!"

"You're wearing a big coat, no one's going to see anything. You can put your books in the cage on the back wheels. It's a cinch."

"Some cinch. I haven't ridden on anyone's handlebars since I was nine. If anything bad happens, Joey, I'll never speak to you again."

"The Prince will deliver Cinderella home promptly and in good health."

"You better!"

Remarkably, the most beautiful girl in Pennsylvania was sitting snugly on my handlebars, her silky, lustrous hair six inches from my face. What a glorious sight and smell! After traveling about ten feet, my bike wobbling precariously, I wasn't so sure it was such a great idea. Peaches wasn't that heavy, but she wasn't light, either.

She looked back and said, "Do you want to stop, Joey?" It actually sounded like a pretty good idea, but I shouted, "No!"

By the time we got to Stewart Avenue, things were feeling better. My bike had stabilized and we were moving smoothly. As we glided downhill, Peaches threw her head back and whooped. We reached the bottom of the hill and I made a left turn onto the sidewalk. I started singing, "Davy, Davy Crockett, King of the Wild Frontier," wobbling the bike like I was drunk. Peaches was laughing so hard, I thought her appendix was going to burst.

I wanted to drive back to Greenwood Avenue and drive Peaches behind one of those big houses with the trees in front and lay her down on the ground, kissing her, touching her and doing whatever I wanted to her. Instead I pedaled forward, smelling her hair and continuing to let my imagination run hog wild.

When we reached her apartment house, Peaches slid from the handlebars, while I sweated and panted, happy that I had done what I said I was going to do. I expected her to get her books, say goodbye and go tromping off to her mother. Instead she threw her arms around my neck and started to kiss me all over my face, saying, "You're the best, Joey Garden, just the best!"

Then she took my cheeks in her hands and planted the wettest, sweetest, most glorious kiss I've ever received in my short little life. When she tried to pull away, I wouldn't let her. I felt her body go slack and she made this soft purring sound; I thought I was going to drench my pants. The kiss ended. Peaches laughed and said, "I have to go, Joey Hot Stuff, see you tomorrow in school."

As I watched her wave goodbye before turning to go inside, I felt an ache so strong, I thought I was going to faint. If, at that moment, God had come down from the sky and said, "Joey, I will let you have Peaches any way you want her, but in exchange, you will have to give up eating for the rest of your life," I would have agreed on the spot, no problem whatever.

I rode around Lansdowne for a very long time, Peaches' kisses radiating through my body and soul. I'd kissed girls before and done a few other things as well. In fact, I had spent the entire movie "Tammy" with my hand on Diane Baxter's left one. Of course, she had her elbow jammed against my wrist so I couldn't move it. The girls my age were little ponds; Peaches was the Atlantic Ocean.

As I drove home to Mansfield Road, it was impossible to restrain certain thoughts. I was totally in love with Peaches Davenport, that was without question. If we started to go out, would she ride everywhere on my handlebars? I would be the hero of the freshman class. Peaches would be laughed at and called a "cradle robber" everywhere she went. When we wanted to be alone, would the dirt and weeds underneath the grandstand be where we went? These thoughts were depressing, because the answers to each were: no, no and NO! What good was love if it had nowhere to go? It was easy to see how Romeo felt after being banished.

I remembered a phrase I'd heard, probably on a stupid soap opera: *Love Conquers All*. I wanted to piss all over those words but maybe, just maybe, there was some truth inside them. Peaches did not just kiss any old guy; I knew she enjoyed it just as much as I did.

Pulling my bike onto the front porch, I opened the front door and went inside. My father was waiting, the *Philadelphia Bulletin* coiled in his right hand. "You're late for dinner, Mr.Big Shot," he said, whacking the paper against the arm of the easy chair. "It's too dark to be playing basketball, so where the hell you been?"

The part of me that was disgusted and pessimistic felt like saying, "Mind your own damn business," while the *Love Conquers All* side was worried about being restricted and not being able to be with my True Love. As both parts warred, I could think of nothing to say. Worried that my silence might mean to my parents that I did something really bad and couldn't talk about it, I blurted out ,"Making out with Peaches Davenport."

Sometimes if you look real close, you can see a whole bunch of emotions going through a person's face, one after the other. My father knew who Peaches was, and that she was not some cute little pig-tailed thing that I sat beside in English class. At first, he looked surprised, then shocked, but when his eyes bulged a little I knew he felt jealous. He covered this up with a "What am I gonna do with my idiot son?" expression.

Banished to my room, I got out my Vaseline and an old sweat sock and thought about Peaches. Just remembering her lips on mine made me shoot off like Sputnik. The pile of homework on my desk kept me from doing it again.

I finished a page of algebra, conjugated some Latin verbs and answered six questions about Poe's "The Gold Bug." There was a social studies report due in two weeks; I'm a firm believer in planning ahead, so I pulled out my book and scanned the map of Africa. I looked it over three or four times when I found myself at the bottom of the continent at the squashed-up shape of Tanganyika, which looked like it was being squeezed by Kenya on top and Mozambique from below, all the while being pushed from behind by Uganda and the Congo right into the Indian Ocean. I decided that it must be a strong country just to survive.

My "T" encyclopedia volume said that Tanganyika was the home of Mt. Kilimanjaro, the highest peak in Africa and Victoria Falls. Its Serengeti Plain was filled with lions, cheetahs, giraffes, wildebeest, elephants and literally hundreds of other animals. Most of the people made their living by farming, and its main exports were cashews and coffee beans. The major city was Dar es Salaam, and Tanganyika had about 25 million inhabitants. That country seemed so exotic and fascinating. I couldn't wait to start looking for other sources.

Weariness from the excitement of the day overtook me and when I went to bed, I fell asleep as soon as I put my head down. When I awoke, my sheets and pajamas were soaked with sweat. An encounter with Peaches can have that effect on a guy.

Over Rice Krispies and bananas, I apologized to my parents and told them that Billy Matlock, Tim McCall and I got into a game of horse and when nobody was making any shots, we just kept going on and on, forgetting all about the time. I said that Peaches was a very nice girl, who would never do anything like that, at least with a guy three years younger than she was.

My mother looked at me with a blank expression; my father harumphed and said, "You're right about that." I thought it was a very stupid story, but they seemed relieved to hear it.

School and Peaches were about twenty minutes away. I tried to visualize how things were going to go between her and me. Naturally, we wouldn't make any big scene in the hallway, perhaps a quick peck or two by the lockers, then I could suggest lunch in the bleachers with no one else around. Maybe after we ate, we could continue what we had begun yesterday. I parked my bike in the rack in front of school and tried to feel as calm as possible as I walked to my locker.

After getting my books, I turned around and there was Peaches with a big, huge grin covering her face. This was much more than I had ever hoped. My heart was ready to burst like a geyser.

I thought I was going to get another big fat one right in front of the whole school. Instead, she grabbed my arm, leaned over and said, in a voice swollen with excitement, "Joey, I have to tell you something. Last night after you dropped me off, my mom sent me out to get hoagies for dinner, and when I was coming out of Sam's, this really groovy guy bumped into me. I tell you, Joey, we looked at each other and it was clickeroo! His name is Otto Sinclair, and he's 20 years old. We went to his car and talked for so long, my mother had to come out looking for me. We're going to the drive-in Saturday night. I feel like he's the guy I've been looking for my whole life. Isn't it great!"

I don't believe in crying, it's for girls and babies. But if I didn't fight with myself, I'd have started bawling like a three-year-old.

"Congratulations," I said, "I always thought you were way too mature for high school guys."

The comment really seemed to please her. "You're the greatest, Joey," she said, bubbling over. The bell rang; it was off to class.

Otto. Had a dull, stupid ring to it. He was probably an Elvis lover who mumbled about two words every half-hour. He smoked Luckies and had tattoos on both arms. His idea of dressing up was dungarees and a tee shirt. His hair had a pound of grease in it. What the hell was Peaches thinking? Didn't our kiss mean anything to her at all?

At lunch, my friends motioned me to join them in the caf, but I wanted no contact with either Peaches or her mother.

Walking out of school to the top row of the grandstand, I first watched a bunch of starlings peck at the grass on the football field and then two fat swollen clouds inching their way across the sky. It was so peaceful up there, so calm. Hurt was going from my stomach up to my brain in long, hot waves. I still refused to cry, but wanted to scream," Fuck you, Peaches!" at the top of my lungs. I thought about cutting Latin, but we were going to be covering the ablative absolute and I knew that was going to be on the big test. If I couldn't score with Peaches, at least I could score in class.

Walking back into school, I felt like a big bag of nothing. I mean who the hell was I to think that I could go with Peaches Davenport? I wanted to change my name to Joey Scarecrow because that's what I felt like; a stiff wind could have blown me to Tanganyika. I wondered how I was going to hide my feelings well enough from Peaches so that she wouldn't know how much her news had shattered me.

When the last bell rang, I walked down to Terry Malseed's locker. He had almost anything a guy would need: card decks with couples in different sexual positions, handlebar knobs with pictures of topless women, Lucky Strikes and Camels, rubbers and fireworks. You had to be careful what you bought from him, though, because his mouth was as big as an elephant's. Sometimes guys bought things from Terry just to make themselves look cool — that was pathetic.

"Yo, Joey," he said, "what can I do for you?"

I handed him three dollars and asked for two cherry bombs and an M-80. He looked around, reached into his locker and slipped them into the pocket of my parka. Running my fingers over the circular and cylindrical shapes, it made me feel better knowing I had some explosives. Whenever I feel frustrated, I try to shoot off fireworks. Sometimes I'll put them into an empty peanut butter jar just to watch the glass fly, or throw them down a sewer hole to hear a loud, ringing echo.

When I got to work, Old Man Sandler was really on the rag. He yelled at me for being fifteen minutes late and told me that after I finished stocking the cigar case, I was going to have to scrape gum from the bottom of the counters. Of all the things he paid me to do, this was the worst. It was very difficult to get that stuff off, my clothes got real dirty and I felt like a real gorp, lying down on the floor with a scraper in my hand.

About fifteen minutes into the job, I heard this breathless feminine voice call, "Joey!" I knew who it was, but didn't move. A few moments later, Peaches was tugging at my sleeve and there was nothing to do but come out from under. Otto was right beside her and boy, did I have this guy pegged. He was about six feet tall, with big arm muscles and a d.a. so pointy he could have stabbed someone with it. He was wearing a dungaree jacket and pants and dirty engineer boots. He looked like Elvis' third cousin. All happy and bubbly, Peaches did the introductions. Otto didn't extend his hand, just said, "Hi, kid," and stood there like a sullen statue.

"You've got to come and see Otto's car," Peaches said. "It's sooo cool!"

Outside on Lansdowne Avenue, I was prepared to see some old beat-up '50 Ford with nothing on it. What I did see was a candy-apple red '55 Chevy with skirts, silver mag wheels, two glass pak mufflers, white leather tuck-and-roll upholstery, four on the floor and a gold-plated steering wheel. The radio antenna was about fifteen feet tall with a beaver tail on the end, all the better to listen to the Geator with the Heater and Hy Lit. Two red dice hung from the rear view mirror. Who knows what he had under the hood, probably a jet engine or at least a 406. I had to admit it was the most cherry car I'd ever seen in my life. God Himself could have made it. Why do all the stupid-ass guys have the best cars?

"Pretty neat," I said.

"Beats the fuck out of anything in Deerfield County," Otto answered, shrugging.

Knowing that she really didn't appreciate that kind of language, I looked over at Peaches to see her reaction. Smiling away, she looked like Otto had just recited Shakespeare. He had to show he was such a big shot by saying "fuck" not "crap," like everyone else. A real numb-nut.

Back in the drugstore, Otto played "Don't Be Cruel" and "Be Bop A Lula" on the jukebox and started to pound the counter like it was an imaginary bongo, probably just the way he pounded his imaginary dick. He ordered a fried egg sandwich, "with a cuppa joe," smiling at Peaches like he was some kind of gourmet. They ate, for what seemed like forever, and when the Magic Couple got up and left, I heaved a great sigh of relief.

I was in love with Peaches Davenport because she was beautiful-looking, but I also appreciated her soul. The only soul Otto knew was on the bottom of his boots. I felt like she and I were like two wires, joined together, ready to conduct beautiful electricity, despite our age difference.

Obviously, she felt a much stronger charge with Otto, probably because of that damn car, and acted like a brainless jackass around him. I liked the fact that she was secretly smart. I liked the fact that she didn't want guys to curse around her. I liked the fact that it was a mystery as to whether she was doing it or not. The thought of these things would never occur to Otto. *Romeo and Juliet* honored two young people who died for love, but from what I'd just seen, love wasn't worth a walk down the street.

Going home down Baltimore Pike, I drove my bike behind the Wildman Arms apartments. There were some big metal barrels by the parking lot filled with trash. I lit a cherry bomb and threw it in; paper scattered everywhere and started to burn. I stood and watched the flames dart through the air, not caring if they caught on to something bigger, not caring if I got caught.

A week drearied by. I must have seen Peaches and Otto twenty times. He waited for her every day after school; they always went to Sandler's. When they weren't eating, they were sitting silently, driving around and around the main streets of Lansdowne. I've seen this phenomenon many times, and I just don't get it. Not saying anything at all is the new sexy thing? Geez.

Basketball season began, and the freshman team won games against Yeadon, Springfield and Interboro. I scored twelve points against Yeadon, all from outside jump shots. My report was coming due on Tanganyika.

In the cafeteria today, Becky Blake, one of the best-looking girls in the freshman class, put her hand on my arm and asked if I was going to the Lansdowne Theater on Friday night. And when I said yes, she smiled and said she'd meet me in the lobby. Under normal circumstances, this invitation would have sent me into a state of ecstasy. Becky was easily the best-looking girl in the ninth grade. All of the freshman guys lusted after her. She had long, sleek auburn hair that she always wore in a ponytail that went halfway down her back. Each day she tied it with a different color ribbon; today it was yellow. Her eyes were a dazzling brown and her skin looked shiny, soft and lustrous.

Becky was also very smart, a cheerleader and vice-president of the Ninth Grade Student Council. I've never seen a person as sure of herself as Becky. She never seemed to get upset about anything much. No running to the girls' bathroom with a Kleenex in her hand like the other girls.

In addition to all of these wondrous qualities, was her extremely hot body. Not voluptuous like Peaches, Becky was perfectly proportioned, her bust and ass sticking out at perfect angles. One day last month, she was wearing a translucent blouse and a sheer bra, and when she leaned back in her desk to yawn, showed two round, perfectly-shaped nipples. It was all I could do to keep myself from immediately running into the boys room.

Thinking about my good fortune, I felt like Mr. Blah. Becky was great and all, but she was no Peaches — a real woman in every sense of the word. Otto was too much of a jerk to last very long with her. She'd come back to me in a few weeks, all upset about something horrible Mr. Pseudo Elvis had done or said.

Friday night rolled around. I still didn't know whether I wanted to go to the movie or not. The old man was going to be watching Friday Night Fights, drinking beer and yelling at the TV. No fun at all.

After I bought my ticket, I saw Becky waiting for me in front of the concession stand, a big smile on her face. She was wearing tight Levis, a long-sleeved white blouse and a black belt with a big, gold buckle. After I bought a large bag of popcorn, she took my hand and we headed up to the balcony.

The movie was *Sweet September*, starring Troy Donahue and Tuesday Weld. Tuesday is hotter than the dog days of August, but Troy, I just don't get it. He's kind of fat and his goofy-looking hair hangs across his forehead like a big shaggy dog's. Girls still go gaga over him, just because they think they're supposed to, I guess.

Reading my mind, Becky said, "Troy Donahue always looks like he's constipated."

I laughed and added, "Is there a doctor in the house? That young man on the screen needs a laxative before his intestines come flying out of his stomach."

Becky started giggling like crazy. I thought she was going to lose it, but she pulled herself back together after about a minute or so. She turned and gave me another big, wonderful smile. She smelled like a forest just after a rain. I believe the fragrance was "Woodhue," a perfume that I bought my mother last Christmas.

We watched the show for about fifteen minutes. Becky began leaning on my shoulder. It was torture trying to figure out what to do. This sounds pretty weird, but it kind of felt like I was betraying Peaches. Becky leaned toward me with her eyes closed. I went ahead and kissed her. We started making out, but all I could think of was the woman I loved. When Becky opened her mouth, I stopped, leaned back in my seat and watched the terrible movie.

At Brown and Diller's soda fountain after the show, my friends began pestering me to tell them all the gory details about what had just happened. I told them that I was tired. They kept pushing for juicy stuff. Finally, Steve McChesney, the smartest person I have ever known, looked at me and said, "Nothing happened, and I know why."

Everyone's interest was piqued. I knew what he was going to say.

Mc Chesney straightened up in the booth and looked at me balefully. "It pains me to say this, but Joseph refused to involve himself with the wondrous Becky Blake because he is hopelessly in love with an unattainable senior girl, Peaches Davenport."

An audible gasp emanated from the booth. All the guys were looking at me like I had leprosy.

Jeff Cavendar grabbed my arm and shook it. "Have you gone entirely insane, Joey? Every guy in the freshman class wished they were sitting where you were tonight. You're like Captain Ahab, on a ridiculous quest that's going to end in disaster."

The discussion went on for another half-hour. I didn't agree or disagree with what was being said, and I didn't defend myself. It took a lot of will power not to open my ordinarily big mouth. The guys were still badgering me as we walked down Lansdowne Avenue. Maybe they were right, I thought as I walked home. There was only one Becky Blake. If she and I started going together, I would be King Shit of the Ninth Grade. Even if we broke up, which we probably would, I would have had the distinction of being with the Best of the Best. Intoxicating as that thought was, it didn't excite me much. Deep down as far as I could go, Peaches was the only woman I wanted. Impossible things happened all the time. Lindbergh flew across the Atlantic. Liz Taylor married Eddie Fisher, a Jewish kid from South Philly, where my father grew up. I *had* to follow my heart, even if, like Ahab, it led to a catastrophe.

On Monday morning, I passed Becky at her locker. She was looking very chipper, as always. When she saw me, she giggled and got a biology book and binder. Two other girls, Babs Lockhart and Trisha Madsen, came up to her. There seemed to be no point in stopping and trying to talk.

As I walked down the hallway, I heard a chorus of *"Joey, Joey Garden, King of the Make-Out Boys."* Turning around, the three of them were laughing hysterically. I guess I deserved that. Nobody said that being in love was easy.

In the summer, Darby Creek was hopping, but no one went there much at other times of the year. It was the best place I could think of to be entirely away from the rest of the world. Maybe I could figure out this Peaches deal or at least throw my M-80 at a frog or something. Pedaling my bike to Scottdale and Baltimore, I saw the creek: muddy and brown, moving slowly, like syrup and molasses mixed together. Leaping from rock to rock, I got over to the other side and sat down on an old log right by a clump of bamboo. The sky was gray. The whole place seemed unnatural and strange.

Pretty much out of sight, I was in full view of the railroad trestle. Someone had put a thick iron cable across the lowest support, which was about ten feet over the creek, so that people crossing could hold on and walk across without falling and hurting themselves. I was getting ready to light the big fire cracker, when I heard laughter. Looking through the bamboo stalks, I saw Otto and Peaches on the girder, making their way to the other side. She was in front, shrieking, pretending to be on a high wire.

About halfway over, Peaches stopped suddenly. Otto came up behind her and began to run his hands all over her breasts. I knew she was going to turn around and deck him, knock his ass right into the dirty water. Instead, she stuck her butt into his crotch and began to wiggle it around. If they could have done it on that narrow iron strip, I'm sure they would have.

I sat there immobilized, feeling like I'd been shot. This love stuff was no joke. Glowy feelings are great, but they don't last. My life was miserable. I had my friends thinking I was totally ludicrous. The ninth-grade girls thought I was a complete joke.

Peaches was in love with an absolute moron. I felt like an escaped convict surrounded by the state police.

There seem to be times in life when whatever secrets you've been keeping get put out like plates for dinner and however you might want a situation to turn out, it won't mean diddly-squat. This was one of those times.

Walking out from the clump of bamboo, I looked across Scottdale Road and saw Otto's candy-apple red chariot about a hundred yards away. It's still hard to figure out why, but I started walking toward it. Maybe I wanted to see Otto and Peaches chastely holding hands, I don't know. As I approached the car, there was some kind of motion in the back seat. When I got closer, I saw that it was Otto's big hairy ass going up and down like a piston. The mystery of whether Peaches was doing it or not was now solved. What was I supposed to do, applaud?

I turned to leave after finding out all I needed to know, but something made me stop. I walked back to the Chevy, took the M-80 out of my pocket, lit the fuse and lobbed it over the car's roof. After about five seconds, a huge boom rang out. Otto bolted out of the car, with his pants down around his ankles, his hard-on blowing in the breeze. I wanted to start laughing my ass off, but didn't want to make a bad situation worse.

Peaches came out from the other side of the car, pulling her underwear up under her skirt. Otto stared at me like a snake about to release its venom. "No little twerp is going to mess with my play," he thundered. "No little shit-ass is going to put his nose into where it don't fuckin' belong." He pulled up his pants, all the while staring at me like I was a gallon of puke.

Before he could launch another tirade and start kicking the shit out of me, Peaches got three inches in front of his face and yelled, "You cut it the hell out, Otto. He's just a kid."

"Little bastard followed us. He can't get into your pants, so he wanted to watch someone who could."

I actually started to cry a little bit. The last comment of Otto's threw Peaches into a fury and she started screaming at him. He yelled back and they really started to argue. I hightailed it out of there.

After dinner, I put the finishing touches on the report about my little African country, translated Latin from the Gallic Wars and finished three pages in my Spanish workbook. I fell asleep pretty easily and when I woke up, couldn't remember any of my dreams.

The next morning in social studies, the teacher called on me to give the report in front of the class. I brought up some maps and pictures of animals that I had cut out of *National Geographic*, put them on the chalk ledge and began my speech, "Tanganyika is a small country in southeastern Africa. It is the home of many wild animals like the giraffe, wildebeest, impala, elephant, cheetah, lion, leopard, and (to great laughter) the dik dik." After I mentioned each one, I showed how I thought they walked, loping across the front of the room for the giraffe, stalking like a cheetah. When I got to the dik dik, which is a small antelope, I did some short little bunny hops. Then I talked about how the people lived, the capital and all that other stuff. The class and Mr. Patrick loved it. He gave me an A+.

My friends wanted me to join them in the lunchroom to share in my triumph, but given what had happened yesterday afternoon, I didn't want to be with anyone.

As I sat in the last row of the bleachers, munching on my baloney and cheese, Peaches appeared on the other side of the field and began walking very slowly along the fifty-yard line. The sun was hitting her beautiful hair and powder blue sweater at just the right angle; she looked like a radiant star, Juliet coming to see her man, dumping a creep for true love. But as she got closer, I could see that her face was glum. She trudged up the stands, stopping at the third row before mine.

"Joey," she said, sitting down and facing the field.

"Hey, Peaches."

Pulling half a hoagie and a cream soda out of her big leather purse, she began to eat, taking very small bites. Without turning around, she said, "I guess you think I'm a real skank."

This made me feel very sad. "I could never think that way about you, Peaches. And I won't tell anyone what I saw."

"I know I was really dumb," she sighed, "usually I'm real careful. We broke up after you left. He wanted to go kick your ass, but I told him I'd track him down with Gully and his boys if he did. Guys... I just can't figure them out."

The picture of Romeo whining his little butt off, when he was banished after killing Tybalt, instead being grateful that he wasn't put to death, flashed into my mind. "I hope you're not pregnant," I said. "You're the greatest girl in the world. Nothing bad should ever happen to you."

She blushed, moved up three rows and sat right beside me.

"People think you're dumb, Peaches, but I know it's just an act. You're a good person. You're going to do a lot with your life. I wish I was your age so we could go out together."

By then, Peaches had tears running down her cheeks. "Why don't the guys I go out with talk to me like you just did, Joey? They just care about my body, not about me."

We started to hug. My kneecaps began to wobble.

"Let's go underneath the stands," she said. Taking my hand, we walked down about ten rows until we were on the track. We went to the back of the grandstand, with no one else in sight. The grass and weeds under the stands were still high.

Without saying anything more, Peaches took off her sweater and began unbuttoning her blouse. In a few seconds, she was standing less than a foot from me, wearing only a tight navy blue skirt and a white bra. My armpits began to fill up with sweat. Peaches unhooked her bra and took it off in one motion. Two perfectly shaped melon-sized breasts with large red nipples announced themselves, waiting for my touch.

"Come over here, Joey," she said, "and let me take care of you."

She held up her breast. For the next ten minutes, I sucked and sucked and sucked.

Part 4

Just A Game

Yesterday I had the Lansdowne High outdoor court completely to myself, unusual for a Saturday afternoon. The air was crisp with a few oversize clouds hanging around the pale blue sky. I dribbled to the right side of the basket and launched a jump shot fifteen to twenty feet away from the hoop. It would have been nice to have a bag of basketballs so I wouldn't have to run after the ball after every shot.

The first shot felt true when it left my hand and made a beautiful parabola, as Mr. Winters, my old geometry teacher, might have said. And down it went, right through the center of the hoop. I ran for the ball, took another shot and had the same result. Again. And again. Until I'd done something I never thought possible, make ten shots in a row that hit nothing but the cords. I stopped and listened to my breath softly inhaling and exhaling, and wondered if there was some invisible presence nearby. Man, this was spooky. I started to laugh out loud. How long could this go on? I tried again and the ball went through perfectly.

At that point, I was frankly bothered, so I took a haphazard shot with my left hand and it clanged off the rim. Sighing with relief, I continued to shoot the way I usually do, hitting one out of two, or close to it. Perfection is pretty frightening when you think about it; once you reach it, there's nothing left. One gets used to half-good and half-bad, all jumbled together. When a flash of pure brilliance occurs, like it just did for me, it can be discombobulating. An ordinary humdrum life can be kind of reassuring sometimes.

Zack Bolton was the only person I know who'd believe what had just happened. Zack is the kind of person who thinks that if you dedicate yourself and work hard, any goal is attainable. He's the best basketball player in the history of Lansdowne High. Better than the "Hawk," Jim Brady, who was All-Ivy at Princeton, or Archie Dryden, who was also All-Ivy for the Tigers. He weighs about 215, is exactly 6'4 inches tall and has perfectly defined biceps and thickly muscled legs. His black hair is long in the front but crewcut in the back. Zack's eyes move around a lot and his lips are often pursed, like he's always about to say something. I'm proud to call him my good friend.

When I reached his garage, Zack was trying to bench press three hundred pounds. His face was bright red and looked like a balloon ready to explode. Damn if he didn't do it — three times in a row. On the last one, he grunted like a water buffalo about to give birth.

"You're gonna kill yourself, Zack."

He slid off the bench, took a towel and rubbed it across his face.

"Nah. People who say that weightlifting is bad for basketball players are wrong. I can jump a lot higher than I used to and when someone from the other team challenges me under the boards, they're gonna remember it."

He worked out for about another half-hour. I know lifting, calisthenics and jumping rope are supposed to be very useful exercises, but they're as boring as homework. I benched a few and did some squats. Mostly, I spotted for Zack on his lifts. I decided to tell him about my encounter with perfection.

He nodded and smiled nonchalantly. "If you can pump them in like that in real games, we'll be that much tougher."

"You don't think I'm bullshitting you? I made over ten in a row, all nothing but net."

"I have never doubted your shooting ability, Joey. If you took yourself more seriously, worked out and played better defense, you'd challenge Tim Martin and become a starter."

"Easy for you to say, Zack."

"He's been bullying you for years. I know you outsmart him a lot, but that's not enough. A fat lip, a broken tooth or a black eye is a small price to pay for standing up to that jerk."

There it was again, hard work and courage, wonderful virtues that solve everything. I've never been very excited about getting my ass kicked, which is what Martin would surely do if I stood up to him. My talent in basketball is shooting, period. It's the only athletic skill I've ever had. Plus, I'm also kind of interested in my studies, as well as my girlfriend, Marilyn Thompson, my friends the Mugwumps, world politics and a bunch of other stuff.

During the summer, Zack worked out in the gym four hours a day, five days a week. He shot hundreds of jump shots, dribbled around chairs, dribbled with a ball in each hand and wore sunglasses to practice not looking at the floor when he dribbled. And he ran one court sprint after the other. The weirdest thing my demented friend did was jog up and down the stairs in the football bleachers with a twelve-pound shot put in each hand during a blistering heat wave. After he finished, he told me, "I felt like I had turned into a breeze, weightless, just flowing easily in every direction."

In the evenings, he played in two summer leagues, one in Southwest Philly, and the other in Upper Darby. He knows all the good high school players in Deerfield County and is better than every one of them.

Out of the blue, he said. "Lansdowne has never gone past the second or third round of Regionals. We gotta win the State championship. It's now or never."

A vision of Hercules carrying the world on his shoulder appeared in my mind. So many factors were involved in winning something that huge. I shuddered to think of what might happen to him if the team failed for some reason. "You make it sound like winning State is solely your responsibility, Zack."

"Aim high, think big, Joey. Otherwise, what's the point?"

I shook my head. *It's just a game*. Last time I told him that, he almost bit my head off. Nothing I said was going to change his attitude anyway. Zack is the anti-Hamlet, no dithering, brooding or overanalyzing for him.

He smiled a little and put on his sweatshirt. He said that the janitor was going to let him into the gym tomorrow, even though it was Sunday, and did I want to join him? I demurred. I had three essays due next week, three pages of *Candide* to translate and Marilyn wanted me to spend part of Sunday afternoon with her.

We said good-bye and as I walked home down Lansdowne Avenue, I wondered what it would be like to be as driven as Zack Bolton, focused on one goal at the expense of everything else in his life. I could not picture myself ever being like that, even a little bit. There's a singular purity about him that I don't see in many other people. Most others, myself included, were a mishmash of various qualities; he streaked through life like a comet, blinding everyone with his light.

Then I started thinking about all those balls I'd shot, the perfect arcs, the way they fell right through the middle of the hoop, like I was releasing birds from my hands into a welcoming sky.

At dinner that Monday evening, I mentioned that basketball season was going to start on Friday night. Mother regards basketball as a harmless little hobby of mine in which she has no interest. My father, who doesn't like any sport but boxing, sees me as an egghead with a superiority complex, who will never learn to do anything practical, like how to fix a transmission. I shouldn't have brought up the subject.

"Last year your mother and I went to a game. I don't think you played for more than five minutes."

"I didn't say you had to go to the games. The team is going to be very good this year, that's all."

"That's very nice, dear," Mother said, passing me a bowl of mashed potatoes. "We'll try to get to a game or two. But you can't forget about your academics. You have to get your application in for a National Merit Society scholarship and do extra studying for the SAT exam."

Same old Mother, she's been harping on this stuff since I started junior high, if not sooner. She even has my school picked out, the University of Pennsylvania, otherwise knows as *Penn*. It's in the Ivy League and about half an hour away, which makes it perfect in her eyes. She's way more invested in Penn than I am, but I think I might enjoy going there. The scholarship is important, because my parents couldn't come close to paying for an Ivy League school on a car mechanic's and assistant bookkeeper's salaries.

After putting a huge slab of meat loaf on his plate, Pop stared at me and said, "I hear you got a colored kid on the team this year."

"Yes, Pop, Calvin Newsome. He left Archbishop O'Connell because the coach there called him a nigger."

"Yeah, maybe the guy had a good reason. How good can a team be if one of the starters is a goddam moolie?"

"Wilt the Stilt Chamberlain seems to have done pretty well."

"You prove my point, hot shot. Wilt never won a title in his life, not in high school or college. He's just a showboat playing with the Globetrotters now."

Dear old dad was far from done. " Just to prove my point, this big-ass jungle bunny comes up to me today at the end of his shift, smelling like a gin mill and a sewage dump. It was all I could do to not vomit all over myself. 'Mr. Victor,' he said, 'I needs a new cab tomorrow morning. This one ain't working so well.' Excuse me, but maybe, Spook, if you didn't ride the clutch and strip the gears, it would be running just fine. What really fried my ass is that O'Malley, the head dispatcher, went along with it. He's a real nigger lover if I ever saw one."

At this point, my mother said, as she usually does when Pop goes off the deep end, "Victor, not at the table."

I learned long ago that when my father is in the middle of one of his rants, the best thing to do is leave him the hell alone. Tonight, though, looking at his smug, tired little jaw chomping on the food, made me furious. In old vaudeville shows, when an act was bombing, the stage manager would send out a big iron hook and yank the stinker from the stage. This was as good a time as any for my father to get the hook.

"If they didn't do that kind of stuff, Pop, you wouldn't have a job," I said, sounding as nonchalant as I could.

He mushed potatoes and peas together and looked at me. No challenges to Mr. Psycho allowed here.

"Maybe, one day, Smart Ass, when you have to get your head out of a book and actually work for a living, you'll understand what I have to go through every day to put food on the table for this family."

By now, Mother was just about wrenching her neck trying to signal to me to shut the hell up. I ignored her.

"At the A&P last summer, I swept the floors, got carts, stocked shelves, bagged groceries. It's not like I'm always at a tea party. If you're so *frustrated*, why don't you find another job, one with just *Italian* guys. It shouldn't be too difficult. You're always saying what a great mechanic you are."

I felt like Alice in *The Honeymooners* waiting for Ralph Kramden to bop her right in the kisser. But I was kind of enjoying watching him seethe. He moved the fork back and forth across his plate, trying to figure out a response.

"Go up to your room before I blow a fuse, Joey."

"Why? I was just asking a question."

Mother glared at my father and said, "Why does everyone have to walk on eggshells around you, Victor? Joey actually made some good points, a few of which we've discussed ourselves. He's going to sit here and finish his dinner, whether you like it or not."

My mom is a soft-spoken person, but when she feels like it, she can be as hard as pig iron. Pop knows that all too well. Why in the hell does he keep doing this over and over again? The color slowly drained from his face. He bent his head down and resumed eating very slowly. The explosion had been postponed, not cancelled.

My father comes from South Philly with the birth name Gardini, which Mother prevailed upon him to change to Garden. I've never been able to find out why. She did, however, agree to the first name of *Joey*, not *Joseph*, or *Josef*, or *Joe*, after the boxer Joey Giardello, who was from the old man's former neighborhood.

My best friends, Jeff Cavendar, Steve McChesney , George Williams and I have eaten lunch together almost every day since the beginning of freshman year. We call ourselves the Mugwumps, after a group of Republican senators who, in protest over financial corruption, supported a Democrat, Grover Cleveland, for president. To us, a Mugwump is a person who considers himself a cut above everyone else. We really believe that about ourselves. The four of us rank in the top ten of our class of 264. Steve is first, Jeff fifth, I'm ninth and George tenth. McChesney has applied to one university: Harvard. He got eight hundred in both SATs last year and has never gotten a grade lower than A+. School is ridiculously easy for him.

Ches spends a lot of time reading books of his own choosing on topics as diverse as military strategy, physics and astronomy. Jeff Cavendar, a clothes horse who would never be caught dead in dungarees, wants to go to Penn and eventually become a thoracic surgeon. George Williams is a math and science whiz, who barely tolerates subjects like English and Problems of Democracy.

The worst thing you can call a Mugwump is "bourgeois," which in our eyes means being conformist and shallow, unthinkingly going along with the crowd. Things we consider bourgeois are: fist fights, *American Bandstand*, *I Love Lucy*, *Life* magazine, cursing (most of the time), Betty Crocker cakes, Dinah Shore, Pat Boone, and much much more. We admire: JFK, J.D. Salinger, astronauts, Little Richard, Chuck Berry, the Skyliners and television dramas *Naked City* and *Playhouse 90*.

Many people at Lansdowne High find us to be a group of deplorable snobs. Before we begin lunch, we stand up and bow to each other before shouting "Mugwumps forever," crossing each other's arms and shaking hands before beginning to eat. If that isn't bad enough, we all started wearing brown Homburg hats with matching vests and ties last semester. George and I handled dressing like this for exactly one week. Getting called "sissy," "fruit," and "asshole" twenty times a day got old fast. Ches and Jeff, after a brief holdout, went along and grudgingly discarded the costume.

I'm the only one who plays a sport, which means I have to endure an unending stream of grief. Today, Jeff advised me once again that basketball is a "simian pursuit" and that "running around a gym in my underwear was beneath someone of my advanced intellectual stature."

"Girls like it," I answered as the other two chortled. Jeff and I are very competitive. I know that he is jealous of my relationship with Marilyn and with me being on the team, even though he has no athletic ability and has not gone to a Lansdowne sporting event since he was a freshman.

"Speaking of girls," George said, "Isn't Jacqueline Kennedy a real dish?"

"I wouldn't kick her out of my *boudoir*," Ches added in a regal tone.

"You'd have to get a bulldozer to pick up all the Tastykake wrappers off your bed first," Jeff said, to great laughter.

McChesney, in response, opened his third package of Tastykake chocolate cupcakes. Steve was about sixty pounds overweight; it's the only thing that kept him from taking over the world. When we got on him for his eating habits in the past, his response was always, "Genetics, genetics," meaning that since his parents are both quite hefty, he is too. It's nonsense. He doesn't need to eat those goddam cupcakes. As much as we chided and ridiculed him, Ches remained an impregnable fortress who allowed no one, least of all the Mugwumps, to get under his huge folds of skin.

"Going along with what Jeff just said," McChesney added, "I think you should give up basketball and join the High-Q team, Joey. With your knowledge of literature and history, Jeff and George's expertise in math and the sciences, along with my extensive acumen in just about any field, we could be the best team on the whole East Coast. That will look a lot better on your resume than basketball."

I could see his point. Despite Zack's belief that I could be a starter on the team, I *know* I can do well at Hi-Q, and that we would be genuine contenders for a state or national title, a great thing to include on my college applications. Mother would be ecstatic with the change.

"Too bad there are scheduling conflicts, Ches," I answered, "otherwise I could do both. I'll give you an answer in a few days."

"Oh, by the way, Joseph, how's Victor?" he asked, wiping chocolate from his lower lip. "Every time I come into your house, I think he wants to kick the holy bejesus out of me."

Jeff ran his hands up and down his stomach like my old man does and barked, "Hangin' around with those goddam Mugwumps alla time, Joey. Pretty soon you're gonna turn into a dictionary and they're gonna put you up on a shelf. Whyn't you hang out with some normal kids? Sometimes, I think you'd be better off going around with niggers than those fruitcakes."

For a few seconds, I thought I *was* listening to my father, Jeff was that good. The other guys were in hysterics.

"Screw you guys," I retorted, "George, your parents look like they haven't had relations in at least ten years. People in your family don't walk, they waddle, McChesney. Jeff, your parents have the worst taste in the world, an entire basement decorated with zebra skin wallpaper and huge pictures of Frank Sinatra."

Even though I felt I gave as good as I got, I did not like it when the Mugwumps made fun of Pop. They often compare him to Curley of the Three Stooges. Physically, Curley and my father are a lot alike, short and bald except for two patches of steel wool on either side of their round domes. I don't tell the Mugwumps that their ridicule hurts my feelings. And I surely don't tell them that I think Curley has a lot more class than dear old Dad.

Being a virgin has become a huge annoyance, kind of like still having an appendix, a useless organ that's not missed when it's gone. Last spring, I could have gotten rid of my virginity, but didn't. Maryann Montrose invited me over to her house, saying that her parents were out of town. She'd liked me for a number of years. When a girl looks at you constantly and hangs on every word you say in class, it's a pretty strong clue. I've always thought she was okay, but I was just starting to go out with Marilyn.

She invited me up to see her bedroom to "see her paintings." I had heard some talk that Maryann was kind of loose, that it wasn't too difficult to get her to take off her shirt and maybe some other garments. Maybe I was too much of an idealist, but I needed more of a reason than simple lust to walk up those stairs. Maybe it was a bad decision, but I said I had to get home for dinner. She doesn't talk to me much any more and looks away whenever I walk by.

Marilyn hit me like a sunbeam at high noon. I always liked her and thought she looked great with her long shiny black hair, tight skirts and white blouses. We were in a lot of classes over the years. One day, I grabbed her books and walked her home from school. Something happened; I'm not sure exactly what. That Friday night we made out in the balcony at the movies and have been pretty much inseparable ever since. Whenever we're together, life becomes much more vivid and alive. I can tell her just about anything. She never puts on airs or acts phony. Sometimes she'll suddenly get emotional, like when she sees a dead bird on the sidewalk, but otherwise, she's usually on a pretty even keel. Marilyn likes to take charge of what we're going to do or where we're going. I don't mind at all. If being in charge makes her happy, I'm fine with it.

I can't hide my real feelings from her by getting sarcastic or clamming up. She will have none of that. Marilyn will challenge teachers when they cop an attitude and avoids jealous spats with other girls. She doesn't like it at all when I put down other people. I don't know why, exactly, but lately I've begun to worry that I won't be able to live up to her expectations and that she'll dump me. Even though I know that's probably not really true, I can't shake the feeling.

As far as the physical stuff goes, she's a Catholic and doesn't want to commit any big sins. We kiss and hold hands for long periods of time. I can't say I don't want to do more, but up until recently, making out has been enough for both of us. A few weekends ago, as we were sitting on her living room sofa after her parents had gone out, she put my hands on her breasts. I thought we were both going to explode.

Last Tuesday, when we got to her house, both of her parents were gone. That meant, according to an agreement I made with Mrs. Thompson, I had to leave the house. Instead, we sat down on the sofa in her basement and began torridly making out. I put my hand inside her blouse and unhooked her bra. Things accelerated from there. Both of our shirts were soon off. Marilyn got up from the sofa and unzipped her skirt, letting it fall to the floor. "I just can't wait any longer, Joey," she said, pulling me down on top of her. I got up and removed the rest of my clothing. The moment I'd been waiting for had arrived. I must have wondered what she looked like naked a thousand times, and now there she was, ready to open herself to me in every way.

I simply couldn't go through with it and sat frozen on the edge of a sofa cushion, a million thoughts racing through my mind. What would happen if she got pregnant? Was I really ready to take this big step? Was I ugly with my clothes off?

My hesitation killed the moment. Marilyn stared at me like she'd just been stabbed before saying, "Joey, this is what I thought you wanted." She turned her head away and began to cry. For someone who is usually pretty glib and verbal, I had no words at all.

As we started to put our clothes back on, we heard Mrs. Thompson pull into the garage. When she entered the basement carrying two grocery bags, we were both sitting on the sofa with Marilyn's powder blue panties lying on the floor.

"The two of you are going to have to come upstairs," she said, trying to keep her voice even, "and we're going to have a nice long chat about this."

I decided to make the worst decision of my life, got up, put on my coat and walked out the cellar door. Marilyn's sobs when I jogged down her driveway were like metal spikes driven into my soul. As I made my way home, the picture of her lying naked with her legs open was so beautiful it made me weep. Unable to walk any further, I sat down at the base of a sycamore tree in front of the Ruess's house. Sobbing, I felt like the raw sewage that ran through nearby Darby Creek. There was no way Marilyn or her parents would ever forgive me for my cowardice. My value in the world was less than zero.

When I saw Marilyn in school the next day, she pulled me into an empty classroom. "I thought you were the man I was going to be with for the rest of my life, Joey," she chastened. "The way you left my mother and me yesterday was something I didn't think you were capable of. But she and I talked about it for a long time, and we both agreed that if you came over and discussed what happened, she can overlook you being so afraid, and we can keep seeing each other."

I should have felt enormous relief, sucked up my courage and agreed to the plan. Instead, a weak, reedy voice came out of my mouth and to my utter disbelief, I said, "I'll have to think about that, Marilyn."

She stared at me, rolled her eyes and stormed off. I left for class. Three days have passed and I've not been able to muster up the courage to go and see Mrs. Thompson. I think I'm ready to walk over to Albemarle Avenue and get it over with, but every time I start, a giant fist comes out of my stomach and holds me back. I know it's the right thing to do, even if I never go out with Marilyn again.

A man will do anything to keep the woman he loves. I have a long way to go before I reach manhood, if I ever do. Maybe I'll be a virgin for the rest of my feeble existence. My life right now is a pile of stinking crap. There's nothing inside me. Joey Garden is 100% Scarecrow. The Mugwumps wanted my answer about the Hi-Q team tomorrow. I haven't been able to figure out anything. Nothing seems to be the only thing I'm capable of right now.

Lansdowne High won its first basketball game, no problem. Even though Montclair High hadn't been any good for years, Zack paced the locker room like a death row prisoner waiting for the electric chair. "We gotta shut them down on defense," he almost shouted. "Don't give them a point." He needed to calm down. No one said anything to him, not even Coach.

Montclair was down by fourteen at the end of the first quarter. Martin was hitting his jump shots, the twins were stealing the ball, Smooth had two dunks; Zack drove the lane for three layups. It was poetry. Hard to imagine any other high school team in Pennsylvania playing better than we were.

Coach put me in right before halftime. Zack and Dave Irwin set screens and I made three jumpers in a row. Very exhilarating. The guy I was guarding, who was pretty quick, gave me a head fake and went right down the lane for two. Zack gave me a dirty look as I brought the ball upcourt. I don't know what he was so worried about; we were ahead by 24 points.

"Defense, defense, Joey," Zack snapped at me as we headed for the locker room at halftime. The team had played great. I hadn't missed a shot. After the game, I was going to have to talk to him about his nit-picking.

During the first four minutes of the second half, Lansdowne scored sixteen straight points before Montclair called a time out. Dan Irwin and I came into the game. I made four long-range shots, but my man got past me a few more times. At the end of the third quarter, we were up by 30 and Coach cleared the bench. We won in a walk, 72-36.

Inside the locker room, Zack looked like his mother had just died. "You played no defense tonight, Joey," he steamed, his face burning red. "Number Eight dribbled right past you and scored every time he came down the court."

"Hey," Dave Irwin chimed in, "We all know Joey's strength is scoring, Zack. If you haven't noticed, we just kicked Montclair's ass."

He smacked a locker door shut and stomped into the shower.

"What a psycho," Martin said, taking off his uniform and tossing it onto the floor.

Dan Irwin was having none of it. "Zack may have been overreacting, Tim, but he just wants everyone to play their best game every night."

I saw Zack in the lobby and motioned him over to the trophy case.

"I'm just not that good on defense, Zack," I said. "The game was never in doubt. How are you going to react when we play one of the tougher teams? You need to learn to calm down."

"You should quit the team if you don't want to play defense, Joey. Because if you keep playing like you did, I'm going to make your life miserable. Tonight was just a warm-up."

"Zack, *it's just a game*."

He looked at me like I was some kind of mass murderer. "For a person who's supposed to be so smart, Joey, you're pretty damn stupid."

He had really gone off the rails. I started to think about another answer, but before I could say anything more, he'd turned around and left. I wasn't going to run after him, the hell with it.

Walking down Essex Avenue toward home, Tim Martin came running up behind me.

"Zack Bolton's a maniac, Joey," he shouted out. "He never should have gotten on you like that. Every game isn't for the state title. Montclair was a pushover, and everyone knows it."

There are things in the world I just don't want to exist, such as mosquitoes, acne, dandruff, halitosis, Dick Clark and Tim Martin. I've hated him since we first met in kindergarten, and he was the bossiest kid on the playground. He's stupid, narrow-minded and only out for himself. But one thing Martin has going for him is that he is a good athlete. At about 6'1" and 180 pounds of solid muscle, he is a starter on the football, basketball and baseball teams. His parents go to all the games and cheer obnoxiously for every miniscule thing he does. It doesn't help that Mr. Martin is the head of the Lansdowne Borough Council. They think their precious son is the greatest kid ever to walk the earth. I think he's about the worst.

"He was right, Tim, I should have tried harder to guard my man. It's a bad habit to get into, even against an easy team."

A sneer crawled slowly across Martin's face. " I knew you'd say something like that, Joey. I was trying to be your friend."

A first. I guess I should have been honored. "I'll handle it on my own, Tim," I answered, hoping to end this quickly.

Martin shook his head before saying, "You're not just a pussy, Joey. You're like a pussy when a girl is having her period, all smelly and useless. You'll never have any balls if you let people walk all over you like that. "

Usually, Martin's phosphorescent bullshit bounces right off me, but given all that's happened with me lately, his words bothered me. Maybe for the first time in his life, Tim Martin was right about something. I haven't been measuring up. As each day passes without talking to Mrs. Thompson, I dig myself deeper into a hole. The Mugwumps continue to badger me about the Hi-Q team. And with Zack justifiably dragging me over the coals tonight, I'm a total zero in every area of my life.

When I got home, Pop was the only one up. He was watching a replay of the Jake La Motta/ Sugar Ray Robinson middleweight championship fight. He thinks La Motta is the greatest fighter who ever lived. I think Sugar Ray is the most graceful, fluid athlete I've ever seen.

As I sat down beside him on the sofa, Pop was taking swings in the air, yelling, "Thatta way, Jake! Tire the black bastard out. He can't knock you down; he'll never get you down!"

It didn't seem to matter that he knew Robinson was going to win the fight. Even though he was never knocked out, La Motta had lost four out of his five fights with Sugar Ray.

A commercial came on for Gillette Blue Blades. Pop leaned back on the sofa and took a long swig of Ballantine beer. "La Motta, Joey," he said in a nearly breathless voice, "the guy's indestructible. Robinson's been hitting him with uppercuts to the chin, jab after jab to the kidneys, left hand smashes to the head, even a few low blows. And after fourteen rounds, he's still standin'."

"His face is covered with blood; it looks like he can barely walk. Is that the secret of life, being able to get off the canvas?" I asked.

He smiled as he drained the bottle. "It might be, kid. It just might be."

"Well what's the damn point? When you get back on your feet, you just get knocked down again. It's like Sisyphus pushing a boulder up a hill and when it just about gets to the top, it rolls back down again."

"Anything's better than lying down and giving up, that's all I gotta say, Joey. And who the hell is this Sizefuss, any way."

The old man began watching the fifteenth round. Why in the hell was I trying to discuss this stuff with him anyway?

I was the first one at the table for lunch. McChesney soon arrived with a tray of food and his standard three packages of chocolate cupcakes. Jeff was next, natty in a brown corduroy blazer with a striped dress shirt and solid green tie. George was next, sitting down and taking an egg salad sandwich, a bottle of apple juice and an orange out of his bag.

I'd been looking forward to our meeting because I wanted to find out from Ches what was going to be on the big Trig test. He knows without fail what Mr. Duncan is going to ask before he asks it. Without him, my grades in Math would be below sea level, instead of the solid gentleman's "B" I've been maintaining.

"So, pray tell, Grand Mugwump," I asked, turning to him as he chomped on a cupcake, "what hoops is Duncan going to have us jump through on tomorrow's test?"

"I think he's going to emphasize inverse sines, for sure. His pea brain will think that's rather adventurous. And, of course cosines and valences, as a way of being generous to the slower students."

George chortled. "His jaw dropped down to his navel when you finished the last test in less than ten minutes."

"I was thinking of holding onto my paper for a little longer so as not to make him feel badly. But, you know, fellow Mugwumps, *noblesse oblige*. Of course, Duncan is Einstein compared to that joke of a Physics teacher, Walter Trump. The guy has never even heard of either the Manhattan Project or neutron beam spectography."

"I've never heard of them either, Ches," I said. "Not everyone knows about physics like you do."

"A teacher of physics should know about the atom being smashed, Joseph. It happened during World War II. Trump went to some backwater teachers' college upstate that's fifty years behind the times. They needed someone here to take over physics after Bollander retired, and he was available. An utterly pitiful choice."

Ches smiled at us sanctimoniously and put a whole cupcake into his mouth. He's an egomaniac, but backs up everything he says. Duncan is always looking at him during Trig class, worried that he just made some kind of mistake. Mr. McChesney is a physicist for General Electric and taught his son the basics of calculus in seventh grade. The two of them have chess games that go on for days on end.

Jeff chugged some chocolate milk before asking, "Hey, Joey, are you and Marilyn on the outs? I've seen the two of you walk past each other in the hallway three times with nary a wayward glance."

Jeff's interest was not suprising. I'd like to think that because we are good friends, he won't make a move.

The Mugwumps, especially McChesney, have always been way too interested in my love life, given that I'm the only one who's had girlfriends. This was too raw to get into and besides, it was none of their goddam business.

"It's really nothing to be concerned about, Jeff."

"Just asking, Joey."

"You know, Joseph," McChesney added, "Mugwumps stick together; your problems are our problems.

"If you would stop eating cupcakes and go out on a date, Ches, you'd know that some things between a guy and a girl are private."

He emitted a long sigh. "Oh, aren't we prickly and thin-skinned today."

"Yes, we are," I answered.

I don't know why I blurted this out at this moment, but I did. "Oh, and by the way, gentlemen, I've decided to stick with basketball. We're going to be very good this year and I want to be part of that."

The three of them looked at me like I was some kind of weird animal in the zoo they had never seen before. "Joey," George said, in an exasperated tone, "we can be Hi-Q champions for the entire East Coast with you on the team. We all know you're going to be spending most of basketball season on the bench. You need to reconsider your choice."

"Well, that's what I'm doing and you guys are going to have to deal with it."

None of us said very much for the rest of lunch period, a very unusual occurrence. George had hit the nail on the head. I probably wasn't going to be making much of a contribution to the basketball team. Being on a winning Hi-Q team would help my chances for an academic scholarship. It'd be the smart move to drop hoops. Sometimes, though, you make decisions and don't know the reason why.

As a result of the discussion in the cafeteria, I decided that today was the day to go and see Mrs. Thompson and take care of the mess I had created. We had a game that night, so there was no basketball practice. I went over what I was going to say as I walked to Marilyn's house: *I'm very sorry about all of this, Mrs. Thompson. You put your trust in me and I let you down. And I especially apologize for walking out on you and Marilyn. That was a cowardly thing to do. I'm sincerely sorry about all of this and hope you will allow us to begin seeing each other again.*

It was plenty cold as I walked to the Thompson house with a scarf around my neck, earmuffs and my gloved hands jammed into my pockets. Marilyn and her mother were compassionate, forgiving people; they were sure to be understanding.

Standing in front of 147 Albemarle for a few moments, I jumped from one foot to the other. I started up the front steps and stopped. My emotions were paralyzed. Mrs. Thompson would open the door and I'd be tongue-tied. I might even start drooling. Not only would she see me as a coward, but as a blithering idiot as well. Walking backwards down the steps, as soon as I felt the sidewalk beneath my feet, I took off. Running across the Ardmore Avenue Field all the way to Willowbrook Avenue, I knelt down by a telephone pole, feeling naked and ridiculous, tears gathering in the corners of my eyes. Had I become a person with no character at all? Someone whose entire life was going to be a wretched failure? I remembered a line from *Hamle*t as I began walking home submerged in gloom: "…'tis bitter cold, And I am sick at heart."

Right after I got inside my house, the phone rang. It was Marilyn. "You're such a guppy, Joey," she said and hung up the phone. Mother called for me to help in the kitchen. I wanted to jump inside a garbage can and stay there.

It was a good thing there was a game the next day, because if I continued to brood, I might not have made it through the night. Plymouth was a rich school near the Main Line. Their sports teams usually weren't very good. I can't remember the last time we lost to them. Yet Zack was sitting in the last row of the bus with his arms folded across his chest, not interacting with anyone. We hadn't talked since the blowup. And I've been trying harder to play defense. In practice, on Wednesday, I even blocked Martin's jump shot, a first. But it's not coming easily. It's hard to start doing something you've avoided for a very long time.

Coach put me in at the beginning of the second quarter. We were only ahead by eight points. My man, number 14, was their leading scorer. I got down in a crouch when he got the ball and looked at his navel as we've been taught to do. I tried to make myself aware of where the ball was at all times. *See the ball*, as Coach said over and over again in practice. Fourteen hit one jump shot. Otherwise, I dogged this guy so hard I was drenched in sweat. The problem was that I was concentrating so much on defense that it affected my ability to shoot. After missing five jumpers, Coach replaced me with Martin.

In the second half, the same pattern continued. My man didn't score and I had only one fast-break layup. Zack sat down beside me on the bench. Lansdowne was up by 20 and the game was no longer in question.

"That's more like it, Joey," he said. "The shots will come. Just keep doing what you're doing."

His words were like a warm balm over my body. Finally, I had done something right.

At the beginning of Advanced English, Mrs. Childress stood in front of the class and asked, "What makes Hamlet a tragic hero?"

We'd been reading the play for two weeks. I'd never been so entranced by a work of literature. The Mugwumps and I had already had a few skirmishes about the Dark Prince. This was going to be interesting.

McChesney spoke first as he usually does, leaving the rest of the class to try to keep up with his deep, complex thinking.

"I vote a resounding no," he said, imperiously. "Aside from being eloquent beyond belief, he spends most of the play picking at his wounds, twisting his mind into a thousand knots, showing enormous disregard for everyone but himself. At the end, he finally acts and it leads to the death of almost all the major characters. He's a self-absorbed weakling. There's nothing heroic about him, nothing at all."

Ches' tirade had upset me. I tried to think of a counter argument.

Before I could speak, Jeff chimed in. "Yes, I agree. Even after hearing from his father's *ghost*, he can't act. He prolongs everything for such a long time, by the time he actually kills his uncle, I could have cared less. And asking his mother, Gertrude, if she enjoys French-kissing Claudius, if that's not sick, nothing is sick."

Now I was genuinely pissed off. "Wait a minute, here," I almost shouted. "Who wouldn't be paralyzed if someone found out, three months after their father died, that their uncle had killed their father so he could marry their mother. Hamlet was living in a moral cesspool and was just as infected as everyone else. So it took him a while to figure what to do. Hamlet is a hero, because even though he had to struggle against weakness and fear and took forever to accomplish his goal, he eventually succeeded." I turned and looked at Marilyn, who was sitting in the back of the room. When our eyes met, she looked down at the floor.

"Well stated, Joey," Mrs. Childress said, smiling.

But Ches was having none of that. "Narcissism is never heroism," he exclaimed. Just about everyone in the class took a side, and a heated discussion took place for the rest of the period. Best English class of the year, and I had held my own against a near-genius.

The discussion continued at lunch. George even got into the act, saying, "Hamlet is simply weird, Joey. All those stupid speeches that don't mean anything. Plus, he has no feelings when Ophelia drowns herself or when he kills Polonius, a man who has never done him any harm."

Ches smiled and added, "So correct, George. We could go on and on and on, Joseph. You make a grievously faulty argument."

I was not quitting, no way at all. "What you gentlemen are forgetting is that every single person in Hamlet's life betrays him: his mother, his uncle, his weak girlfriend, his college friends, Rosencrantz and Guildenstern. Think of how you would feel if something like that happened in your lives. Like I said in class, Hamlet eventually avenged his father's death. He's sloppy and he's complicated, but he finishes the job, the only help coming from his father's ghost. I'd like to see one of you guys do something that monumental."

Things were getting a bit heated at this point, and about to get worse. Jeff said, "Did you see the way Childress smiled when Joey stuck up for the Twisted Prince? It's easy to make an argument that the teacher supports."

"If that's the best you can offer, Jeff, just fuck off."

No one had ever talked to another Mugwump in this fashion, even though we insult each other and our respective families to death. My three friends stared at me in stunned silence.

"And another thing, gentlemen. I'm not doing the Mugwump handshake any more; I think it's stupid."

I'd wanted some courage and I'd found some. Hamlet. Hamlet. Hamlet. He's a screw-up and a mess. But like one of the fighters Pop is so crazy about, he perseveres. Perhaps the old man is onto something.

I can't remember the last time I cared about Christmas, maybe when I was ten and got a BB gun. I was only able to use it a few times under strict supervision before forgetting I even had it. We don't go to church. The main Christmas tradition in the Garden household is having a big breakfast before opening presents. Mother gets up at seven and cooks for about an hour. We have fresh-squeezed orange juice, waffles with hot maple syrup, bacon, Habersett's sausage and scrapple, eggs cooked any way you want them, raisin toast and butter, and Pillsbury cinnamon rolls covered with sugary white syrup. I usually eat so much, I can barely get up and walk to the living room, where our presents sit underneath the tree.

I got the old man Ring Magazine's *History of Boxing*. His eyes lit up as he removed the wrapping paper. Mother can be hard to shop for, but she seemed to genuinely like the bracelet filled with multi-colored stones I got for her. I pretended to like the Phillies jacket Pop bought me. It's maroon with brown leather sleeves, instead of the usual red-and-white. I guess he thought it was cool. The Mugwumps would banish me for good if I ever wore something that bourgeois to school.

Mother got me *The Complete Works of William Shakespeare*, which was an exciting gift. I also got a navy blue crewneck sweater, some dress slacks and a pair of black desert boots. It would have been nice to get a check paying for my first year of college, but no such miracle occurred. Pop got Mother a pearl necklace and a jumbo-sized Whitman's Sampler. I could tell she didn't like the candy, but she smiled and thanked him anyway. Mother's been gaining weight and chocolate is her weakness. I'm not so sure how much she's been enjoying life lately. She spends a lot of time reading novel after novel about New York's upper crust by James Marquand and Louis Auchincloss, who is Jackie Kennedy's cousin. All those stories about martinis and stock deals, as if Mother prefers that fictional world to the one she resides in. But this morning, our good mood persisted. I wish every day were Christmas.

Feeling restless, I put on the new jacket and went out for a walk, even though the temperature was less than twenty degrees. After crossing Baltimore Pike, even though I didn't plan to, I walked down Windermere to Albemarle and found myself standing in front of Marilyn's house again.

I could see through the front windows that everyone was sitting by the fireplace, laughing and opening presents. I so badly wanted to be inside there with them. Realizing how ridiculous I'd look if someone noticed me, I got the hell out of there, fast. I may be pathetic, but not that pathetic. Tears started sliding down my face as I continued walking briskly down Windermere. There's definitely a penalty for missed opportunities.

The next day, the basketball team gathered on the front steps of Lansdowne High. A big black charter bus sat on the street, ready to take us to our state capital and the Harrisburg Invitational High School Basketball Tournament. We were going to be staying in a Holiday Inn and eating all of our meals there. I had never stayed in a hotel and I'd never been to Harrisburg, even though it's only two hours away from Lansdowne.

I walked past the cheerleaders to the rear of the bus and took a window seat right before the last row. Zack sat down beside me.

Martin had a transistor radio turned on to the Hy Lit show on WIBG. I hoped he wouldn't play "The Twist" by Chubby Checker, since I'm beyond sick of that song. "I'm Sorry" by Brenda Lee, another tune I hate, came on, followed by two excellent choices, "Tonight's the Night" by the Shirelles and "Wonderful World" by Sam Cooke. Black people have the best songs, with Buddy Holly and the Everly Brothers being the exceptions to that rule.

Zack moved around in his seat, full of his usual agitation. 'This is really big, Joey," he said. "The teams we've beaten so far have been a bunch of patsies. Finally, we're gonna face some real competition."

"Yeah, who's the best team, Zack?"

"McKeesport, by far. They have a center, Curtis Wilkerson, who's 6'9" and a high school All-American. They also have a real good guard, Jim Hall. If we play them, it'll be for the championship."

I half-listened as Zack went on and on about the other teams in the tournament. We passed one farm after another. Even though the fields were dry and barren, the red barns, many with Amish hex symbols over the doors, shone like jewels on the Pennsylvania countryside. It was hard to stop staring at Marilyn's shiny black hair as she chatted animatedly with Barbara Turley. She was probably talking about what a great Christmas she had, and how her mother loved the new terrycloth bathrobe with sunflowers all over it that she bought for her. I'd rather be called an asshole than a "guppy," a tiny little nondescript fish swimming around a little bowl, going nowhere.

The bus pulled into the Holiday Inn parking lot and parked by the main entrance. We disembarked and walked into the lobby, which was very small, with a potted palm tree on each side of the reservation desk and not much else. Coach motioned us over and began handing out room keys. I was hoping I'd be rooming with Zack, but my worst fear became reality; I was stuck in a room with Tim Martin.

He smirked at me before we picked up our suitcases and began walking to Room 108. Inside, Martin took off his shirt and began walking around the room, flexing his biceps. Deciding that he wanted the bed by the window, he collapsed on it and said, "You're really lucky to have Tim Martin as a roommate, Joey. I have to admit that I was kind of disappointed when Coach said your name instead of Mac's. But then I realized that Coach put us together so my toughness would rub off on you."

I stared hard at Martin's face to see if there was a trace of irony or sarcasm, but he was as serious as a car accident. I took my clothes out of my suitcase and filled up the top bureau drawers. I brought along my *Collected Shakespeare* and began re-reading *Hamlet.*

"Aw, man," Barton moaned, "Cindy's with Helene Becker in Room 208 right on top of us. I wish she was sitting on top of my face right now. Oh, baby, oh baby, ooohh baby! It's been four or five days since I've had some hot pussy, Joey. It's killin' me!"

The only things on television were the Pinky Lee Show and soap operas, so I turned it off. Every time I began reading the play, Martin started singing very loudly or made more moronic comments. Coach said we were to stay in our rooms until 4:30, when we were to leave for the pregame meal.

An idea occurred to me, which I immediately dismissed as insane. Then Martin began writhing on his bed, crying out "Cindy," over and over, which quickly made me reconsider. If I was forced to spend any more time with this dimwit, I was going to do something that would get me thrown in jail. Every cell of Martin's body cried out, *I'm stupid!* Something drastic had to be done.

Helene "The Machine" Becker had the worst reputation of any girl at Lansdowne High. The list of guys who said they had her would fill up a bulletin board. My guess was that they gave Helene a line about being in love with her, got what they wanted and split. She probably thought that sooner or later, one of them might be telling the truth, so she kept on trying.

Helene hung around with tough girls: Theresa Mattolini, Gabby Sinclair and Dottie Remlinger. They were usually with Gully and his boys: Tommy DeAngelis aka the Mole, Kit Lambert, Skeeter Fremont. The stereotype was that they were all a bunch of stupid lowlifes, getting ready to live behind bars forever. Helene and the Mole, however, were both extremely intelligent. I knew this from watching them in classes over the years; both were very alert and paid close attention to whatever the teacher said. But they never asked questions or joined in any discussions because in their crowd, they'd be subject to ridicule. Helene would often stop me after English class and ask about why I thought a character did something, or what a line in a Shakespearean sonnet meant.

One thing about her that no one else seems to notice is that's Helene is sad. It's not easy being the school slut. She walks around a bit hunched over, seldom smiles, and usually looks like she's daring someone to mess with her. Maybe the girl's P.E. teacher, Mrs. Cleese, figured this out and got her on the cheerleading squad, giving Helene a chance to redeem her bad reputation.

Martin was continuing to gyrate all over the bed. It looked like he was ready to whip it out and start pounding away.

"Hey, Tim," I said, sitting down on the edge of his mattress. "I can see how much you really want Cindy. And I'm not so enthused being trapped in the room here for the rest of the afternoon. Why don't you call her? She can come down to be with you and I can go see Helene."

Martin bolted up from his prone position and began to laugh like a drunken hyena. "You and Helene Becker? You gotta be kidding me, Joey. She'd break you right in half, if you even figured out where to put that little weenie of yours. That's the funniest thing I've heard since the last Red Skelton Show."

"You're probably right, Tim. But let me worry about that. Our rooms are right at the end of the hallways. I can sneak upstairs, and Cindy can come down here. We have two-and-a-half hours before the team has to meet in the lobby. It's a cinch."

Martin looked like a wolf staring at a pork chop. I knew that he loved getting away with stuff and bragging about it afterwards.

Rolling across the bed, he picked up the phone and asked for #208. It was not a long negotiation. Martin turned to me grinning and said, "You can't back out now, Joey. It's on."

"Great," I said, feeling anything but, and headed for the door.

"Give us at least an hour," Martin said. "That'll give me a chance to get my rocks off two or three times."

Cindy, her large breasts bouncing, kissed me on the cheek as we passed on the stairs.

The door was ajar at 208, so I didn't have to knock. Helene was sitting in an easy chair, looking bored. She was wearing a dark green sweater over a long- sleeved white blouse, and a plaid skirt, not her usual tough chick look. A transistor radio sitting on the end table was playing "Runaway" by Del Shannon. I love that song, especially when he goes into his falsetto voice and sings "*run run run runaway*".

"So, Joey, you want to play some canasta, or maybe parcheesi?"

"Martin was driving me nuts. He's like a water buffalo in heat."

She laughed. "Yeah, Cindy's no prize, either. Those two were made for each other."

An elongated pause ensued. I knew why I was there, and so did Helene. "Tears on my Pillow" by Little Anthony and the Imperials came on the radio.

We started to dance. She smelled great, and I loved the feel of her body against mine. I could sense the softness beneath her tough exterior. Much as I wanted to continue and much as I wanted to avoid being alone with Martin, I realized that my plan was a farce. Helene could get thrown out of cheerleading, the one good thing in her life, if we got caught. And she sure didn't need another guy trying to get into her pants.

"Don't take this the wrong way, Helene," I said, pulling away from her. "I like you and all, but this really does not seem like a good idea. If they catch us, you'll have to stop being a cheerleader. And I could get thrown off the basketball team. The gossip will go on for months."

"You scared, Joey?"

"It's not that, Helene. We both know about your reputation, which I always thought wasn't fair at all. I don't want to put you in any kind of jeopardy."

Her eyes were boring right through me. I had her complete attention. She said calmly, "I think you're scared shitless, which I'm not, Joey. But it's very sweet of you to think about me the way you do. If you leave now, Cindy can get back upstairs before anyone notices."

We hugged and I was gone, as Chuck Berry said, "like a cool breeze."

Cindy and Martin's moans could be heard in the hallway. If I knocked, they probably wouldn't even hear me. And if they did, Tim would start breaking furniture. What the hell, I thought, let Lansdowne High's favorite couple have their fun. I could go down to the lobby and read the Harrisburg papers. Coach would be in his room, figuring out strategy. No way he'd do a daytime bed check.

I took a paper from the front desk and sat down in a black-and-white striped easy chair. The sports section had a big article about the tournament. Half of the space was devoted to McKeesport High and their great center, Curtis Wilkerson. Undefeated Lansdowne High and their star forward, Zack Bolton, had a brief mention. If the sports editor had done any kind of research, he'd have found out that Smooth was almost as good as Curtis and deserved as much space.

As I was reading through the analyses of the other teams, including Carlisle, tonight's opponent, I felt a tap on my shoulder. I looked up. It was Coach.

"I thought I was pretty clear about everyone having to stay their rooms, Joey," he said in a clipped voice.

I guess I should have been alarmed, but I wasn't. I pride myself on quickly extricating myself from difficult situations. I was sure I'd come up with something.

"Yeah, well, Coach, Tim snores like a bull elephant, so I came down here to get some peace. I figured you were probably taking a nap and didn't want to bother asking you if it was okay."

For a second, I thought he bought it. But his face grew suspicious and he said, "Let's go back to your room and check things out."

Coach Johnson, who was my American History teacher last year, is a pretty cerebral, low-key guy. I got an A in the course, and we've always gotten along. At the end of the year, he told me that I was one of the best students he ever had, which was a great compliment. He's been married for years and his twin boys, Frank and Theo, named after the Roosevelts, graduated four years ago and went to Dartmouth and Columbia, respectively. His wife, Eunice, comes to every game, sitting right behind the Lansdowne bench. She is a very formal person, always dressed-up and speaking very fluent English. There have been rumors that she's a bit of a drinker. Even though she is a bit glassy-eyed at times, she's never looked the least bit drunk to me.

It's pretty evident that Coach can't stand the Martins. The parents buttonhole him after every game, complaining if Tim spent too much time on the bench or didn't get enough shots. You can tell from the pained expression on his face that he'd rather be in jail than listen to those two.

I prayed that Tim and Cindy had done the dirty deed and that she was back safely in her room with Helene. Coach had me open the door. I guess God was taking a nap, because we were greeted with the sight of Cindy, totally naked, sitting on the edge of Tim's bed. She shrieked, wrapped a sheet around herself, and ran into the bathroom. Martin, wearing only boxer shorts, quickly picked up Cindy's clothes and handed them to her through the bathroom door.

After Cindy had gotten dressed in about thirty seconds, Coach said that he was very disappointed in her behavior and would be notifying Mrs. Cleese about what had happened.

He ran his hands nervously through his hair and addressed the two of us. "The reason I had a curfew for this afternoon was to avoid situations like this one. Joe, you never should have left the room, and Tim, your behavior is inexcusable."

He told me to wait outside in the hallway; for ten minutes, I listened to their agitated voices coming through the wall. Martin was probably blaming the incident on me, because I was the one who thought up the plan. But Coach had found me in the lobby, while Helene was safely in her room. Martin had no way of proving the whole thing was my idea unless Cindy or Helene told the truth.

Tim barged out of the room, looking ready to destroy something. Coach put his head quickly out the door and motioned me inside. I sat down in the chair right opposite his.

"Tim says that you planned the whole thing and that you went upstairs to be with the Becker girl. Is this the case?"

There was no way I was going to sacrifice Helene on Tim Martin's altar. Hard as it was to admit to myself, being on the team had started to become very important to me. I felt like one of those divers from Mexico getting ready to dive off a ridiculously high cliff. If the girls contradicted my story, the team and I were finished.

"Coach, I really don't like implicating one of my teammates, but that's not what happened."

"Did Tim force you to leave the room? I've seen him bully people to get what he wants many times."

"I wouldn't say that. I agreed to do it."

"And the Becker girl was not involved in this?"

"Not at all, Coach."

He sighed and looked away. I felt badly for my part in causing this mess. Coach didn't need to be concentrating on anything but getting ready for tonight's game.

"I'd rather not punish you, Joe, but the Martins will raise holy hell if I don't. Although I must say that you showed very poor judgment here. I'm going to keep you on the bench for the first half. Tim is suspended for the entire tournament. You and Jim McWilliams are going to switch rooms. Zack will be your new roommate, so pack your stuff. Mr. and Mrs. Martin have come up for the tournament. They're probably out in the hallway as we speak. Don't say anything to them or Tim, if they provoke you. We have to concentrate on winning a basketball tournament."

"Sorry for all this trouble, Coach."

He nodded. Just as he said, the entire Martin family was waiting out in the hall, looking like cougars ready to pounce on a fawn. Mrs. Martin's ridiculous beehive hairdo started to shake and her husband's prodigious beer gut began to shimmy as they began to rip into me. Tim was leaning against the wall with his arms folded, glaring at the floor. I sensed that he wasn't looking at me because if he did, he might lose control of himself.

"If it isn't Mr. Smarty Pants," Mrs. Beehive shrieked, "you think you're so brilliant, setting up Timmy so you could play more."

Her husband added his two cents. "You think you pulled a fast one, Garden, but you're not going to get away with this.

Superintendent Adams is on his way up here as we speak. And I'm going to call your parents when we finish our meeting with Johnson. They'll both be very interested to hear what went on up here."

Following Coach's instructions, I didn't respond. Walking toward Zack's room, waves of nausea undulated through my stomach. Of course, the Martins would have to involve my parents. I forced Tim to call Cindy. I forced Tim to take off his clothes. I forced Tim to fuck his brains out. Obviously, the whole incident was entirely my fault. Mother is very impressed with things like Tim's father being President of the Borough Council, so she'll be mortified and will try to drown me in her shame. Helene and Cindy just *have* to back up my story.

Zack surprised me with his answer after I told him what happened. "Maybe this is a blessing in disguise, Joey. Coach has the opening he needs to keep Martin on the bench and start you."

Tim was not at the pot roast dinner or on the bus. Everyone on the team assumed that he had gone home with his parents. I doubted that very much. This story hadn't reached its conclusion; I was sure of that.

After arriving at the Harrisburg Armory, an old, musty building with about 5,000 seats, the team sat down beside the scorer's table. In the first game, McKeesport was going to be playing South Harrisburg, who I assumed was the hometown favorite. We would go into our locker room at the beginning of the second half to get dressed for our game against Carlisle.

Dan and Dave Irwin sat down beside me.

"Hey, Joey, we heard about what happened, " Dan said, putting his arm on my shoulder. "Tim fucked Cindy and you got a blowjob from Helene. We didn't think you had it in you."

"Joey Garden, Casanova of Lansdowne High," Dave chimed in.

"I don't know where you two heard that, but Helene and I didn't do anything. I went down to the lobby, that's it."

Both of them winked and Dan poked me in the ribs with his elbow. Neither of them had a serious bone in their body.

The cheerleaders in their garnet sweaters and gray skirts came and sat down at courtside right in front of us. Helene turned around and motioned for me to sit down beside her. Dan and Dave started laughing the moment I got up.

She put her head down and began talking in a hoarse whisper. "Coach Johnson called Cindy and me to his room. I felt like I was in the police station, Joey. At first, Cindy was going to tell the truth, but remembered that Tim said she looked fat. Plus, she didn't want to drag me into it. I wasn't sure she would hold up, but she supported our version all the way."

"How did you know I didn't say exactly what happened, Helene?"

"Because of what you said to me in the room, Joey. I thought you'd try to protect me and knew you hated Tim."

"So I guess we're both still on the varsity."

"Guess so. Get back to your teammates. People are going to start talking."

Helene's words should have made me feel great, but they didn't. My life had changed in the last few hours. No one who knew me would ever expect I was capable of doing what I'd just done. I've been caving in to Martin for years. Might makes right in this jungle of a world. But Zack's words had finally sunk in, so what if he kicked my ass?

The game started. I sat down with the rest of the team to watch. From the opening tap, it was clear that South Harrisburg had no chance. Curtis Wilkerson was a giant among pygmies. Built like a battleship, he moved across the court like an antelope, swift and graceful. His legs and arms were one big muscle and when he blocked out for a rebound, no Harrisburg player could even get close to the backboard.

McKeesport's star guard, Tim Hall, had obviously figured out a way to work hand in glove with Curtis. He'd lob the ball into the pivot, where Curtis, with his back to the basket, would push his man backward and either put up a right or left hand hook or pass it back to Hall for a jump shot. The only way to stop them, as far as I could tell, was to deter Hall from making the pass or put a man in front of Curtis who could intercept it. Even Smooth, who is a great defender, wouldn't be able to stop this imposing big man once he got his hands on the ball.

The half ended with McKeesport comfortably ahead 48-22. I stared at Zack and shook my head in disbelief.

"First, we have to beat Carlisle, Joey," he said, "then we'll worry about Curtis."

After the two teams came back on the floor, we left the court to get changed. Inside the locker room, a nightmare vision greeted me: Tim Martin sitting on a bench with his uniform on, Superintendent Adams standing beside him. Sweet Jesus. Looking at the other players, they all seemed as stunned as I was. Guess screwing a cheerleader was not a serious offense.

Coach asked for everyone's attention before saying, "Our superintendent has a few words to say."

Dr. Adams cleared his throat and began to speak. "I'm sure you all know about the problems that occurred this afternoon. After careful deliberation, I've decided that because this is Tim's first offense, Coach's Johnson's suspension will be lifted, with the stern admonition that if Tim breaks any more rules, he will be expelled from the team."

I looked at Coach. His face betrayed no emotion, but I knew he was torn up about being overruled. Our leader was wounded. Everyone in the locker room knew exactly what had happened. If any player other than Tim Martin was caught with a cheerleader in his room, they were done. It was easy to figure out what had gone down. Mr. and Mrs. Martin blamed me and said Tim was just a young kid feeling his oats, and that Coach had a vendetta against their son. Blah, blah and blah. Coach knew enough to keep his cool.

Zack's leg was going up and down like a pogo stick. I knew he was about at his boiling point. He admired Coach as much as he hated Martin.

"And one more thing, boys," the superintendent added, holding his hat in his hands, "at Coach Johnson's request, Joey Garden will be fully reinstated as well. Now go out on the court and make Lansdowne proud of our Lancers."

Coach followed the superintendent out the door. Tim was smiling a victory grin; I don't think he knew how to be anything other than a complete jackass.

Zack got up and walked over to him and bent down about three inches from his face. "You know you should be thrown off the team, Martin, and so does everyone else. What the hell would you do if your parents didn't bail you out all the time?"

Martin put his head down.

"You have to know this, Tim. If you cause Coach one more problem, I'm going to come after you. If you threaten or harass Joey, I'm going to stomp you in half." He stopped and scanned the room. "As Captain of the team, I'm telling each and every one of you guys, if Tim causes you any problems, let me know."

The locker room was deathly quiet. Guys started getting undressed and putting on their uniforms. Tim was scowling. He and his parents cut the Coach's legs out from under him and Zack returned the favor. Hard cheese. I really appreciated what he said about me, because there was no doubt in my mind that Martin was going to try to skin me alive. I knew from experience not to underestimate his titanic ego and capacity for revenge.

Zack motioned me over to the shower room. "You have to play your ass off, tonight, Joey. If I know Coach, Martin won't play. No way we can let him down tonight."

If Zack was right, in a few minutes I was going to be in my first game as a starter in front of 5,000 people, not hiding on the end of the bench as I usually did. I'd have to play good defense, and when Carlisle double-teamed Zack, make them pay by hitting my shots.

We left the locker room and waited underneath the wooden stands. Everyone was nervous. This was our biggest challenge of the season. The buzzer sounded. McKeesport had won in a walk, 82-44. We ran onto the court and started our layup drill. South Harrisburg entered from the other side of the gym and the place erupted.

As we huddled in front of the bench, Tim removed his warm-up jacket, expecting everything to be the same. Coach looked at his clipboard and announced, "Starters tonight will be Dave Irwin and Joe Garden at guard, Zack Bolton and Tim Mac Williams at forward, Calvin Newsome at center. Take the man you line up with at mid-court. Let's show them what we're made of, boys."

Walking out for the center jump, I felt weightless and insubstantial. I was not ready for this. The crowd was cheering like crazy for South Harrisburg. My man, who also had number six, was about an inch taller and ten pounds heavier than me. He got the ball and whizzed right by me for an easy layup. Bringing the ball upcourt, I dribbled it off my foot and out of bounds. After we finally settled in on offense, Zack set a pick for me, springing me for a wide-open jumper. The ball went over the backboard and out of bounds.

Zack took over and scored three baskets in a row on a beautiful reverse layup, a corner jump shot and a hook from the middle of the lane. It was a relief knowing he could do most of the scoring. My biggest problems were on defense. My man was turning out to be much faster and stronger than me. South Harrisburg was pretty expert in setting picks. He scored ten quick points.

When I finally hit a shot, it hit the back of the rim and bounced about four feet in the air, going in the basket and rolling around about three times before finally going in. "Great job, Six," someone yelled from the stands, "at least you did one thing right."

I expected Martin to come in to replace me and that I'd be relegated to the bench for the rest of the game. Instead, it was Dan Irwin. Coach was not going to budge.

He motioned me to sit down beside him and said, "I realize that it's hard to start your first game in front of such a big crowd, Joe. If you can figure out a way to relax, I think you'll be fine. I'm going to take Mac out of the game in a few minutes. Dan and Dave will be the guards, and you can start getting corner jump shots at forward. You're man is bigger than you, but he's slow. Pretend you're playing in our gym. Everything will be okay."

Martin looked like an A-bomb ready to explode. What a spectacle that would be, Tim's peewee brain splattered all over the court. Mr. and Mrs. Martin were sitting right behind their beloved son, looking very grim. Coach had taken a great risk. I had to come through for him.

I was substituted for Mac, which made me nervous, because I've never played forward in my life. The next quarter changed my basketball career forever. My man was slow, as Coach said, and he didn't shoot much. South Harrisburg wasn't able to figure out that Dan and Dave don't have much of a role in our offense and that Zack and I could be double-teamed.

We started to press and the twins were magnificent, harassing the opposing guards to distraction, stealing the ball over and over again and making Harrisburg throw their passes out of bounds. On offense, we played almost perfectly, moving the ball around with great efficiency, scoring at will. South Harrisburg did start to double-team Zack, which left me open in the corner. I felt totally relaxed when I let my first shot go, and watched in delight as the ball went straight through the hoop.

On the next possession, I did the same thing. Then I did it once again. South Harrisburg called time out and when they returned to the court, I had a man on me so tightly, I thought he was going to propose. Dan and Dave started driving into the lane and hitting Calvin in the pivot. He hit four shots in a row. Then Zack got into the act from the other corner. I was part of a magnificent ballet. The crowd started to ooh and aah. We were up 44-28 at half, and in full control of the game.

Tim smacked his fist into his hand and yelled, "Motherfuckin' Coach," as soon as we got into the locker room. Zack glared at him, and Martin quickly shut up.

The second half was a cakewalk. South Harrisburg had no answer for Lansdowne High. The final score was 82-52. When the buzzer rang, the crowd gave us a standing ovation. The announcer started reading the stats and when he said, "Joe Garden, sixteen points," my heart leapt. My best performance ever. And in such an important game, what could be better?

Zack saw me grinning in the shower and said, "One more to go, Joey. Don't get too excited."

I knew what he was saying, but it was hard advice to follow. I never thought I could feel so good playing basketball, and what was really intoxicating was that the season was just beginning. Zack's vision of a state title was starting to seem real.

Whatever Tim was doing, I wasn't paying attention to it. But Mr. and Mrs. Martin's glares when I entered the hallway were impossible to ignore. I brushed right past them, letting them stew in their own juices. Marilyn and Barbara passed by me in the hallway. "Nice game, Joey," Barbara chirped, "Maybe we can win the tournament."

When I opened the door to my room, Zack was sitting tensely on the edge of his bed. Damn, didn't that guy ever relax? We could at least bask in the glow of our victory for a few minutes. A few compliments from our Captain would have been pretty nice as well.

"You did good, Joey," he said, "just as I thought you would. Mac isn't going to be happy sitting on the bench, but I think having you and the twins in the game at the same time is a good strategy. If Smooth is able to cover Curtis, we can beat McKeesport. Then we'll all know anything is possible."

Curtis Wilkerson strode into the coffee shop the next morning like a king walking among his humble servants. I don't think I've ever seen anyone exude so much confidence, smiling at everyone, totally relaxed. He walked over to our table, shook everyone's hand and said, "Don't y'all beat us up too bad tonight, Lansdowne."

Then, what was utterly flabbergasting to me, he said, "Hey, Six, wish we had someone on our team with a jump shot nice as yours."

Curtis had noticed me? The hair on the back of my neck rose.

"It'll be there tonight, Curtis, if you don't shove it down my throat," I said.

He laughed. The guy was so smooth.

He shook Calvin's and Zack's hands, waved and was off.

"You gotta hand it to the guy," Zack said, smiling, "trying to lull us into believing tonight's game will be a cinch."

"He can't think we're that stupid," I answered. "He was just Curtis being Curtis. He's talked to national sportswriters, had some of the best college coaches in his living room and has about twenty girlfriends, if not more."

"Don't get too awed, Joey. He's is an obstacle we have to overcome. Don't make him into Superman."

We hung out in the lobby for a while before going back to our rooms. There was a lot of time to kill. I started reading *Hamlet* again but couldn't concentrate very well. What I really wanted was to be back in Helene's room, holding her in my arms. Her skin was so soft and she smelled so good. It was preposterous to think of us being together, brainy good kid Joey Garden and the toughest girl in the school. One thing I found out in our brief encounter, though, was that Helene was a real person, not some useless slut. Crazier things have happened. After all, South Philly Jew Eddie Fisher ended up with the queen of the movies, Elizabeth Taylor.

Coach got us together after dinner and mapped out a strategy. Smooth was going to guard Curtis, but he was every other player's defensive responsibility as well. Each time he got the ball in the pivot, the guards were to double back and harass him. Zack was responsible for neutralizing Tim Hall. He continued. "We have to hope the other three starters are as ineffectual as they were against Carlisle. If they aren't, we're going to have to change the plan.

"On offense, move the ball around, three passes before every shot, unless we have a fast break or a tap-in. They have to know that there's no easy way to shut us down."

My nerves were getting frayed. The one thing I knew was that when we were on offense, I didn't want to be anywhere near Curtis. Goliath shook all of our hands before the center jump, a politician to the core. Smooth looked tense as the ref got ready to toss up the ball. I didn't envy him in the least. Curtis tipped the ball to Hall, who sped to the basket. Just as he got ready to make a lay up, Zack reached over and knocked the ball out of bounds. The crowd cheered. Hall threw the inbounds pass to Curtis, who shot it over Smooth's outstretched hands for two.

My man, number twelve, was a dream come true. He bit on every fake I made and was at least a step slower than I was. I started to relax and began telling myself, "Don't think: just react." Zack set a pick on the top of the key and Dave hit me with a chest pass. Twelve was slow getting to me. The basket looked as big as a washtub. I shot the ball into a high arc and it went right through the hoop without touching iron. There was a roar from the crowd, and I was the reason.

The score teetered back and forth for the entire first quarter. Calvin was dripping with sweat, but he'd limited Curtis to only eight points. Zack held Hall to one basket. The other three

McKeesport players remained inconsequential, although they scored a few baskets on fast breaks. We were ahead 22-12, and seemingly headed to the championship.

Coach put Dan in the game. I sat on the far end of the bench beside Martin, who sneered as I sat down.

"I guess you're real happy, Joey, making me ride the pine. But we both know that you're a weak little candyass that Çoach likes more than me because you're smart in school. The fun is going to be over for you very soon. Enjoy it while it lasts, jerk-off."

I was going to make a comment about Martin needing to start worrying about the team and not so much about his dumb-ass self, but realized it would be pointless. I kept my mouth shut and watched the game. Smooth was really struggling as he tried to contain Curtis, who was starting to back him farther and farther toward the basket. Dan and Dave were being their usual pesky selves, harassing the big center every time he got the ball. Even so, McKeesport had cut the lead to six.

When Smooth got back on offense, he was breathing very hard , but there was no one on the bench to replace him. Zack began carrying the team, scoring on a reverse layup and hitting three jumpers from the top of the key. Coach motioned to me and said, "I'm going to put you in for Calvin, Joe. Zack is going to be our center, you and Mac will be forwards. The twins will stay at guard. Get us a few baskets. Someone other than Zack has got to score."

We made all the adjustments. My man turned his head as Dave tossed the ball to Zack, Curtis looming over him like Mt. Everest. I knew I was going to get the ball, and when the bounce pass came my way, I was already moving. Picking up the ball in rhythm, I went straight up and released. I started to go back on defense, knowing the ball was going in. Such an intoxicating feeling, like I was a wave moving toward the shore.

The next play was the greatest I've ever seen on a basketball court. Hall dribbled past Dan and around Mac, lobbing the ball to Curtis. He moved into the lane and put up a left-handed hook that looked like a sure two points. Zack shot up far into the air and grabbed the ball before it reached the rim. When he came down, Curtis, with his massive hands, tried to wrench the ball away. Zack refused to let the big man take it. They were fighting like two grizzly bears. The crowd let out a primal roar as Zack kept the ball and began dribbling up the court.

Dave got the ball to me in the corner just as I left my feet. I caught the ball in one motion and drilled in a jump shot. I had never done anything like that in my life. The ball went right through the rim, no questions asked. At this point, given my shot and Zack's defensive heroics, the entire gym was in bedlam. McKeesport called for a timeout. As I walked to the bench, I wondered if we had just cut the heart out of McKeesport. Adrenaline was racing through my arms and legs. I took a few deep breaths and tried to calm down.

Everyone on the bench had gotten up and was pounding Zack and me on the back. It felt a bit strange, but I liked it.

In the second half, Smooth got his second wind and began to slow Curtis down. Hall was tired and started clanging jumper after jumper off the rim. It looked like Lansdowne was fully in charge when Curtis suddenly found God. No matter what strategy we tried, he was unstoppable. Going through Zack and Smooth, not letting the twins disrupt him, he scored basket after basket, bringing his team within four points. Then it was Zack's turn to make McKeesport look ridiculous, hitting four jumpers in a row from the right corner, then driving into the key and putting in three acrobatic layups over Curtis' outstretched hands, Final score: Lansdowne 76, McKeesport 68. Zack had thirty-four points and Curtis thirty-eight. It was impossible to tell who was the better player, but *Lansdowne* had won the Harrisburg Invitational.

We mobbed Coach as he accepted the winner's trophy at center court. The crowd was on its feet, cheering wildly. This had been one exceptional high school basketball game. Our cheerleaders were hugging us. Helene grabbed me and kissed me on the cheek; seemed like I had made an impression on her.

THREE DAYS BEFORE New Year's Eve and no date. I guessed I'd be spending the night alone. Mac was having a party in his rec room, an annual tradition. The whole team was invited, as well as all the cheerleaders. No way I wanted to be anywhere near Marilyn when midnight rolled around.

Zack had gotten the custodian to open the gym; a few of us were going to join him.

Walking down Stewart Avenue before turning onto Highland. I heard a horn beep. It was Martin, in his father's blue Ford Fairlane.

"Hey Joey," Tim yelled, sticking his head out the window. "Get in, I'll drive you to the gym."

Looking at that mule face, I had the grim realization that I was going to be dancing in the trouble patch very shortly. I had no desire to get in the car with him, even though wet snow was starting to come down like sodden confetti.

"No thanks, Tim," I answered.

He continued to drive beside me, "Stop and listen to me, Garden, you stupid little son of a bitch."

I ignored him.

"We both know you suckered me into having Cindy come down to the room. You've been jealous of me since kindergarten. And now you've got me in Johnson's shithouse. You had your fun and got to play in the tournament, while I sat on the bench. Go tell Coach the truth and we'll be square."

In the past, I would be looking for ways to wiggle out of the situation. Years and years of being humiliated by this dumb-ass were officially over. No. No and Double No.

"And don't think you can hide behind Zack's promise. If he lays a hand on me, my parents will have him thrown in jail."

"Whether I tricked you or not, Tim, you went along with it. If you didn't have your parents make the superintendent overrule Coach, the whole incident would be yesterday's news. Get over it."

"You planned the whole thing so you could see Cindy naked, Garden, you fucking little degenerate. I could bury you so deep in the snow, no one would ever be able to dig you out. Scumbag motherfucker. And if I do, I'm sure you'll rat me out to Coach, coward."

There was no choice but to fight back.

"I'm not saying anything to Coach, Tim. I'm not saying anything to anyone. It's over. IF YOU WANT TO GET OUT OF YOUR CAR AND KICK MY ASS ON HIGHLAND AVENUE IN BROAD DAYLIGHT, GO RIGHT THE FUCK AHEAD. I'M SO SICK OF YOUR DUMB FUCKING ASS."

I proceeded down Highland. If he was going to jump me from behind, I was going to kick, bite and punch him. After about a minute of nothing happening, I turned around. Martin and his father's car were nowhere to be seen.

We did a layup drill and played three on three. My mind was elsewhere. When you get as angry as I did, it takes a long time to calm down. Martin was such a chickenshit, why had it taken me so long to figure that out? The ball went through the rim, or it didn't. I sleepwalked through the workout.

Zack offered to drive me home. When we got there, the Martin's blue Ford was sitting ominously in front of my house.

"When is this nightmare going to end?" I muttered. "The entire Martin family is waiting for me in my living room, Zack, mark my words."

"You want me to come in, Joey?"

"Nah, I'll just have to deal with it."

My premonition proved correct, as I was greeted by the phantasmagoric sight of Beehive, Beer Gut and their loving son sitting on our sofa, drinking coffee.

Pop was in the easy chair; I couldn't tell what he was feeling. Mother was sitting in a dining room chair, a decidedly unhappy expression on her face. I went and got another chair and sat down between my parents. Mother turned to me and said in a very unpleasant tone, "Joey, the Martins have been telling me a very interesting story about what happened up in Harrisburg. I'm sure I don't have to repeat all the details. I think if what they say is true, you owe them all an apology."

Pop was staring into space. Because just about everyone has more education than he does, he feels like he doesn't have the right to say much of anything.

Mr. Martin took a long swig of coffee and started to speak, "I don't mind saying this, Alice; we don't appreciate Joey screaming at Tim this afternoon. Our son was manipulated by your son in Harrisburg and has a right to be angry. Joey knew that Coach Johnson didn't like Timmy and was just looking for an excuse to sit him on the bench."

"Yeah," Tim added, "we won the tournament in Harrisburg and I didn't even get a chance to play. I'm a much better player than Joey. Everybody knows that."

It was Mrs. Martin's turn to chime in. "Victor and Alice, we know you're good people, but that boy tried to pull a fast one that he shouldn't be able to get away with."

I knew one thing. If it took all the strength I possessed, I was not going to give in to these people. I sat up straight and said, "Mr. and Mrs. Martin, you can continue to smear my character, you can scream in my face, my parents can punish me, the Superintendent can force Coach to kick me off the team, but I'm never going to apologize."

Mother looked like she was going to fall out of her chair. The Head of the Borough Council and his wife were sitting in her living room, and her son was speaking to them with enormous insolence. She sat up as straight as she could and eyed me coldly. "You need to answer the question, Joey. Did you make up the plan as Tim said you did?"

"No one forced Tim to call Cindy. Maybe I should have stopped him, but I didn't."

Mr. Martin was on his feet, wagging his finger at me. "Stop trying to weasel out of this, you little ingrate."

His wife jumped up as well, "Smart aleck. You've always looked down on Timmy. You look down on everyone, you little snob."

Tim started to scream; they all began to yell at me in unison. I felt a strong urge to cry, just break down and crumble as if all of my braggadocio was a big act. I got up and walked around the dining room table and into the kitchen saying to myself: *I just can't cry. I just can't cry. I just can't cry.*

Pounding my fist into the wall by the breakfast nook, I walked back into the living room. Everyone was staring at me. I said, "I'm not admitting to anything, and I'm not apologizing."

Expecting another onslaught, I sat astonished while the Martin clan got up, put on their coats, and stormed out of the house. Mother hurried after them. I could hear the their loud, agitated voices as they got into the car.

Mother came back and slammed the front door. "I never believed that my only son could be so disrespectful. I'm so humiliated, Joey." She took out a Kleenex from her purse and began to cry. I couldn't remember the last time I'd seen her like that. There was nothing I could say that was going to make her feel better, so I didn't say anything.

No one spoke during dinner. Mother was really suffering. Pop looked befuddled. There were going to be repercussions.

I was reading the scene from *Hamlet* where he figures out how he was going to write a play to show how Uncle Claudius killed his father, when there was a knock on my bedroom door. It was Pop.

"You really upset your mother tonight," he said. "It'll be a long time before she's over this."

"The Martins are horrible people, Pop. Tim was found with a naked girl in his room, and it's my fault? They got the Superintendent to make Coach reinstate him, which he shouldn't have had to do, and they're still making trouble. Mother's so impressed with this Borough Council crap, it makes me sick."

"I was proud of the way you stood up to them, Joey."

"Thanks, Pop. I felt pretty lonely down there. Just because you didn't finish high school doesn't mean you don't have a right to express your opinion."

There were tears in his eyes. I was the only one who didn't cry tonight.

Mother was obviously still upset as she gave me a fried egg sandwich for breakfast. Why can't she see the Martins for what they are? Mother has always been obsessed with social status; she spends hours reading the society pages. I bet if someone asked her, she could recite verbatim who the latest debutantes are and where and when their balls are being held. I think if our house was picked up by a helicopter and dropped into the Main Line, she'd be ecstatic.

My favorite times with her when I was younger were when I brought home a good report card and we both went to Saul's Pharmacy to get sundaes. It was great, just sitting and enjoying my time with her. Such a distant memory.

It was probably best to keep my mouth shut and try to let the whole thing pass, but I couldn't.

"I'm not sure why you are so upset with me, Mother. Tim Martin has been a thorn in my side for years. No one likes him. His parents bail him out of situation after situation. The whole family's a blot on the town. Even though Mr. Martin is Head of the Borough Council, Lansdowne would be a lot better off with them gone."

She was holding a spatula on her hip and looking at me with disbelief. "I've always had very high standards for my son. Is there anything wrong with that?"

"I'm not perfect, Mother, much as you want me to be. Being alone in a hotel room with Tim Martin was torture.

He's stupid. He's doesn't respect anything. He can't have a conversation without saying how great he is a dozen times. He's a mollycoddled disgrace."

"Did you make up the plan?"

This was so frustrating. I was on the verge of pounding my fist on the wall once again. "Can't you ever be on my side, even if I'm wrong, which I'm not saying I was?"

"I think you'll have a fine career as a lawyer, Joey. I want you to answer the question, did you or did you not make up the plan?"

"You make me ill."

There may have been another time in my life when I spoke to Mother this way, but I could not remember it. She grabbed the edge of the kitchen sink with both hands, breathing in short, deep bursts. Pop came into the kitchen and asked, "What the hell is going on here?"

"Mother and I were talking about the Martins, and things got a little heated. I'm going over to Zack's."

I was out the front door in seconds before my parents were able to tell me to go to my room. Walking down Mansfield Road, my stomach churned and churned. The person who brought one into the world demanded a huge amount of respect. But Mother did make me sick. I guess that's been true for a while, but this was the first time I've expressed it. Where would we go from here?

Zack lives on Windermere Terrace near Stratford Avenue, in a third-floor apartment in what used to be a mansion at the turn of the century. His father died when he was five, so it's just Zack and his mom, who's a secretary for Dr. Phillips, Lansdowne's most popular physician.

He was vacuuming his living room rug.

"You should be wearing an apron, Zack." I said.

He walked into the kitchen and came back wearing a yellow-and-white striped apron. I wished I had a camera. One picture of him dressed like this, and I could bribe him for years.

"You want me to help with the dusting?"

"If I don't do my chores, my mother will have my hide. Mac called me about an hour ago. He saw the Martins going into Green Avenue School, probably to see the Superintendent. What happened yesterday?"

"They wanted me to admit I set up Tim. I think they figured that if I confessed, Coach would make their darling son a starter again. All of them started screaming at me when I wouldn't go along. Mother took their side. It was quite an afternoon."

"Don't give Coach any reason to put you back on the bench. Martin can die there for all anyone cares."

Both of us were hungry, so we headed up to Sandler's Drugs on the corner of Lansdowne and Baltimore. I used to work there when I was a freshman, stocking shelves and sweeping floors. They have a soda fountain that runs about the length of the store. The food is cheap, but tastes pretty good.

Officer McMahon, taking a break from directing traffic, was sitting right by the entrance, drinking a cup of coffee. Millicent McDade, the town crazy woman, was staring at a tuna salad sandwich, wearing a multi-colored scarf, her poodle on the floor beside her. Maria Tedesco and Janie Gilmartin were drinking Cokes, smoking Luckies, chomping on their gum, deeply involved in some juicy gossip.

Zack and I ordered cheeseburgers and black-and-white shakes. While we were waiting for the food, I said, "We're going to win State just like you said, Zack."

Before answering, he took a huge bite of the burger, grease and cheese dripping onto his plate. "The teams in our schedule are a big bunch of nothing. We could get soft and overconfident playing them. I'm trying to figure out a way for us to face more serious competition."

Was he thinking about taking on some of the local colleges? Our schedule was set in stone. But I've known Zack for twelve years, and when he says he's going to do something, it usually gets done. The burger beckoned. It tasted fantastic, particularly when I washed it down with the shake.

A hand was on my shoulder. It was Helene, with her good friend, Theresa. She was wearing a black leather coat and a brown skirt. I hadn't realized how good-looking she was until we danced in Harrisburg. We miss a lot of things in life because we don't look at them closely enough. Her jangly earrings, bright red lipstick and matching nail polish added to her sexy good looks.

She motioned to the cigar case with a nod of her head. From her nervous smile and the way she was holding on to her purse strap, I could tell she was pretty anxious about something.

Helene got a piece of Wrigley's Spearmint gum from her purse, unwrapped it and jammed it into her mouth. She began to talk but stopped herself. I grabbed onto her wrist and told her to relax.

Finally, she began to speak." I didn't think this was going to be so hard, Joey. But Tommy Cuccinelli's having a New Year's Eve party, and I wanted to know if you would be my date?"

A big smile spread across my face. This tough-looking chick was shaking like a tree in the rain.

"You're probably already going to the MacWilliam's party anyway. And I know that I'm not the kind of girl you usually go out with, but..."

"I'd be delighted, Helene. I was wondering what I was going to do New Year's. That sounds great. Who's going to be there?"

"Oh, the usual, Gully and his boys, Theresa, a few other people. Tommy's mother isn't very strict, so there'll be some beer, maybe some other stuff."

"Not my usual crowd, but so what?"

"I was gonna call, but when I saw you and Zack at the counter, I figured what the hell. Pick me up about 9:00, 36 Rigby Avenue."

Taking out a cigarette and lighting it, Helene left quickly, looking relieved to have gotten it over with. I guess it's very difficult for girls to make the first move. I can't remember that ever happening to me before. The Mugwumps were going to rake me over the coals when they found out about this development. They were going to think I was a slut. Already, I was thinking about the midnight kiss.

Back at the counter, I told Zack what had just happened. He looked at me like I was a creature from the moon.

"Don't get mixed up with that crowd, Joey," he said, frowning. "I know Helene has a hot bod, but the Martins are looking for any kind of ammo they can use against you. Coach might quit and the team might fall apart if Tim becomes a starter again."

"You act like I'm going to be involved in a murder plot or something, Zack. I'll probably have a few beers, maybe make out with Helene. If she wants to do more, we'll just have to see what happens."

"A few beers?"

"Yeah, Captain, a few. I like the taste, and the way it makes me feel. Not everyone can be a saint like you."

"I would never do anything to jeopardize the team, and neither should you."

"Did you ever think that being so single-minded and fanatical, *you* might be jeopardizing the team?"

We went on like that for a good while, and parted with no resolution. But Zack's warning made me think a bit more about my decision. Certainly, I was not going to have much in common with the people at the party. Rumors had been circulating around school that Gully and his crew were stealing cars on a pretty regular basis. God knows what else they were up to. And was I really ready for the scrutiny that going out with Helene could bring? But damn, I genuinely liked her; it wasn't just lust. People get put into boxes for one reason or another: how much money their parents have, their race, how well they do in school. Why can't everyone move easily from one box to the other without getting a ton of grief?

The Beckers lived in one of those big, old-fashioned houses that are all over Lansdowne. It needed a few coats of paint. There was a strong smell of piss and baby vomit permeating the stairway, as I made my way up to the third floor. I rang the bell and a big, burly guy with a bald head and a huge belly opened the door. He was wearing a gray flannel shirt, tan pajama bottoms, and tan slippers with holes on the sides. The shirt might have had stains on it, but it was hard to tell in the dark hallway. We walked past stacks of old newspapers and cases of empty beer bottles stacked into haphazard piles. I plopped down in an old easy chair in the living room and looked around. The walls were completely bare and there was no TV. My house was no palace, but I felt badly for Helene, having to live in this mess every day.

Smelling some very strong, fragrant perfume, I turned around and there she was, looking fantastic in black nylons and a tight dress with thick black-and-white curvy,vertical stripes with gray on either side. She had on ruby-red lipstick and blue eye shadow. Her sandy hair was wavy, probably held together with a lot of hairspray. Even though Helene looked pretty hard, as she usually does, I thought she was beautiful. Obviously, she'd spent a lot of time fixing herself up, which made me feel flattered all over again.

As I was helping her put on her coat, her parents came into the living room. Her father was smoking a cigar and holding a can of beer. Mrs. Becker was wearing an old house dress, smiling uncomfortably behind a thick fog of cigarette smoke.

"Helene says youse is a big basketball star," she said.

"I play on the team, Mrs. Becker, but I'm no star."

"Don't you be drinkin' no beer, Helene," Mr. Becker admonished.

"Yeah, pop, I'll be sure to follow your example."

When we got out to Rigby Avenue, Helene looked a bit surprised. "You don't have a car?"

"My father says I can't get my license until I learn how to fix brakes and do tune-ups. And since working with car engines is my least favorite thing in the world, I haven't gotten it yet."

I could tell she was disappointed, but the Cucinellis lived only four blocks away.

Inside the house at Greenwood and Wycombe, the first thing I noticed was the pungent smell of cigarettes and beer. Helene wasn't kidding when she said Tony's mother wasn't strict. There was a big pile of sandwiches on the kitchen table, as well as bowls of potato chips and pretzels. Someone told me once that eating a lot helps to keep you from getting drunk. I reminded myself to make sure to stuff myself all night long.

I followed Helene into the kitchen, where Theresa Colanetti, Trudy Jenkins, Ann Pyrninski and Viv Hopkins were all sitting at the table, Luckies in their mouths. Theresa rolled her eyes when I entered: the other girls looked at Helene and smiled. I wasn't sure what that all meant, but guessed they were telling Helene "great going, girl." Seemed like getting a smarty boy who was not a hoodlum was some kind of a coup.

It became readily apparent that the girls wanted to have their own private conversation, so I split. The guys were in the living room, smoking and drinking. Kit Lambert was sitting by himself at the end of the sofa, and I sat down beside him. I've always liked Kit. He played the tough guy, but really wasn't, although I think he could kick some serious ass if he felt like it. One of the counselors enrolled him in the senior honors English class; he didn't say much, but I could tell he was soaking it all in. He dropped out right before Christmas break, and I never understood why. I was helping him with the essays and he was passing, for sure.

Kit took a long swig of beer and said. "I'm a nobody; who are you?"

"I'm a nobody too."

We both laughed. Mrs.Childress was obsessed with Emily Dickinson and the class spent two periods discussing that poem.

"You know, Joey. I really liked that one. It was short, but really deep. She likes hiding out. I hide out all the time, but I'm not sure I really like it."

"Join the club, Kit. I've felt like that my whole life. That might be changing, though. Hey, why did you drop out of honors English?"

He leaned forward, stubbed out his cig and put his beer bottle on the coffee table. His tone got serious before he said, "If I tell you something, Joey, you gotta promise you'll keep your mouth shut. I've been dying to talk to someone about it, but Gully, Skeeter and The Mole think I'm completely full of shit when I try."

"Your secret is safe with me."

"I popped Marcie Taylor and she dumped me."

"What? You and Marcie...."

"Yeah, I know. I'm not her type, just like Helene is not your type. We did it, then she cut it right off like I was some kind of experiment. Her parents study native tribes or something. I think that had something to do with it."

"Yeah, they're anthropologists. I'm sorry, Kit. That must have really hurt. Marcie? You think you know someone and you don't know a goddamn thing about them."

"Watch yourself with Helene, Joey. She's not stuck up like Marcie, but that girl has a few screws loose, especially if she thinks you're two-timin' her."

Over on the other side of the living room, Mole was holding court. He was talking very loudly; it was easy to hear what he was saying.

"I was at Lansdowne Avenue and Garrett Road. This jerk-off pulls up beside me in a '57 Chevy. It probably had a Corvette engine, 406 cubes, at least two hundred horses. He had four on the floor, mag wheels that looked like they'd been polished for three hours each, dual glass pak mufflers, tuck-and-roll upholstery, every fuckin' thing."

Mole paused and looked at the adoring throng. He had everyone's attention, including mine. "The motherfucker revs his engine and gives me the 'Show Me What You Got, Asshole' look. I smile at this shitbag and start revving up the Merc. It sounded like a hiccup, compared to his car. The guy kept staring at me and lookin' at the light. Oh man, he was fuckin' ready. We were making so much noise, we could have waked up the dead. The light turned green and I....

He stopped to take a swig of beer and a drag from his Lucky before finishing the sentence, "turned right!"

The guys erupted. I smiled; greaseball humor at its best/worst?

"I just wish I could have seen the fucker's face when he turned to see how he was doin' and realized he was having a race with NOTHIN'!!!"

That line *really* drove them nuts. Kit had momentarily escaped from his gloom. Mole was a real spellbinder. Feeling pretty lost, I wandered back into the kitchen. Helene gave me a big hug and announced to the other girls, "I got the smartest, cutest guy in the school." I guess I blushed because everyone started laughing uproariously. Theresa said, "Don't be embarrassed by Helene, Joey, she has a heart of gold." They all started laughing again, at what, I did not know.

Arms around each other, we went back into the living room, and found an easy chair, where Helene plopped right into my lap. We started kissing. Helene's tongue almost touched my tonsils. I loved it, but hoped I didn't explode into my pants. When I looked up, two other couples were on the sofa, going at it fast and furious. Gully had one hand squeezing Viv Hopkins' left tit, while his other hand was halfway up her skirt. Tony Cuccinelli was with Trudy Hopkins, doing pretty much the same thing. Was there the possibility of an orgy, like in ancient Rome? Hell of a way to lose my virginity. Loud moans started coming from one of the bedrooms. My guess was that it was The Mole and

Theresa; boy, was she a screamer. I could see Mrs. Cuccinelli smoking a cigarette and staring vacantly at the wall. Nothing remotely close to this was happening at Mac's, where everyone would be jitterbugging, drinking Pepsi and eating chips. Helene took my hand and put it on her breast.

Suddenly, a fist smashed into my eye, throwing me back on the sofa. When I looked up, Frank Stampler was looming, looking like a homicidal maniac. "Big basketball star, piece of shit, think you can take my girl?" he cried.

Stampler was getting ready to hit me again, when a huge hand reached around his neck and pulled him to the ground. The next two minutes seemed like two years, as Gully kicked Stampler in the ribs and punched him over and over again, saying, "I told you not to do this, Frank, fucking asshole!"

Mole and Kit pulled Gully off of Stampler, who got up, blood streaming from his nose, and fell into a chair. Calmed down a bit, Gully walked over to him and said, "Sucker-punching somebody is for pussies, Frank, which is what you are. Get your fucking coat and get the fuck out of here."

Stampler flung his head back and moaned, "Aw, Gully, don't be like that, man. He was bird-doggin' my girl."

Unable to take any more, Helene rose to her feet and yelled, "It's over, Frank. I told you about twenty times. WE ARE DONE!!!"

Mole handed Frank his coat. But before he got out the door, he turned around and cried, "I want you so bad, Helene. You gotta take me back!"

This was too much for Gully, who pushed Stampler through the door and down the stairs. I though he might have killed him, but screams of "Helene, Helene, Helene," started ringing out.

"Go out and say something to him," I said to her. "If he keeps this up, Gully is going to kill him."

She smashed her cigarette into an ashtray and walked down the stairs. Mrs. Cuccinelli brought me a dishtowel filled with ice cubes. I thanked her and collapsed back onto the sofa. I was going to have a shiner that covered the whole left side of my face. Mother was going to be furious. Frank Stampler. I barely knew the guy. We didn't acknowledge each other in the hallways. The only thing I knew about him was that he looked sullen all the time. It kind of impressed me though, how over the moon he was about Helene; his whole life depended on being with her. I suddenly felt stupid, out of place, like I was the Easter Bunny sitting on Santa Claus's lap.

Mole handed me a beer. "Bitches," he said. "Use 'em and lose 'em, that's the only policy."

"You seemed like you were having a good time using Theresa, Mole."

"It was an exceptional time, Joey. And now it's over, until I feel like doin' it again, which may be tomorrow, next week or never. Girls got something you can't get anywhere else, and they know it. Give 'em a line of bullshit, take what you need and that's the end of it. I know you didn't come here with Helene just to hold hands. You got something on her now, Joey. Take advantage of the situation."

What a true cynic the Mole was. I had the feeling that he was going to be that way for the rest of his life. Why do some people become hard-asses and others aren't that way at all? Mole confided in me one time that he'd read a whole set of Encylopedia Brittanicas from Aardvark to Zygote. I believe he did. He's always been quick-witted and intelligent, just never did any schoolwork. Maybe I'd be like that, if Mother hadn't gotten on my case in the early grades to get my homework finished before I went out to play. Taking weekly trips to the Lansdowne Public Library before I could go on my own and going to various museums in New York and Philadelphia also got me interested in learning new things. Next year, Mole will be working in some gas station and McChesney will be at Harvard. I guess a lot depends on whether your parents give a shit about school or not.

Gully sidled over to me and put his arm across my shoulder. My eye was throbbing like crazy and I thought that if I had one more beer, I was going to puke all over the living room rug. "Don't leave before midnight, Joey," he said. "I know you're a classy guy and all, but we got our own way of doin' things. Helene'll be back in a few minutes. You shoulda seen the two of you. It's about time somethin' good happened for that girl."

His words made me feel guilty, because all I wanted to do was get up and get the hell out of there. I know Helene needed a break. But what I needed was not to get the crap kicked out of me.

There was some loud pounding on the stairs. Helene was back, looking very concerned. She came right over to me and put her hands on my cheeks. "I can't tell you how sorry I am, Joey," she moaned. "I told Frank before the party that we were over. Going with him was a big mistake, it was like carrying a lead weight on my back. He never said much and wouldn't leave me alone. I was much nicer with him this time; I think he finally got it."

She started to kiss me, but I pulled away because my eye hurt so badly. Gully was right. I should wait until midnight before I left. Helene put her head on my shoulder. She looked like she was going to cry. I patted her on the hand; I guess it really wasn't her fault.

The TV set was turned on to Times Square and when the ball came down, everyone started whooping. Helene and I kissed, but it hurt. She wanted more. I shook my head "no." I blew a plastic horn and yelled a little bit before saying to Helene, "You can stay if you want, but I feel so lousy, I just want to go the hell home."

She went and got our coats, which I appreciated. After thanking Mrs. Cuccinelli for being a good host, and saying goodbye to everyone, we were out in the cold night air. Helene's head was down.

"Look, Helene, don't look so sad. I know you didn't want this to happen. It's just one night."

"Are we going to go out again, Joey?"

When I hesitated in giving an answer, she blurted, "Nothing ever good happens to me. A loser like Frank is the only kind of guy I'll ever get."

I wanted to make it better for her, but the way I was feeling, I just wanted to go home. "I was very happy when you asked me out, Helene," I said. "Most girls wouldn't have the guts to do something like that. We can talk about it next week."

She became silent as we walked down La Crosse to Wycombe. When we got to her house, Helene gave me a hug. I told her I'd see her at school. The wind was whipping through me as I walked down Baltimore Pike. Maybe we do all belong in boxes, even though it's often unfair. Gully and his boys would not have fit in at Mac's party any more than I did at theirs. As for my virginity, the hell with it. I'll lose it when it's ready to be lost.

When I awoke at 8:30 and went to the bathroom, the left side of my face looked like it was covered by a giant scab. No way I could avoid explaining what happened.

Mother was making pancakes and Pop was sitting in the breakfast nook staring out the back window when I entered the kitchen.

"Oh, my good Lord!" Mother shrieked.

"Holy geez," Pop added. "What a shiner!"

I sat down beside Pop and slumped down on the table.

"The girl who asked me to the New Year's party's old boyfriend saw us and hit me when I wasn't looking. I know I look horrible, but it's not that big of a deal."

This was the absolutely wrong thing to say. A human's face could not have gotten any redder than Mother's was at that moment.

"Not a big deal? Not a big deal? You've *never* had anything happen like this to you, Joey. *Never.*"

"I think he looks good with a shiner, Alice. Shows that he's finally becomin' a man."

Pop's words were the *coup de grace*. She picked up a pot from the stove, walked over to us and began pounding it on the table over and over again. Mother was breathing so hard, it took about a minute before she was able to speak.

"It was that Becker girl the Martins were talking about, wasn't it?"

Overwhelmed by her onslaught of rage, I nodded.

"I told you who she was, Mother."

"So you did come up with the plan in Harrisburg?"

I looked at her and shrugged.

Pop, looking surprised, said, "I thought you were goin' with Marilyn."

"We broke it off, Pop."

Mother raised her fist into the air and slammed it down on the wood.

"This is ending TODAY," she screamed. "I did not spend seventeen years raising you to become a crude, dishonest person. You are going to stop with the lying. Stop with the evasions. Stop with the manipulation. As long as you are living under my roof, these new developments of yours are *over*!!"

Pop and I sat frozen as we watched Mother storm out of the kitchen and up the stairs. She slammed the door to her bedroom, opened it and slammed it again. My father had a shell-shocked look on his face, and I'm sure I had one as well. Mother has gotten angry many times over the years, but she'd never detonated like this before. I could get put on restriction for infinity. She could give me the cold shoulder for months. At the moment, I wasn't sure whether that was a good thing or not. A cold chill ran up my back and across my shoulders. *She could make me quit the basketball team.* I thought I was going to be sick.

The old man put his hand on my shoulder and smiled. "Your mother will get over this, kid," he said. "Just try to keep from gettin' under her skin for a while. "

Although I appreciated Pop having his own point of view, his words were of no comfort. Mother always got her way. "She's not going to be getting over anything, Pop. And if she makes me quit the team, Tim Martin will be starting again. And when we win State, it'll just kill me not to be a part of it."

"Just sit tight, Joey. Everything'll be okay."

It felt like most people at school knew why I had a black eye about fifteen minutes after I walked in the front entrance. They were gawking at me like I was some kind of sideshow freak. Whenever anyone asked me about it, I just shook my head. Zack gave me a horrifically dirty look when we passed in the hall. What the hell did he care about a black eye? I was ambulatory. I could still play. Helene walked right past me with no acknowledgment whatsoever. If she was pissed at me, I had no idea why. A basic tenet of Mugwumpism is that physical violence is absurd. I agreed with that, but there was something pleasing about walking around with my wound on display. After this, maybe I wouldn't be so easily categorized.

As I sat down with the Mugwumps at lunch, Ches spoke first. "I'm sure Victor was very pleased with you, Joseph."

"My shiner elicited the first kind words I've heard from him in months, Ches. Mother, however, has not been very sanguine about the new direction my young life has taken."

Okay, irony. This was the way we usually dealt with each other and, obviously, today was not going to be any different.

Jeff took a bite of his Lebanon bologna sandwich before laying into me. "I can't believe you'd put yourself in that environment, Joey. Helene the Machine? Give us a damn break. Pretty soon, you'll be playing pinball five hours a day and breaking into houses."

"Don't call Helene that, Jeff."

"Helene Becker's a skank of the first order, Joey. You know it, she knows it, and the whole rest of the school knows it. What is making you risk your good reputation for that utter piece of trash?"

McChesney, the Grand Mugwump, intervened; he cannot stand emotionality of any kind, particularly anger. "The two of you better watch yourselves before this turns into a major brouhaha. Joseph, you had your little sojourn into the wild side of town, which is now over. And Jeff, a little empathy might be in order for your compatriot. He tried an experiment and it failed. There is no need for vilification of any kind."

Ches leaned back on his stool, confident that his wise counsel had saved the day. Jeff was having none of it. "One more thing you should know, Joey. I asked Marilyn to Winter Ball, and she accepted."

Jeff's words hit me as hard as Stampler's punch. There are some things friends are just not supposed to do, and this was one of them.

"You've been salivating over Marilyn ever since we started going together, Jeff. Everything I have you want. That's always been the case, and you know it. Why do we call ourselves friends anyway?"

Jeff's face was red, and I could tell he was trying to formulate a response as he sucked milk through a straw. The sight of Jeff's perfectly knotted red-and-blue tie, Penn's colors, the college he can never stop talking about, drove me into a fury. I reached across the table, grabbed the lapels of his blue blazer and dragged him toward me, knocking food all over the place. An audible gasp rose from the rest of the cafeteria. I didn't have to worry about retaliation, because Jeff was too much of a chicken. George and Ches looked stunned as he tried to wipe off his clothes.

It felt like the walls in my brain had collapsed. I bolted out of the cafeteria at breakneck speed and started walking up and down the hallways. After a few minutes, Helene emerged from the girl's bathroom and stood in front of me, looking ready to do battle. "Hey Joey," she said. "What's the deal with your goddamn mother?"

I stared at her incredulously. "What are you talking about, Helene?"

"She came over my house last night and called me a 'trashy person, who was never to associate with my son again.' The bitch is lucky me or my old man didn't kick her ass sideways. What did you say to her?"

"Just what happened on New Year's. She blew her stack when she saw my eye. She heard about you from the Martins and put two and two together."

"For Christ's sake, Joey. We didn't *do* anything."

I went into the boys' bathroom and found an empty stall. Mother had never done anything like this. I guess this is why Pop always shut up when she clamped down on him. Sweat was running down my arms. My head was spinning. I wasn't sure I was going to make it to class.

Right before the final bell at 3 o'clock, I was handed a note that told me to report to the Superintendent's Office. *Mother told the Martins that I'd lied about what happened in Harrisburg.*

Zack stopped me in the hallway and asked if I was going to practice. When I told him what was happening, he grabbed me by the shoulders and said, "Don't admit a goddamn thing, Joey. The hell with those people."

The Lansdowne School District offices were right across the street from the high school, in Green Avenue Elementary School. I told the Superintendent's secretary who I was, and she motioned me to his office.

I was in the lion's den with no one on my side. Zack's words provided grim solace. Maybe if I fell on the floor and began groveling, screaming, "I'm sorry, I'm so sorry!" they'd be satisfied and I could go back to the ruins of my life. The Martins were on one side of Superintendent Adams' desk with smug smiles on their faces. Mother was clutching her purse like it was a life raft. Pop, who'd left work early, was slumped over, a sullen expression on his face.

When the Superintendent began to talk, it occurred to me that if someone cut off the top of his head and turned him upside down, a big pile of black ashes would fall onto the floor. He had a big job and a big salary, but was nothing more than a marionette. And Mother, what did she hope to get from this fiasco? Her little boy back to his compliant, docile self? That wasn't going to happen. That the Martins would see her as a good mother, not responsible for her smartass liar of a son? No, just another person they could bully.

Pop almost shouted, "Joey may have lied, but he didn't bring no girl into his hotel room. This whole thing has been a big deal over nothin'."

Mother, in an icily disdainful tone, said, "You're not being at all helpful here, Victor. Joey is guilty of being a manipulator and a liar, and there must be consequences."

Pop was moving his hands across his knees, totally on my side for the first time ever. Once again, he was totally out of his element.

"The whole incident would've never happened if your son didn't con Timmy," Mrs. Martin, beehive waving to and fro, added.

The Superintendent raised his hands in an effort to calm things down. "I think there's been enough discussion," he said in a soothing voice before looking directly at me. "Joey, if you can simply apologize to the Martins for all the trouble you've caused, we can all put this behind us and go win the State Championship."

I looked at everyone's expectant stares: Mother wanting quick redemption; the Martins wanting revenge, Adams wanting to go home and have three martinis. If I started to tear up, look weak in any way, I might as well have gone out and shot myself in the head.

After about a minute of intense silence, the Superintendent spoke again. "I hoped it wasn't going to come to this, Joey," he said gravely, leaning back in his chair and pressing his fingertips together in front of his face. "But if you don't apologize to the Martins, I'm going to have to remove you from the basketball team."

Adams's solemn tone, like a Supreme Court Justice, struck me as completely absurd. A pygmy defending pygmies. I couldn't keep myself from laughing.

The Superintendent was playing chess. He figured appeasing the Martins was his strongest move. My job was to convince him that it wasn't. "I'm not going to apologize, Superintendent Adams, because I'm not sorry about anything. You're right, Lansdowne High has a great chance to win the first State Championship in school history. We've been doing fine with Tim on the bench. If I'm forced to leave the team, a lot of people from this town will be upset about your decision."

A mini-riot broke out. Adams's secretary must have thought a wrestling match had started. Pop kept repeating, "Joey shouldn't have to apologize." The Martins were yelling in unison like they had at my house. Mother looked like she was about to have a stroke. The Superintendent stood up behind his desk and said, "I'm going to apprise Coach Johnson about what has transpired. I'll contact both families this evening about my decision."

Mr. Martin jumped out of his chair and pointed his finger at the Superintendent. "Whaddya mean, make your decision,

Adams? You said if Joey didn't apologize, the little bastard was through."

There was no point in staying one second longer. I had said what I wanted to say. Let them argue their heads off.

Zack and the twins were waiting for me at the bottom of the steps. I could have kissed each one of them on the lips. Before I could open my mouth, Mother came behind me, grabbed my collar and yanked me toward the car. Pop clutched her hand and pulled it away. It looked like they were going to start punching it out, but they just glared at each other before stomping toward the Chevy.

Pop turned and yelled, "There's no decision, Joey. Go to practice, where you belong."

They both slammed the car doors as hard as they could and sped off. I told the guys what had just happened. "Nothing's gonna break up the team, Joey, " Zack said, putting his hand on my shoulder. "We just spoke with Coach. I don't want to get into any details, but you've got no reason to worry."

At home after an exhausting practice, I sat down to dinner and began to eat. Mother gave me a baleful stare and spoke. "You've utterly disgraced me and everything our family stands for, Joey. I hope you're proud of yourself."

"He didn't disgrace nothin', Alice. Except for the laughin,' I was proud of our son standin' up for himself today in front of all those big shots."

Mother started to chew very, very slowly. Her words came out of her mouth like bullets. "You can be proud or ashamed or indignant about Joey, Victor. But you know and I know that ultimately, he's not really your concern."

Of all the denigrating, insulting things Mother said to Pop over the years, this was the worst. A father isn't supposed to care about his son?

"I'm not Pop's concern. What do you mean by that, Mother?"

"I've said all I'm going to say, Joey. Your father and I know what I'm talking about."

"Leave it alone, Joey," Pop said, looking crestfallen. The guy had finally been a real father to me and got cut down for his troubles. I did what he asked but damn, I wanted to find out what this was all about.

The phone rang. Mother walked into the living room and answered it. I knew it was the Superintendent. Mother made a few terse responses before returning to the kitchen.

"You've been suspended for one game," she announced. "Evidently, basketball has become more important than moral principles."

Pop smiled. I wanted to shout, but there was no sense rubbing it in.

I thought the next thing Mother was going to say was: *Since the Superintendent isn't willing to pull you off the team, I'm going to do it myself.* Instead, she said nothing and began to clear the table.

I woke up remembering the expression on Pop's face after Mother said I was "ultimately not his concern" burning in my brain. Since I was not going to be at practice, I could come home while both of them were at work and do some snooping around. There was something rotten in the state of Garden. I could smell it.

Zack grabbed me in the hallway before first period and began to talk excitedly. He looked as happy as a robin with a worm in its mouth. "Man, I wish you could have been there, Joey. After Coach and I sat down, Adams explained what had happened and that he was thinking of throwing you off the team. Before he could say another word, I said, 'If Joey goes, we all go.' Then Coach chimed in, 'And I'll hand in my resignation.' Adams knew he was beaten. Finally, he said, 'I think a one- game suspension will suffice. Thank you for your trouble, gentlemen.'"

Having Zack, Coach and the whole rest of the team back me up brought a few tears to my eyes. The basketball team could win State without me, I was sure of that, yet they decided to take a giant risk on my behalf.

"One game's no big deal, Joey. We're playing West Highland on Friday night, the worst team in the league. They're so bad, even Martin will get a chance to play."

Even though I felt deep down I didn't deserve it, Coach and my teammates had genuine love for me. Dizzy, I leaned against some lockers. Sometimes the best news can be the hardest to take.

Arriving home right after school, I took off my coat and went right upstairs to the attic. It's a very dirty and musty place. I haven't been up there in years. You get in by pulling down a door in the ceiling right at the top of the staircase. A set of wooden stairs came down after I yanked the chain. In seconds, I was in the neglected room. Boxes and boxes of old books were piled haphazardly on the floor, along with my old Lionel train set and a few pieces of wooden furniture we no longer used. If there were any secrets to be found, this is where they would be.

Looking around, I saw an old metal box in a far corner. I pressed my thumb on the lock and opened it easily. Inside were lots of papers: stock certificates for the Pennsylvania Railroad, life insurance policies on both my parents, the deed for our house and at the bottom of the box, my parent's marriage license, along with my birth certificate. The license certified the union of Alice Ann Townsend and Victor Anthony Gardini on October 12, 1942. It was signed by both of them and notarized in Media, Pennsylvania, the Deerfield County seat.

I stopped and thought for a moment. My parents celebrated their anniversary on July 10th. It was easy to remember because it was right after the Fourth of July. Some years they didn't even acknowledge it, but last year we had ice cream and cake.

I put the marriage license in my shirt and walked slowly down the wooden steps as quietly as I could before folding them up and pushing the door closed. Mother had come home from work and was stirring in the kitchen. As I lay on the bed, my armpits were filled with sweat. Mother was pregnant with me for three months before she and Pop got married? The morally upstanding woman who never did an immoral thing in her life and expected the same from me? This was nuts, goofy crazy and went against everything I thought I knew about my parents.

This new information started to sink into my brain. Mother and Pop, the great mismatched pair, would never have gotten married if he hadn't gotten her pregnant. It also explained why Nan and Grandpa Joe were never shy about showing their dislike for my Pop. I'd always thought the main reason they moved to Florida and gave us the house was so they wouldn't have to be around him. Yet, something was very wrong with this scenario. How could it be that the first man Mother gave it up to was Pop?

The two of us were going to Lit Brothers to buy me some new clothes after dinner. Even if we got into a fistfight, I was going to get the truth out of him.

Dinner passed uneventfully. After we'd been driving for about fifteen minutes, I told Pop to pull the car over to the Elgin Diner parking lot in Upper Darby.

I glanced over at him and started talking very slowly. "I couldn't stop thinking about Mother's comment about me not being your concern, Pop. So, today, when I got home from school, I went up to the attic and found your marriage license. According to the document, the two of you were married on October 12, 1942, not on the tenth of July, which is when you celebrate it. What in the hell is going on?"

Pop looked like he had just been hit in the face with a shovel. "Some things are better off left alone, Joey."

"I *deserve* to know about the basic facts of my life, Pop."

"Your mother will murder me if I tell you the truth, son."

"Stop acting like Mother's cocker spaniel and be my father."

Pop sighed and tears began to run slowly down his cheeks. This was one of the few times I'd ever seen him cry. "Okay, Joey, you asked for it. But when you hear what happened, you might wish you never asked. I told you how I met your mother when we both were working in the Clam Shack down Beach Haven. It was during the War, everything was upside down and crazy. Alice was the best and prettiest waitress in the joint. It seemed natural that this blonde-haired lifeguard rippling with muscles would ask her out. All the other waitresses were jealous, and so was I. She got all dolled up and acted very excited before he'd pick her up. This lasted for about two weeks. Your mother started moping around the restaurant and almost got fired. Turns out the guy dumped her for no reason."

"Yeah, so?"

"This is the hard part, son. The lifeguard, a total jerk, came back into the Clam Shack about a week later, a new girl on his arm. Your mother, when she saw this, ran out of the restaurant, crying her eyes out. I followed her to the back steps where she'd sat down, wiping her eyes with her apron. Turns out the guy gave her a big line telling her how beautiful she was before he took advantage of her. We talked and went walking on the boardwalk almost every night after that. When summer ended, I thought I'd seen the last of her."

"So why did you lie about your anniversary?"

" I called her in September to see how she was doing and she told me she had gotten pregnant and didn't know what to do. She was frantic about your grandparents finding out. It had been about three months, and she was starting to show."

These words were an anvil blow to my head. This guy with his half-bald head with bristly hair on the sides, his bad English, and who'd been with me since the day I was born, wasn't my real father!

"So you married Mother to protect her reputation?"

"In a way, Joey. As you get older, you'll come to realize that not much in this world is simple. I cared a lot about Alice. And she was a lot classier than any girl in my neighborhood. I also saw this as an opportunity to get out of South Philly, which I thought I would never be able to do. My parents didn't believe me. They thought I knocked Alice up. Grandpa Joe and Nan also thought I was the one who got their daughter in trouble, even when Alice told them the truth. And they hated the idea that their only child was marrying an Italian who got his hands dirty at work."

My father put his hands on the steering wheel, pulled out the choke and turned the key in the ignition. He started to cry so hard, he couldn't even back the Chevy out of the parking space. I patted him on the back a few times, but it didn't seem to help much.

After he regained his composure, Pop turned to me and said, "I just wanted to protect you, Joey. Now you know why your mother has been so difficult lately. The idea of you goin' up to that hotel room in Harrisburg was like a hurricane coming through the house."

"You gave up a lot to be with her, Pop."

"Yeah, but I got a lot back, kid. I wouldn't trade the life I've known for anything in the world. I can't tell you how much it's meant to me seein' you grow up. Even though you didn't come from my seed, I know deep in my heart that you're truly my son."

Now it was my turn to cry. We sat in the car for at least ten minutes, not moving or talking.

Waking up the next morning at 5:30 a.m., I realized that I had fallen asleep in my clothes, my arms wrapped around a basketball. Got dressed, went downstairs and ate a bowl of Rice Krispies. Many thoughts, running at breakneck speed, were racing through my mind as I walked to school. My father, who wasn't really my father, had become more of a parent to me than the woman whose body I lived in for nine months. Mother, with all of her self-righteousness, let a guy she barely knew get her pregnant. I knew what she'd say when I confronted her: *I don't want you making the same mistakes I made.* And who in the hell was my real father anyway? Was I like him in any way? He sounded like Tim Martin, someone I will never be like. Did he change? Did he have a family? If I saw him on the street, would I know it was him?

I wished I had an off switch for my rampaging brain. When I got to school, I knew Ches would be in the library. I found him looking closely at a big atlas opened to the map of Sicily.

He looked up before saying, "Did you know Sicily has many active volcanoes, Joseph? Mt. Etna is the largest, but there are many others. There used to be sulfur mines in the 19th century in Sicily, until they were depleted. I try to learn about one new country a day, get all the information I can, then move on to the next one. Albania awaits tomorrow."

He paused and his tone became serious, "The Mugwumps miss you, Joseph. A short apology to Jeff and the group will be as good as new."

"Jeff should apologize to *me*, Ches. Then maybe I'll consider it. If I tell you something, you must swear to complete secrecy."

"My lips are permanently sealed."

"I found out yesterday that my father is not my real father. Some lifeguard impregnated Mother down at the shore and Pop married her, mostly out of pity, I think. I feel like my whole life has been a bogus lie."

Real sympathy shone in McChesney's eyes, "This certainly explains why you and Victor are so dissimilar. I wouldn't be so hard on your parents; it's almost impossible to reveal something like that to a young kid."

"They could have cared enough about me to tell me the truth when I got older."

"How important is it who your parents are? We're all related to Adam and Eve or Cave Man and Cave Woman anyway."

Ches always saw into the deeper meanings of things. One good thing about this shocking revelation is that I appreciate Pop much more that I ever thought I would. Maybe we can finally get beyond our mutual sniping matches. But Mother was another story. She'd tried repeatedly to sell me out to the Martins. Mother's always acted like a grand and mighty empress, ruling the family. As of today, I was no longer her little flunky.

The bell rang for first period. I started walking slowly into school, oblivious to the people around me, simmering with anger. I walked down the stairs to where the shop classes were. There was a fire alarm in a little alcove beneath the stairway. Not bothering to see if anyone was looking, I took the little hammer hanging on a chain, smashed the glass door and pulled the alarm. The sound of loud persistent bells rang throughout the entire school. I joined the rest of the students walking hurriedly outside onto Green Avenue.

Zack and the rest of the team were standing on the sidewalk in front of the hockey field. Tim Irwin punched me in the arm, laughed and said, "No first period, wowie."

After milling around for about ten minutes, Vice Principal Kaufman's voice rang out from the loudspeaker. "To the person who set off the false alarm, we know who you are. Turn yourself in to the front office to avoid expulsion. Others report immediately to their first period classes." The twins started laughing hysterically. "Yeah, right," Dan chortled, "we know who you are, which is why we haven't nailed your ass to a tree."

Going in the right side entrance, Ches was standing at the bottom of the stairway. I could tell by the disappointed expression on his face that he knew exactly what'd happened. His reaction bothered me. I knew he wouldn't turn me in, but he was sure to ask why I did such a dangerous, stupid thing. A Mugwump was supposed to be above this kind of thing. What

I was finding out about myself was that I wasn't above much of anything at all. Maybe I never was a Mugwump at heart. Maybe I didn't fit in anywhere at all.

As I walked to class, the feverish cloud that had taken over my mind started to evaporate. Setting a false alarm was a felony. People could have gotten knocked down and hurt leaving the building. If a real fire occurred sometime in the near future, kids might think the alarm was just a joke, which could lead to someone getting seriously hurt or killed. But who else in this goddamn school just found out that their parents had been lying to them for their entire life? Chuck Berry was right: *Too much monkey business for me to be involved in*. Just as Dan said, if the Administration knew I did it, I'd be in a police van headed out to Youth Camp right now, which was probably where I belonged.

Instead of going straight home after school, I stopped by Sam's Hoagie Shop where Gully, Mole, Kit and Skeeter were playing pinball. God, I love the smell of Sam's: provolone, olive oil, oregano, salami, ham. I ordered a regular Italian hoagie. Gully nodded to me as he flicked the flippers. Kit smiled and Mole gave me no recognition at all. I joined them, watching the ball ricochet beneath the glass.

The game was called "Cycle Babes" and had a picture of a hard-looking woman, with huge breasts and blinking lights on her nipples, sitting on a huge red motorcycle. I used to play pinball a lot in junior high, but it got boring. Every time the ball would hit one of the targets, Gully moaned, "Give it to me, momma, sock it to me, baby, all night, honey," while the other two looked on, grinning.

Mole finally regarded me and said, "How 'bout that false alarm, Joey? Too bad that fucking place didn't burn right down to the ground. Think about it, no more bullshit about the Constitution and being a good citizen, no more dressing for gym, no more stupid-ass pep rallies. Kids from Lansdowne just aren't lucky. Thank Christ, there are only a few more months in that shithole."

Kit looked at Mole reproachfully. "Don't put Joey in the same bag as us, Mole. He's gonna be going to some hot shit college next year, gettin' good grades so he can make a lot of money and pay us to fix his Cadillac."

What Kit had just said is something I'd been hearing for my entire life in one version or another. I'm sure he was trying to make me feel good, but, as far as I was concerned, I was worse than the three of them multiplied by ten.

I had to add to Mole's little tirade. "Why stop at the high school, Mole? Burn down every square inch of this idiotic, boring town. Think about it, huge, giant flames devouring Horn and Hardart's, the A&P, all the churches, the big houses on Owen Avenue. The flames could rise hundreds of yards into the air. Make the Burning of the Greens look like a backyard barbecue."

I took a big swig of a Chippy's lime soda and watched as looks of incredulity passed over their faces. "Holy fuck, Joey, you're too much. Get a black leather jacket and join the crew. And speaking of fire, I happen to know Helene's still carrying a torch for you."

I shrugged. Mugwump to Greaseball, what I used to think was an impossible transformation.

"You know, guys, some stuff happened at home that really pissed me off, so I broke the glass on the alarm and pulled the switch."

Gully looked like he had just seen a unicorn. "Get the fuck out of here, Garden."

Mole added, "Don't bullshit bullshitters, Joey. The only person who could have pulled that alarm was somebody like us."

Kit took a long drag on his Lucky and said nothing, still processing what I'd just said. If any one of these guys would be able to realize I was telling the truth, it would be him.

We talked for a while about which girls had the biggest tits in school, whether "Don't Be Cruel" was Elvis' greatest song (it's the only one of his I ever liked), whether it was a good idea to go into the Army or Marines after graduation. While we were talking, I started thinking about how I'd spent my life wanting to do certain things like shoplift and cut class but didn't, because I wanted to avoid the consequences. Well, guess what? There were no consequences.

The guys seemed to appreciate this new attitude of mine, so they offered me a ride home in Kit's Merc. I dearly hoped that Mother would be in the living room and see my hoodlum friends dropping me off, but, as usual, she was in the kitchen fixing dinner. As I left the car, I turned and shouted, "See you later, motherfuckers!"

Bounding up the stairs, I put my books on my desk and got the marriage license out of the middle drawer. I put it back and then took it out again. Staring at the dreaded piece of paper, I began walking downstairs, my stomach feeling heavier and heavier.

"I'm not used to you being home so early from school," Mother said as she put a casserole into the oven. "I kind of like it."

I put the license on the table. She picked it up and looked at it. "What in the world are you doing with our marriage license, Joey?"

"Maybe, Mother, you can explain to me why the date on the certificate is October 12, 1942, instead of July 10, 1942, which is when you and Pop celebrate your anniversary."

I had a strong feeling that she was getting ready to give me some kind of razzmatazz, so I cut her off. "I talked to Pop about this last night, so I know exactly what happened. Who is my real father, Mother?"

Her entire body started to quiver and, for a moment, I thought she might faint. She slid onto the bench in the breakfast nook and stared straight past me, her face churning with consternation. "I swore to myself many years ago that I would never let that man's name pass my lips again, and I see no reason to break that vow now, Joey, " she said.

There was a fragility in Mother's eyes I'd never seen before. "Mother, I know bringing this up must be very painful for you," I went on. "But it's been very difficult for me to realize that I'd been lied to my whole life, and that the version of how I came into this world was a complete falsehood. "

She got up, rubbed her hands across her apron and walked back to the stove. "The truth isn't all it's cracked up to be, Joey," she muttered, her words barely audible. "That man was a conceited, shallow, immoral creature who took delight in destroying young girls' lives. He refused to admit he got me pregnant. He wouldn't even call me by my first name after he found out. Is that the kind of person you would have wanted as a father?"

Her response got me even more riled up. "It's not that I would *want* him to be my father, he *is* my father." I exclaimed. "Why couldn't you trust me with the truth, Mother?"

Violent sobs convulsed her frame, wave after wave of agony. She walked slowly into the dining room, opened the china cabinet, took out a ceramic soup tureen covered with beautiful hand-painted roses and held it to her chest.

"This was a gift from Nan and Grandpa Joe. It's the most beautiful thing in this house and I've never had the heart to use it. That was the only time in my life I went against their rules. *One time!* It ruined everything between us. I was so ashamed of myself. ASHAMED!"

"At least you got me out of the deal, Mother."

She turned her head away and responded in the same faint, sandpapery voice, "Oh, I always wanted you, Joey, but by a man with a college degree. *I wanted to go to college.* Life sometimes takes a certain turn and there's no changing it. I tried to make the best of the situation. Your father is a good man who loves you very much, Joey."

"Imagine what would have happened if he didn't offer to marry you. I would have been born in a home for unwed mothers."

Mother put the tureen back into the china cabinet and walked back into the kitchen. There were so many things I wanted to say and find out about, but I could tell she was talked out. People walk around with all of these incredible things going on inside them, pain that won't go away, guilt about mistakes they made, fears about all kinds of things. Mother, on the surface, seemed like a very intelligent, competent woman, which she was. I had just gotten acquainted with her hidden side. One thing was certain: I was a bastard, pure and simple.

After walking upstairs, I opened my desk and took out the application for the National Merit Scholarship. This was something that was Mother's idea, not mine. I went to the section *Personal Info* and wrote the first thing that came into my warped mind: *Greatest Achievement:* Whacked off five times in one day. *Greatest Strength:* I am seldom constipated. *Future Goals:* To massage Annette Funicello's tits and get Jerry Lee Lewis elected president. *Things You Would Like to Improve about Yourself:* I'd like to stop kicking old ladies when they're trying to cross the street.

The hours I'd spent in my young life thinking about the future Mother wanted me to have, when I could have been shooting a basketball or unbuttoning a girl's sweater, were done. I took the application form, shredded it into two dozen pieces and threw them into my wastebasket. No more future for me.

The rest of the evening went by in slow motion. After quickly falling asleep, I had a dream where I was climbing up a beanstalk that never stopped growing. I was attacked by a swarm of giant bees and fell into a large pond filled with water so clear, I could see everything that was going on beneath it. When I landed, my body didn't go below the surface. Instead, I skittered on top, past lily pads, huge frogs, a hippo and an orange-and-black spotted crocodile. No matter how hard I tried, I couldn't stop myself from heading toward the croc's open mouth. When I woke up, I was relieved to be back in my room, with posters of Fats Domino and JFK on my walls. McChesney has read Freud on how to interpret dreams; maybe I should ask him about this one. One thing I did know, my life was careening around like a merry-go-round gone amok.

When I woke up on Saturday morning, the sun was beaming through the blinds right onto my face. It was one of those real brilliant winter days, very cold, but bright and clear like a mirror that'd just been polished.

At breakfast, raisin bran and toast, Mother and Pop were acting like everything was the same. I didn't see any reason to challenge the status quo. The doorbell rang. To my great surprise, Zack and the twins were standing there, big wide grins on their faces.

After they came into the living room, Pop asked, "To what do we owe this honor, gentlemen?"

Dan began to walk around, looking behind the sofa and easy chair. "Gentlemen, I can't seem to find any of those, Mr. Garden."

That brought a big laugh.

Zack looked at Pop and asked, "We were wondering if Joey can come with us to the gym at 57th and Parrish. Our center, Calvin Newsome, has some cousins who live around there, and they agreed to get a team together to play us. We beat Plymouth 72-28 last night. Some Philadelphia Public League all-stars will be there, and I think it will be a good challenge for us."

"Yeah," Dave added, "we just moved from that neighborhood last year; it'll be fun."

Seeing Pop's frown and furrowed brow, I knew he was dead set against me joining my teammates. A lot of whites had fled West Philly, including Dave and Dan's family, to escape living in the same neighborhood as black people. The homes were still pretty nice and the streets clean. For the ten thousandth time, I wondered why living with black people was such a horrible thing.

Pop looked at me and said, "Come into the kitchen, Joey. I'd like to have a word with you."

I didn't want say no to him in front of my friends. But I was going, no matter what he said.

Pop brought his face about two inches from mine and began spitting out words. "No way are you doing this, Joey. I know these are your friends and they're nice kids, but no son of mine is going to play basketball in the middle of Ubangiland. Those people will slit your throat, steal your wallet and laugh about it afterwards. Go back to the living room and tell your friends you have chores and won't be able to go."

Mother, having overheard this little speech, asked, "What is this about, Victor?"

I ran up to my bedroom and packed my gym bag. Pop was waiting for me at the bottom of the stairs, his eyes glistening with rage. He pushed his finger into my chest really hard and said, "You're not going, Joey."

"The hell I'm not," I answered, brushing right past him. The guys followed me out the door, and in just a few seconds we were heading down Baltimore Pike in Zack's station wagon. My head was pounding and I was breathing in short, quick bursts. I'd never been so openly defiant of my father. But his prejudice had always felt like an anchor around my neck.

Dan and Dave started laughing like crazy. "I thought the two of you were going to start wrestling," Dan said. "Your father's just like my old man, everything is *nigger nigger nigger*. At least when he's not shit-faced drunk with his head on the kitchen table."

They both started laughing, maybe a bit too hard. When the laughter subsided, Dave leaned over the front seat and added, "If me and my brother had a dollar for every time we had to drag that sorry son of a bitch upstairs, we could buy a new Impala."

Dan turned to Zack and asked, "Was your father like Joey's and ours, Zack?"

Zack turned onto Nyack Avenue before answering. "He died of a heart attack when I was six, so I don't remember much. My mom says he was a real nice guy, a hard worker who didn't show his feelings very much."

We were on Bartram Avenue, the only street in Lansdowne that had Negroes living on it. I usually had no reason to come down here, but Peaches Davenport, my freshman year crush, lived nearby. One Sunday morning, I got bored waiting for her to come out of her apartment building and rode my bike down to Bartram just for the hell of it. The Baptist church was having a service. The power of the music froze me on the spot. It felt like the ocean was pouring onto the street. This is where rock 'n'roll came from. If Pop knew I went there, he would have blown his stack, but I came back every Sunday. I'd get there right as the service was starting and leave right before it ended, overwhelmed by the glorious sounds. I don't know why I stopped going; guess I got interested in something else.

Calvin lived at the end of the street near Union Avenue in a small, brown, wooden frame house with a tiny front porch. His mother was a secretary and his father was the head custodian at a big office building in downtown Philly. There were three other kids, all girls and younger than Smooth.

After we got inside, Mrs. Newsome came bustling in, wearing a long brown dress under a white apron. She was a husky woman, broad-shouldered, with very dark skin and straight black hair that flowed down her shoulders. Gushing over us, she offered sodas and cookies, but we didn't have the time. Putting her arm across Smooth's shoulder and kissing him on the cheek, she said, "Tell Leemoore to let Aunt Myrelle know we'll be at their house tomorrow evening around six for dinner. And if she's making chitlins to let me know, so I can bake a ham."

She smiled at us and explained, "The last time my sister made chitlins, our whole family got diarrhea."

Smooth grimaced and said, "They tasted *really* nasty."

I thought it would be bad manners to ask what chitlins were, so I didn't. As I walked to the car, I realized that this was one of the only times I'd ever been in a black family's home. The only difference I could tell was the unique smell from the spices Calvin's mother was using in the kitchen.

I moved to the back seat with Dave and Dan so Calvin could have more leg room.

"Yo, Calvin," Dave asked. "Do the guys at the rec center know about our team?"

"Yeah, they sure do. Guys from Philly don't usually pay much attention to what's happening in the suburban leagues, but when we beat McKeesport and Curtis Wilkerson in Harrisburg, Lansdowne's reputation was spread far and wide."

"Tell me about Frank Ward, Calvin," Zack asked. "He's the leading scorer in the Public League and some of the sportswriters say he's the best player to come out of West Philly since Wilt the Stilt."

"Frank's 6' 7", and can dunk easily with either hand. His jump shot is killer and he can drive on anyone. On defense, he blocks shots and steals the ball all game long. The two best high school forwards in Pennsylvania will be playing against each other today."

We pulled up to a gray, two-story building that had a sign over the front door, *Cobbs Creek Recreational Center*. Inside the lobby, there were little girls jumping rope, young boys playing with yo yos and three quartets of teenaged guys singing doo wop. The place was jumping.

The players challenging us were standing at the middle of the court, dressed in white shorts, white tee shirts and white Converse high-tops. I figured the guy with light brown skin and a pencil-thin mustache was Frank Ward. There was another player who was taller than Ward, but he was kind of chunky and didn't have the presence of a star. The rest all looked like guards, below six feet, some muscular, some not.

We shook hands and went underneath the stands to change. Calvin had us put our wallets into his gym bag, which he gave to his cousin. Can't be too cautious anywhere you go, I guess.

We walked out to the center of the court; the gym was three-quarters full. When people saw us they started jumping up and down and whooping. Calvin was right; we were famous! Zack had us huddle around him. "Let's play tough man-to- man, and keep moving the ball on offense. Don't try anything fancy, just play our usual game."

Since there was no ref, we were given the opportunity to bring the ball in first. Calvin tossed me the ball. I dribbled past my man and flung a line drive pass to Zack. He dribbled into the lane and jammed the ball through the basket with both hands. Cheers echoed through the rafters.

I kind of had the feeling that Ward was not going to let that one pass, and he didn't. He got the ball in the corner, backed Zack in, faked left then right, spun around 360 degrees and banked in a fadeaway jumper. This was going to be interesting. My man, mesmerized by our Captain, started to cheat a little bit, sagging off me to help defend Zack. I hit three jumpers in a row: no net, no rim, no backboard.

The crowd was eating it up. Certainly they wanted their guys to win, but if you did something good, they appreciated it. Zack and Frank were like two elk locked in mortal combat. My man's job seemed to be to get the ball to Ward. I stopped worrying about guarding him and ran to the half-court line. Smooth got a rebound and hit me with a long pass. I went in for an easy layup. This happened two more times, and we were ahead, 16-6. Lansdowne High was killing the best West Philly had to offer. Zack came and said, "You're going to score the rest of the points, Joey." Sounded nuts, but who was I to argue?

Getting behind Dan and Dave's screens, I threw up two arching jump shots, both of which went right through the rim. Zack got free for an easy layup, but before he scored, turned around and threw me a pass. No one expected this, so I was wide open. Another bucket. The game went to 24; we needed one more score. Ward hit a jumper from the corner, then ran back and started guarding me. It was flattering to have a star like him take me so seriously; he was so tall and so quick, I knew I had no chance to score over him. Zack or someone else could make the final basket.

After Dave got me the ball, Zack yelled, "Take the shot, Joey, it's yours." I dribbled to my right, Ward stole the ball and raced down court for a thunderous dunk. Anticipating what I was going to say, Zack ran up to me, put a hand on my shoulder and said, "You can do it."

Unlike Zack, I realize I have serious limitations as a basketball player, but here went nothing. Ward was right in front of me, sweat glistening off his face onto the gym floor. As soon as I got the ball, I turned sideways and began bouncing it with my left hand. Ward reached in with his long arm, ready to flick the ball away. I turned my back to him and made a quick movement, threw a bullet pass to Dan and broke for the basket. Dan got the ball to Zack, who hit me in stride at the top of the key. I knew that if I shot a simple layup, Ward would shove the ball so far down my throat I'd look like I was pregnant. Instead of shooting, I drove underneath the basket and threw the ball up without looking. When I turned around, the ball was rolling and rolling inside the rim, before dropping through. The guys came up and mobbed me. I had scored 20 of our 24 points! Ward shook my hand and said, "You got some serious game there, little man."

This couldn't go on for the rest of the morning, and it didn't. Zack took over the second game, which we won as well, 24-20. Agreeing to play one more, even though every player was drenched in sweat, Frank Ward bombarded the basket with left- and right-handed jumpers, virtuoso dunks and poetic hook shots. The guy was a phenomenal talent. Final score: West Philly 24, Lansdowne 18, the first time we'd ever lost a game.

Zack was beaming as we walked through the crowd.

"I thought you'd be pissed, Zack. We lost."

"You can't be angry when basketball is played like that, Joey. Frank Ward is the best player I ever played against. Today was a total gas."

Most of the crowd had converged at half-court. Everyone shook hands. No one threatened me. No one had gone after our wallets. In fact, we were being treated like royalty.

Headed down Walnut Street, no one said anything for a while as we basked in the glow of a great experience. Finally Dave chirped, "Tell you what, motherfuckers; 1961 Pennsylvania All-State Team is Curtis Wilkerson at center, Zack Bolton and Frank Ward at forwards, Curtis' teammate, Brandon Malone, at one guard and at the other...*Joeee Garden* of Lansdowne High School!"

Amidst the cheers, I had to protest. "No goddamn way. There are dozens of better guards out there. I couldn't even hold their jocks."

The cheers turned to boos. As preposterous as Dave's claim sounded, I was brimming with happiness.

I expected a conflagration with Pop when I returned home, but it didn't happen. He nodded at me and went back to reading the paper when I came in the front door. I could tell he was upset, because his body was rigid. Even though I felt I was in the right by disobeying him, it felt bad to have hurt his feelings.

If he wasn't going to say anything, I was. "We had a great time, Pop. The people at the Rec Center treated us very well. I scored a lot of points. Everyone cheered when we left. No one threatened us. No one took our money. No one even gave us so much as a dirty look."

He put the paper down slowly into his lap and said with great irritation, "Going against my wishes was not enough, now you wanna rub it in?"

"I don't want to rub it in at all, Pop. And I got no joy from defying you." I took a deep breath. If I was going to get into this, I might as well get into it all the way. "You know, I think you're a good father, I really do. But I've been listening to you going on and on about the 'niggers' for as long as I can remember. You're like Harry the Barber. Every time I get a haircut, he starts going on about the jigaboos, the niggers, the jungle bunnies, the Ubangis, when as far as I can tell, they haven't done anything to him. It's always bothered me that my father's racial attitudes were just like my dumb-ass barber. I know you work with some pretty tough guys, but not all black people are like that."

He put his head down and didn't say anything for a while. When he finally looked up, he said, "Now that you know the truth about me, you think you can lecture me about how I'm supposed to think?"

"No, I just don't want to feel ashamed of my father, which is what I feel when you go on about black people. Let that *nigger* stuff go. It makes you look stupid when you're anything but."

"I been thinkin' and talkin' like that for most of my life. The older you get, the harder it is to change. I'll think about what you said. One other thing, young man, you're gonna be restricted next weekend for walkin' out of the house when I told you not to."

"Fine. That's fair."

Pop looked startled when I agreed so readily. I just couldn't find it in me to challenge him again. Winter Ball was next weekend, but even though I'd never missed a big dance before, with all the stuff that's been going on with me, I could have cared less about it.

Lunch followed Advanced English class. After reading the section where Macbeth had Macduff's wife and children murdered, I didn't have much of an appetite. I guess there was nowhere for him to go but down after he killed his cousin, King Duncan. Even though *Macbeth* is just a play, it mirrors real life. When once-good people commit serious crimes like murder, their lives fall apart, just like Macbeth's. Thank God I'd gotten away with pulling the fire alarm; I didn't feel a need to do anything else.

After I got my tray, Zack motioned me to sit with him and the rest of the team, but I felt like rejoining the Mugwumps. I missed Ches and George. If Jeff got uncomfortable, so be it.

When I put my tray down beside McChesney, he said, "Something wicked this way comes," which is what the witches said to Macbeth when he came to see them.

"The prodigal son returns," Jeff quipped.

"To what do we owe this grand honor?" George asked.

"Gully and The Mole were busy."

Watching Jeff very carefully, the stolid expression on his face betrayed no emotion. He'll never forgive me for grabbing him; I won't forgive him for his move on Marilyn. Sometimes one just has to work around things like this and move on. I could tell by the quick grins on their faces that the other two were happy to see me.

For the first time in memory, Ches did not have any Tastykake chocolate cupcakes. A miracle. I congratulated him.

"Our family doctor told me I had to lose weight if I wanted to live past thirty. His speech had the desired effect. No more sweets and, even though I hate exercise more than death, I've been walking every evening after dinner for half an hour. Perhaps, next semester, I may even suck up my pride and take P.E. It's a travail, but there's no sense getting into Harvard if I'm going to croak right after I graduate."

George chimed in, "The Drama Club decided to stage 'Our Town.' I'm in charge of building the sets."

"This is monumentally good news, gentlemen. You've thrived in my absence."

Turning to Jeff, I said, "I see you and Marilyn are competing for King and Queen of Winter Ball. Good luck."

My blasé attitude seemed to flummox him a bit, as it took him a while to compose an answer. "We are, Joey. You may have noticed that Zack and Cindy Devers have entered as well.

It's going to be difficult competing against a basketball star and those two formidable bosoms."

This was pretty shocking news, which made me instantly uncomfortable. Zack never goes to dances. I don't think he even knows how to do a simple fox trot. And since he'd made a solemn vow to swear off girls until the season was over, this could be a serious development. If I knew Cindy, Zack was her ticket back to the limelight after being kicked off cheerleaders for the fiasco with Martin in the hotel room.

"Yes, they're tough opponents. No Winter Ball for me this year, otherwise I may have competed myself."

Jeff took a long swig of his, yes, chocolate milk before asking, "With Helene the Machine?"

He knew this would royally piss me off, and it did. Before I could respond, Ches leaned across the table until his face was about six inches away from Jeff's and began berating him. "The incident is over, Jeff. If Joey's man enough to come sit with us, you should be man enough to not open old wounds. The Mugwumps are not the same with just the three of us. Grow up."

"Easy for you to say, McChesney."

"You got the better of the deal. Let it go."

Emotions were roiling through Jeff's face. I don't think anyone at the table knew whether he was going to take off or stay. My heart was pounding, so I guess I cared about his decision. He got his tray and started walking off, before turning around abruptly and sitting back down.

"Okay, I'll try to forget it."

"Shake hands, you two," McChesney said, "so we can get back to being Lansdowne High School's intellectual elite."

We dutifully shook hands. I'm not sure anything was solved, but at least we were speaking again, and the Mugwumps were now intact. As we talked about *Macbeth* and Problems of Democracy class, I realized how much I had missed our intellectual repartée.

Just as the bell was about to ring ending lunch, Ches arose and said, "I have an announcement to make. Yesterday I received a letter from Harvard University informing me that I've been accepted for the fall semester as an Electronic Physics major. My parents and I will be driving up to Cambridge next month to discuss the possibility of receiving some financial aid."

We all cheered and slapped our friend on the back. Although the news wasn't exactly surprising, it was great to hear. Many Lansdowne High graduates have gone to Ivy League universities, but Ches was the first I've heard of to get into Harvard. He'll take over the place, I'm sure.

Buoyed by that good news, the rest of the day tumbled by quickly. It felt great to be back in the locker room with the guys, getting ready for practice. Two reunions in one day was a pretty good deal.

Right after Zack arrived in the locker room, I asked him about Winter Ball.

He seemed kind of embarrassed talking about it. "My mom kept ragging me about basketball taking over my life. She must have said, 'It's not normal to think only about one thing' about a hundred times a day. I got sick of listening to her, so I asked Cindy to the dance. She entered us in the King and Queen competition on her own. I'm going over her house to practice dancing on Friday night. Can't wait until the whole thing's over with."

Coach lectured us for about fifteen minutes about not taking unnecessary chances on hurting ourselves with so much at stake. He'd found out about the Rec Center. The further we advanced, the more uptight Coach was getting. I don't think he should have interfered. We could get hurt as easily in league games as we could playing pick-up ball. Zack would never disobey Coach. But since he was so worried about the team becoming stagnant, he made us all agree to go to the old gym and practice on Sunday afternoon.

Five people showed up for the workout: Dan and Dave, Mac, Calvin and me. Zack was nowhere to be found. Our Captain being a no-show energized everyone. We did twenty court sprints, twice the usual number, with almost no rest in-between. After the sprints, we ran some fast break drills and played against each other one on one. I wanted to work on driving to the basket, and had the twins guard me. I scored twice, two times more than I'd expected. We finished by practicing our outside shots, three guys shooting and two guys underneath getting rebounds.

As we were toweling off in the showers, Zack walked into the locker room, an embarrassed look on his face.

"Hey, guys," he said. "Sorry I missed the workout."

No one responded.

"Cindy and I had a little problem that had to be resolved."

Dave snickered, "Yeah, six inches worth of problem."

Dan added, "How does it feel to be pussywhipped after just one date?"

Zack usually returned insults very quickly, but instead he just stood there, looking glum. Mac decided to speak, "You know, Zack, we're all happy about your new love life, but when the team Captain doesn't show up to a workout that he arranged, it's a big deal."

"I am genuinely sorry, Mac, like I said. It won't happen again."

We finished dressing and went out into the cold afternoon. Zack and I started walking down Essex Avenue. He seemed distracted, totally lost in thought.

After two minutes of silence, he spoke. "Man, Joey, you won't believe what happened. Cindy and I won King and Queen of the Winter Ball. She loved putting on the tiara, but when I got crowned, I wanted to run out of the gym. We got back to her house and went down to the basement. Before very long, our clothes were off. I don't think you need any more details, just that it happened three times. I got home at 2:30 and gave my mom a "Wake Up Little Suzie" excuse. *We fell asleep, didn't get up until after two, blah blah.* Cindy called about ten, saying that she *had* to see me. I went over there and she wanted me to drive to her cousin's house in Drexel Hill. There didn't seem to be any choice but go along. I had to drag her home just to get to the gym when I did."

My first thought, I have to admit, was pure envy: the guy who had totally sworn off girls had lost his virginity before I did. My second thought was that if Zack stayed distracted, the rest of our basketball season was doomed. We were only two wins from being Deerfield County League champions, a given. Without Zack's maniacal determination behind us, winning State was nothing more than a pipe dream.

"Now you know why you swore off girls until after the season, Zack. Cindy and a lot of other girls will be there once the season is over. Call her tonight and tell her you're going to have to stop seeing her for a while. She'll try to talk you out of it, but don't let her."

My words had clearly agitated him. "I've never experienced *anything* like that before, Joey. After one date, Cindy's a big magnet pulling me away from the most important thing in my life."

"Don't let getting some pussy turn you into one. Remember that Cindy was *Martin's* girlfriend. Just put it aside, man."

For the first time in memory of all my interactions with Zack Bolton, I was the stronger one. It felt like trying on a style of clothes I'd never worn before. Snow started whirling around our heads as we walked down Owen to Stratford. Zack had clammed up and I didn't know what more I could say. When we reached his apartment building on LaCrosse, I astonished myself by saying, "Take care of this, Zack, or I will." The sheepish expression on his face, after these words, made my stomach sink.

During Monday's practice, Zack was playing very sluggishly, with no zip on his passes, taking clanky shots and dribbling the ball off his knees. Coach yelled at him, "Wake the hell up, Zack!" He didn't. As we headed to the locker room, Coach told Zack to run a dozen laps around the court.

We were all dressed when Zack entered the locker room. Dan stood in front of him and said, "That was your worst practice ever, Zack. What the fuck?"

Mac came up beside the twin and put in his two cents, "You're our *Captain*, and you were sleepwalking out there. For Christ's sake, man."

Martin was in the corner, buttoning his shirt, a big smile on his face. He loved seeing us in turmoil. If we failed, he could say that if Coach didn't have a grudge against him, we'd have been State champions.

I could tell by the way Zack had sat with Cindy at lunch, oblivious to everything else around him, that he hadn't heard one word I'd said to him about breaking it off. I thought about going back and talking to him some more, but decided against it. I'd said what I needed to say, and repeating it wasn't going to do any good.

All through dinner I ruminated about this sorry state of affairs. I could sit back and watch disaster unfold, or try to stop it in its tracks. Winning State was my obsession now. I'd fallen head over heels for basketball. Opportunities like this didn't come around more than once in a person's life. If we failed in our quest, the world wasn't going to end, but I'd have a hard time living with myself if I didn't do everything in my power to make it happen.

Upstairs, I looked up Cindy's phone number and dialed it. She was not the brightest girl in the world, and pretty shallow to boot, and would have trouble understanding concepts like integrity, loyalty, sacrifice. My best bet was to try to convince her that her newly found status as the basketball star's girlfriend wasn't going to last very long if we didn't win State.

Mr. Devers answered the phone and said, "I'll tell Madame Queen you want to talk to her, Joey."

After a minute or so, Cindy's husky voice came on the line.

"Are you in a private place?" I asked. "The stuff I want to talk to you about is rather personal."

After a few moments, she came on again. " I want to congratulate you, Cindy, for becoming Queen of the Winter Ball," I said.

"Thanks a lot, Joey."

"It must be especially gratifying to be back in the limelight after you were thrown off cheerleaders."

"Tell me what you want, Joey. My mother's expecting a call."

"Okay, I'll try to make this short and sweet. Zack told me what happened with the two of you after the dance. He missed our Sunday workout because of you. In a thousand years, I never expected he'd do anything like that."

"What happened between Zack and me is nobody's business but our own."

"Interesting, because the same thing that happened between you and Zack happened between you and Martin. What a coincidence! And if you wanted it to happen between you and another guy, Cindy, I'm sure you could arrange that pretty quickly."

"I don't think Zack will appreciate what you're saying to me."

"Our basketball team has a chance to win the first state championship in the history of the school, Cindy. *Think about that.* If you continue to keep Zack distracted, we won't win anything. Trust me, I won't be shy about telling anyone who will listen that we failed because you couldn't keep your legs closed."

"That's the most insulting thing anyone has ever said to me."

"If you think that's bad, wait and see what happens if you don't break it off with Zack."

"You're a real bastard, Joey."

"Just remember what I said, Cindy. Back the hell off."

I hung up the phone, went to my room and threw myself across the bed. It felt like I had just finished two hours of practice. If Cindy had a brain in her head, she would have figured out what I'd just told her and not gone all the way with Zack on the first date. She was incapable of thinking beyond her immediate needs. I felt like an executioner, like I just put a bullet through her right temple. It was a good feeling.

I should have known Zack would nab me the second I arrived at school, which he did right inside the front entrance.

"What in the hell are you trying to do, Joey?' he seethed, pointing an index finger at my eye. "Cindy cried all night after your phone call. Her parents were ready to take her to the hospital."

"Someone needed to clue her in about the implications of what she did. You certainly weren't going to do it."

Zack looked at me in total disgust, saying as he walked away, "Stay the fuck out of my business, Joey."

I ran to the bottom of the stairs and got in front of him. He's six inches taller and forty pounds heavier than me, but I was not scared.

"A lot of people, myself included, thought you were absolutely nuts in your single-minded pursuit of a state title, Zack. But eventually, just about everyone in the school, myself included, has bought into your dream. Then you lose your virginity and turn into the proverbial 90-lb. weakling. Do you think I'd be able to talk to you this way if you hadn't fucked that stupid cow? Do you think I'd have to?"

A lot of student saw us arguing and had gathered around in a semi-circle. I didn't plan to embarrass Zack, but the team needed our Captain back. Walking to first period, my entire body was shaking.

At lunch, Zack walked past me without acknowledging my presence. Hopefully, he'd get over our spat pretty quickly and come to his senses. I thought about joining the Mugwumps, but just didn't feel like getting involved in an intense discussion of any kind. It felt good to pull away from things sometimes, just block everything out and reflect on what was happening. Kind of weird to do that in the middle of lunch period, but that's what I wanted to do. I walked to the end of the main hall, sat down at the top of the stairs and began eating.

About halfway through my salami and cheese, Helene came and sat down beside me. I had a brief impulse to tell her I wanted to be alone, but even though I didn't want company, I was glad to see her. Her sandy hair had gotten a little longer; it looked like she was trying to grow it out, a new look. Usually, she wore lipstick, eye shadow and rouge, but the only make-up she was wearing today was pink fingernail polish. Her face was very pretty without all the glop, with her thick lips, shining blue eyes, pug nose. If I could compare her to a movie star, it would be Jayne Mansfield, without the tumultuous breasts and bleached hair. But there was a kind of hardness around the corners of Helene's mouth that kept her from looking like a total knockout.

She unwrapped a hoagie before saying, "You looked like you needed some company."

"Just kind of lost in my thoughts, Helene. You look real nice without makeup."

"Thanks, Joey. Theresa is trying to talk me into bleaching my hair, but I don't know."

"Big mistake, Helene, your hair looks fine."

"My hair is so boring, not blonde, not brunette, just nothing at all."

"It looks great to me."

She blushed a little before saying, "Gully thinks you're a secret badass. He thinks it was you who pulled the fire alarm. I told him he was full of shit, that you would never do anything like that. He told me to tell you that you can join his crew any time you want."

I had to smile, just thinking about me with greasy hair, black leather jacket, Lucky Strike dangling from my lips was pretty amusing. Helene thought so highly of me; if she only knew. When the bell rang, I gave her a hug and a kiss on the cheek. The hell if anyone else noticed.

Zack was a different person in practice, playing harder and concentrating on the business at hand. He wasn't back to his old self yet, but anything was better than the zombie he was yesterday.

He had his mother's station wagon and offered me a ride home after practice. I hesitated a moment before accepting, worried that he might want to start screaming at me in the car. But it was cold, and I needed a ride.

"I wanted to thank you for this morning, Joey. I needed someone to kick my ass."

"Usually, it's been the other way around."

"Yeah, well, you told me the truth, which I finally was able to appreciate."

We were quiet for a while, listening as Sam Cooke's "Chain Gang" played on the radio.

"I spent most of third period in the counselor's office. My mother watched me moping around the house last night and figured out that something was very wrong. When I broke down and told her, she called Cindy's parents and set up today's meeting. Mr. and Mrs. Devers acted like it was no big deal. Cindy sat there with her arms folded, chewing gum and sulking. My mother *hated* them. Needless to say, no more dates with the Queen of the Winter Ball."

"What a relief."

"Yeah, but there's still the possibility she's pregnant."

"Holy shit, you didn't use a rubber?"

Zack pulled the car over, put his head on the steering wheel and started to pound the dashboard with his fist. When he was able to speak, he looked at me and said, "Man, if she gets pregnant, Joey, I don't know what I'm going to do. Can you imagine me married to Cindy Devers?"

"The hell with that, Zack. Cindy knew you didn't have much experience with girls. I'll bet she planned the whole thing. There are only a few days in a month when a girl can get knocked up. After she gets her period, which she will, you should offer to buy her Kotex for the rest of her life."

"You're one tough little nut, Joey."

"You taught me, man. There's *no way* we win State without our maniac Captain pushing us to the limit."

In my room after dinner, I was having a hard time concentrating on Moliere. And I needed to outline a paper on how the McCarthy Era had threatened the First Amendment. With all that'd been going on, school had seemed more and more irrelevant, like background music in an elevator. I'll get the stuff done, but damn, what if Zack did become the father of Cindy Devers's child? Even if they didn't get end up getting married, he'd have to stay involved with that dumb ass bitch for the rest of his life.

The team won three more games by large margins. The town was starting to get excited about us. Many students watched me as I walked down the hallways and beeped their horns when they saw me walking through town. The shopkeepers in downtown Lansdowne came up and asked how I was doing and whether I thought we were good enough to win State.

Tonight's game was against Conshohocken at their place.

Coach talked on and on about becoming complacent, but I don't think anyone was really listening. We knew we'd kill those guys. The game would be over by the end of the first quarter. The starters were beginning to get a bit concerned about Coach. With every win, he continued to get more and more uptight, even agitated at times. He snapped at Dan and Dave for goofing off in the locker room yesterday, something he'd never done before.

Martin continued to be pretty much of a joke, sitting on the end of the bench, contributing nothing. I thought Coach might play him more as an insurance policy in case one of the starters got hurt, but he didn't. Someone else might have quit in disgust about not being used, but not dear old Tim.

We were ahead 50-28 halfway through the third quarter. Coach called out, "Tim, go in for Zack," but Martin scowled and refused to get up. When Coach realized what was happening, he walked down to the end of the bench and asked Martin if something was wrong. He answered in a very loud voice, "No way I'm going into this game, Johnson. You only put me in during garbage time and I'm not garbage."

Coach walked back to his seat and put me in instead. When the game was over, Martin walked slowly back to the locker room, warm-up jacket covering his head, completely alone, like the leper he was.

In the locker room, Coach told us to stop changing our clothes and pay attention. "In my eighteen years of coaching," he said, putting his foot on a bench and leaning over, "I have never had a player defy me in the middle of a game, until tonight." He looked straight at Tim and spoke in a stern no-nonsense tone. "As of right now, Martin, you are officially off the Lansdowne High basketball team. Leave your uniform here and do not come to any more practices or games."

I thought Martin would be righteously pissed and argue back; instead, he gave Coach a dismissive wave of his hand and answered, "We'll see about that, Johnson."

During the ride back to school, Martin sat in the back seat by himself, singing and whistling. Zack was beside me, getting more and more irate. "If it wouldn't get me into trouble, I'd kick Tim Martin's ass all the way to West Philly. Son of a bitch, humiliating Coach in front of everybody. Thank God he's finally gone. Good riddance to bad rubbish."

"Don't be too sure, Zack. I don't think Martin would have done what he did if he wasn't sure he could get away with it."

Zack looked at me with a look of incredulity, leaned back in the seat and sighed.

At the last home game of every season, the seniors on the basketball team honor their parents in a short ceremony before the game. Mothers and fathers line up on the mid-court line. The player's name is announced and he gives his mother a dozen roses, while the crowd cheers. It's kind of nice. I hadn't been thinking about it much because I've gotten used to not having my parents attending. Tonight, I wanted them to come. It'd be more than a little bit weird to be the only senior whose parents didn't show up.

As I was clearing the dinner plates, Mother was at the sink and Pop was sitting in the breakfast nook, smoking a cigar. I told them what was going to be happening at the final home game, and that it would look strange if they weren't there.

Mother began washing the dishes intensely, before saying, "I've come to accept how important basketball has become to you, Joey. Where you got your ability, I'll never know. P.E. was my worst subject in high school. I simply hated it. No one ever wanted to pick me for a team. I couldn't run very well or throw a ball or do very much of anything. And I don't like being in front of a large group of people. I hope you'll understand if your father and I respectfully decline the invitation."

My stomach sank. I'd hoped that despite her lack of interest, she might secretly be proud of what the team and I had accomplished and want to be there. Pop was sitting quietly, his hands folded In front of him on the kitchen table. Normally, I couldn't count on him to take my side. Once Mother made a decision, it was law.

"I dunno, Alice," he said. "I stunk at sports myself, but our son wants us to be there. And from what I read in the paper, they might actually win that State Championship. I think we should go. Show how proud we are of Joey."

Mother stopped washing. It looked like she had stopped breathing. Even though he was doing it in a nice way, Pop challenging Mother was as unusual as seeing an elephant doing ballet.

"Victor," she answered very slowly, emphasizing every syllable, "I'm just not comfortable in those kinds of situations. I'm sure that Joey will understand."

"It's not going to kill you, Alice."

"I'm not so sure about that."

Pop hesitated and scratched his head. "If that's really the way you feel, I'll go by myself. It'll look strange for him to have only one parent there, but it's better than nothin.'"

"That will put even more attention on me. You'll do no such thing, Victor Garden."

Pop remained steadfast and Mother eventually gave in. Maybe nothing really *is* set in stone.

The next morning, Zack was waiting for me in front of my first-period class. He was clearly agitated. I hoped he wasn't bringing catastrophic news.

"Martin's back on the team, the fucker," he said. "Coach called me into his classroom this morning and told me the news. Coach just said that Tim had to be reinstated on the team. I proposed that we'd all go over to the Superintendent's office and threaten to quit like we did for you, but he wouldn't have it. Coach looked real sad, Joey, totally down in the dumps."

The bell rang before I had a chance to answer. This was horrendous news. I guessed the fact that Coach didn't play Tim festered and festered in the hearts of the President of the Borough Council and his charming wife. The whole incident was probably planned. They wanted to rub Coach's nose in it, figuring he wouldn't quit leading such a successful team. None of us would blame him if he did walk out, but there wasn't a chance we'd win State without him.

Like a big zit ready to pop, Martin sat on a bench in the locker room before practice, looking smug. Seeing him like this was like having to drink a pint of cod liver oil. Most of us were too disgusted to say anything, but Dave walked over to Tim and said, "Don't get smug, Martin. You and your parents won this one, but it's far from over."

Tim started to say something before stopping himself. Good thing, because the twins looked like they were ready to vivisect his sorry ass. Even Calvin, who was usually so calm and placid, looked disgusted.

Coach's voice was lifeless as he called out the drills. Zack noticed, put his hand up and stopped everything. "Before we get started Coach, as Captain of the team, I have a few things to say. We all know that you kicked Tim Martin off the team, and we all know he deserved it. We also know, even though you didn't tell anyone, that Superintendent Adams caved into pressure from Tim's parents and had him reinstated against your wishes. I think I speak for every player in saying that *no one* wants him on our team. As much as all of us hate this decision, in honoring your wishes, there will be no protest. This is just one more obstacle we have to overcome before winning the State Championship."

Anyone with any shame at all would have left the gym after that speech, but not Tim. As Zack said, we'd have to tolerate this miserable state of affairs for the time being. Coach found energy from our Captain's words. Practice became an intense, nonstop slice of hell. I sweated through my gym clothes at least twice and when we finished, my thighs and calves were so swollen, walking to the showers was torture. Martin was the worst off, doubled over in the first row of the grandstand, struggling for breath.

The gym was packed to the rafters for our final home game against Interboro. We'd won the league championship two weeks ago, but even for such a meaningless game, just about everyone in town had turned out. After finishing our layup drills, the players sat down on the bench. Coach walked to the scorer's table, picked up a microphone and said. "Will the parents of the senior players please come to the center of the court for a short ceremony."

The men and women filed out of the stands and quickly assembled at half-court. Calvin's mom and dad were first, dressed in their Sunday best clothes. Mrs. Bolton was next in a tan suit, followed by the evil Martins. Has Mrs. Martin always worn her hair in a hideous beehive? Probably. Mr. and Mrs. Irwin were next. The twins were worried that their father might be too drunk to make it, but even though he was hunched over, he wasn't wobbly. Victor and Alice Garden were last. Mother stood motionless, obviously uncomfortable. Pop had his cap in his hand, moving quickly from one foot to the other.

When everyone was situated, Coach addressed the crowd, "We wish to commemorate the parents of our senior players. They have produced some wonderful young men who are a credit to our school and town. Please let them know how much we appreciate them."

The team manager handed each senior player a dozen roses. The crowd cheered as we gave our mothers the flowers. When my name was called, as I strode up to my parents, I had an impulse to drop the roses at Mother's feet. She'd be humiliated in front of the whole town, which is what she deserved. But I'd look like a nasty little ingrate. After a moment's hesitation, I placed them in her arms.

We went after Interboro like a team of surgeons, exploiting their lack of size and speed. Martin came in halfway through the first quarter and scored eight points. Final score: 72-36. Next stop: a rendezvous with destiny.

THE POT OF gold at the end of the rainbow might be ours by the end of next week. There were no other undefeated public high school basketball teams in Pennsylvania. We were the only one that had beaten McKeesport. Wilkes Barre was supposed to be very good, with every starter over 6'3'. And Chilton, the team that knocked us out of the Regionals in '55, '57 and '59, was back again with a 20-2 record. The whole school was in the throes of State Championship Fever. The players were all being treated like we were visiting dignitaries. Conversations stopped when we went past people. Quite a few kids stood and gawked at us, doing everything but bow down as we walked the hallways. I kept telling myself: *This won't be going on much longer. This won't be going on much longer.*

The team was in great shape. No one was injured. We were all supremely confident about our chances. The only fly in the ointment was Martin.

I got a note that said Coach wanted to see me in his classroom right after school, which I tried not to think about as I walked to the cafeteria.

The Mugwumps seemed surprised when I sat down with them. Jeff's body tightened. Ches smiled broadly. George said "hoorah" upon my arrival; it was unusual for him to be so demonstrative.

"I was wondering, Joseph," Ches asked, leaning toward me, "Do you think Calvin Johnson is being ignored on offense too much lately? Seems to me that if the team wants to go all the way, he's got to score more close to the basket."

Flabbergasting comment. Even the rest of the Mugwumps, who hated all sports, were infected with the fever. Ches had actually gone to some recent games, a miracle. How did I miss seeing him?

"I thought this was the one place in this cafeteria that I could come to and not have to talk about basketball. But I guess there's no escape. In answer to your question, Steve, Calvin hasn't been scoring because our outside shooting has been so good. If the teams we play in Regionals ignore him, they'll be making a big mistake."

George had an embarrassed look on his face as he put his hand on my shoulder and asked, "Hey, Joey. I've been looking at this sophomore, Traci Arnold. We've been talking a little bit, and I'm starting to really like her. Her locker's on the second floor right by the biology lab. It would be great if you could walk by there with me after school. She's bound to be very impressed if she sees that you're my friend. "

"Watch out, George, Joey can have any girl in the school. He might just steal her away from you."

Good old Jeff, always ready to sow seeds of enmity. I had to return the favor.

"Naw, Jeff, I'd never take another friend's girl, unlike some people I know. Of course I'll do that for you, George. But you're probably better off just doing it yourself.

"And yes, Jeff, the whole team of guys running around in their underwear is getting all kinds of attention these days. Dan Irwin had a pair of pink panties stuffed through the slats on his locker door this morning. He said there was a phone number written on them in black marker. It seems that the girl was sending him some kind of message. Who knows what'll happen if we win State? Players will be forced to walk past dozens of naked girls every time they change classes. Orgies for basketball players will be held on wrestling mats in the old gym."

Jeff had no response. I guess I made my point. Ches, however, looked like he had just eaten a piece of moldy bread.

"What is wrong with you, McChesney? I'm just fooling around."

"Watch out that your head doesn't get as big as a helium balloon, Joseph. We don't want you to fly away."

Ches wanted things to be the way they were before. I couldn't change what had happened. It was kind of poignant, though.

"The packaging has changed a little bit, Ches, but I'm still the same old idiot."

George was waiting for me outside of Problems of Democracy class, looking nervous as hell. It was nice to see him getting involved with girls. It was no accident he was interested in a sophomore. I didn't think he had enough confidence to date a junior or senior.

"Tell me about Traci," I asked as we began going up the stairs.

"She's in the Science Club and is interested in things like how to conduct electricity. I think she's a straight A student. Her older brother's a biochemistry major at Penn. I think the whole family's very intelligent."

"Have you talked to her very much?"

"A little bit about science stuff, but I haven't asked her out yet. I spent about an hour last night rehearsing what I was going to say."

About halfway down the second-floor hallway, George pointed to her talking to two other girls. Traci was on the tall side, with long brown hair tied into two pony tails. She was wearing a tight navy blue skirt and white long-sleeved blouse with a red sweater wrapped around her waist. There was a pretty nice figure beneath the clothes. Had to hand it to my friend on that front. Her face was very thin, and pretty in a delicate kind of way.

I followed George as he walked up to her. "Hey Traci," he said, in a reasonably assertive voice, "this is my good friend, Joey Garden. We were just walking by."

If Traci was impressed by meeting me, she didn't show it. Kind of nice to know, though, that there was at least one person in this school not infected by championship mania.

"Nice to meet you, Traci." I said, shaking her hand. "Any friend of George's is a friend of mine."

The whole scene felt awkward; I wanted to get out of there as quickly as possible. I stepped away from them and said, "I think you're right about this girl, George. She seems very special. By all means, ask her out."

Traci giggled and started to blush. Hopefully, George would walk through the door I'd just opened for him. When I turned around, they were talking. I'd find out what happened tomorrow at lunch.

It was time to go and see Coach. His classroom was at the far end of the hallway overlooking Green Avenue. When I walked inside, he was sitting at his desk going over some student work.

"You wanted to see me, Coach?"

He put down his pen and looked toward the window before answering. "Thanks for coming to see me so promptly, Joe. I've always admired your maturity and intelligence. When you hear what I'm about to say, I'm sure you'll respond in a thoughtful, level-headed way."

Uh-oh. Bad news was coming.

"I think as kind of an insurance policy as we get down to our final games, I should make Tim Martin a starting guard, with you coming off the bench. You'll be playing as much as you have been, but I think we need Tim's size in the backcourt."

Coach dropped his head after saying this; he couldn't even look me in the eye. What an ocean of bullshit. He had gone from giant to midget in a matter of seconds.

After an awkward half-minute, I managed to speak. "This isn't going to help anything, Coach. Tim barely goes through the motions in practice. The only thing he cares about is shooting. Plus, we've gotten used to playing without him. All the hard work and dedication the starters put in this season could be ruined by your decision, which, despite what you just said, I know you didn't want to make."

The shock had passed and I began to feel emboldened. What could I lose by expressing my true feelings? Goddammit if the Martins were going to destroy my dream. Coach grimaced, put his hands behind his head and leaned away from his desk, looking very weary and worn-out.

"As you get older, Joe," he answered, "you'll find yourself at times overwhelmed by factors beyond your control. As a younger man, I always felt that I'd be better able to figure out things out and have more control over my life as the years went on. That hasn't been the case."

He was speaking monotonously without any feeling. This was our leader, taking the team into Regionals?

I put my fists on Coach's desk and bent forward. "Everyone hates Tim Martin. I *know* you don't like him or his parents. The whole team will be willing to go back to Superintendent Adams's office like we did after Harrisburg and refuse to go along with this disgrace. He's not going to ruin our chance at the State Title. People will run him out of town on a rail if he does."

"There are things I'm not at liberty to tell you, Joe. I gave you my decision, and I expect you to live with it," he responded, acting like a bookkeeper who'd just finished adding up a column of numbers.

I couldn't decide whether to go on or not; what was the point? Then words just forced themselves out of my mouth. "There's something I want you to consider, Coach. Is giving in to whatever the Martins are holding over your head worth being responsible for the best team in Lansdowne High School's history losing the State Championship?" Too emotionally overwrought to listen to his response, I picked up my books and stomped out of the classroom, drowning in feelings of disgust.

On my way to the gym, I fantasized about making a speech in front of the team, quitting in protest and encouraging the rest of the team to join me. We would broadcast far and wide why we quit. This fantasy quickly evaporated. While that stance might be morally satisfying, I would be giving up the thing I most desperately wanted in my entire life, and play right into the Martins' hands. They'd set this up beautifully. If we actually won State, Martin would get the glory of being a starter on the championship team. And since he didn't really care if we won or lost, he'd be thrilled to get back at Coach and the rest of us for not perpetually kissing his ass.

Zack and the twins were in the locker room, and when I told them what had just transpired, Dan kicked a locker door so hard he put a dent in it.

"Motherfucker!" Dave screamed, tugging violently on the towel that was hanging around his neck. "We gotta go over to that shithead of a superintendent and threaten to quit just like we did before."

Zack stood mute and smoldering.

"Coach squashed that idea, guys. I know the situation is truly screwed," I said, beginning to disrobe. "It's a horrible, infuriating situation. We have a State Championship. There should be one idea in our minds: Don't let Tim Martin or anyone else keep us from our goal."

Right after I finished saying this, Martin strode into the locker room with a cocky, insolent grin on his face. He turned to say something, but before he could utter a word, Dave and Dan were right in his face.

"Don't say one goddam word, dirtball," Dan yelled.

"You're nothin' without your parents, Martin, you fucking scumbag," Dave added, pushing Martin into a locker. "If you do anything to keep us away from winning State, even they won't be able to protect you, asshole."

"You can't even imagine what your life's going to be like if we lose because of you, Martfuck," Dan cut in. "Don't make any mistakes until Coach puts Joey in and maybe you'll survive."

"Can I just say something?" Martin asked.

"*No!*" Dan and Dave screamed.

At that point, Calvin came into the locker room and looked at everyone quizzically. We started to get dressed for practice.

Coach gathered us together at the half court line. He told everyone what he had told me: Making Tim a starter was going to be good for the team, and that I would be a more effective weapon coming off the bench. Tim got up and stood beside Coach. "I just want everyone to know that I want to win State as much as anyone else and I'm going to work as hard as I can to make that happen."

Our silence was deafening until Dan and Dave started laughing and rolling on the floor. Martin's face got bright red, while Coach stared on blankly, betraying no feeling whatsoever. He *had* to know that this misbegotten plan was a total catastrophe.

It was hard to imagine things getting any worse, but they soon did. After we started a scrimmage with Tim, Zack, Smooth, Dan and Mac as the starting five playing against myself, Dave and three scrubs, things got ugly real fast. At first, Dan refused to pass the ball to Martin. Then, after Coach intervened and told him "to get the ball to Tim," he waited until Tim wasn't looking and bounced the ball off his head. After Coach yelled at him again, Dan started to play normally.

A pattern quickly developed. I dogged Tim whenever he got the ball, giving him no room to maneuver at all. When I did this, Dave came over and took the ball right out of Martin's hands. After this happened about half a dozen times, Tim screamed out, "Goddammit, Joey" and threw the ball into the stands. Then he stormed up to Coach and yelled, "You planned it this way, Johnson. You know it and I know it."

But what was Coach to do? He couldn't very well tell Dave and me to stop playing defense. Mr. and Mrs. Martin wanted their son back on the starting five, and they had gotten their wish. Revenge felt sweet, but I wondered whether treating Tim this way was in our best interest. All of this stuff festered during the long walk home to Gladstone Manor. By the time I opened the front door, I was in a very foul mood. Mother had made lasagna, which was somewhat comforting. I nodded to my parents and began eating.

"They hired five new cab drivers today," the old man said, "all jigs. Pretty soon me and Tony Fiarello are going to be the only white guys in the whole garage."

Guess my little lecture about how putting down black people made him look stupid had worn off. If he kept going on this, I was going to excuse myself and go up to my room.

Mother looked at me with a placid smile on her face. "I saw Gladys Martin in the five and ten today and she told me that Tim was back on the starting team. She's been avoiding me since they came over to the house after the Harrisburg tournament.

Today, she was smiling ear to ear and greeted me like we were long lost friends."

Of course, Mother, great basketball fan that she was, would not be able to put two and two together and realize that the player Tim was replacing was her son.

"He's replacing one of the Irwin twins?" Pop asked. "Those two are pretty good."

"No, he's taking my spot," I answered. "And it's probably going to cost us the state championship."

I sank my fork into a piece of lasagna and began to eat. Nothing changes. Every once in a while the wrapping paper is replaced, but the package remains the same.

"Coach Johnson must have his reasons," Mother replied, "I'm sure you'll get a chance to play."

"Your glorious Martins have something on Coach and pressured him to make this move. Tim should have been thrown off the team for defying Coach, and now the laziest, most egotistical high school player in the world has won back his starting spot on the best team in Pennsylvania without doing one thing to deserve the promotion. I think I'm going to puke for an entire month."

Mother and Pop looked stunned, their mouths half-opened, their forks frozen in mid-air. I had a very strong urge to get up and leave the table. They were going to say more stupid shit, which, at the moment, I just did not need to hear.

"I'd like to be excused," I said, getting up and throwing my napkin on the table. Before they could answer, I was halfway up the stairs. I heard Pop yell, "Come back here, young man!" but I was through with them for the evening. State Championship? We were as good as any other team. No one has worked harder than we have. Now the team was covered with a thick layer of rot. And I was the one left to suffer the most because of it.

The next morning Martin was standing in the front lobby, grinning like it was Christmas morning. I walked right past him. He'd love nothing more than to get me into a screaming match or goad me into taking a swing at him. No thank you, moron. This stuff had really gotten to me. I couldn't remember what happened in any of my morning classes; the only thing I could think about was meeting my teammates at lunch.

Four of us got trays and found an empty table in the back of the cafeteria. Dan and Dave showed up about a minute later with a huge bag of Wise potato chips and two bottles of orange soda. Some lunch.

Zack spoke first. "I talked to Coach during his prep period right before lunch. I don't think I've ever been more disappointed in anyone in my entire life. He just kept repeating: 'I think this is the best move for the team, Zack.' No matter what objections I brought up, he never changed the answer. If this happened earlier in the season, I'd have stopped playing for the sorry son of a bitch."

"Like I said before," I stated, "the Martins have something on Coach. What that is, no one knows, but it's something big. He wanted Martin off the team a week ago. I don't think this is really his fault. We're wasting a lot of energy being pissed off at him."

"Okay, Joey," Dave asked, "what the hell do we do, with asshole on the starting five?"

"Tim Martin's going to start and be on the court for big minutes, no matter what we say or do. If we want to win State, we go along. If we decide it's not worth it, we'll go over to Adams's office and quit this afternoon."

I made eye contact with Smooth, Mac, Zack and the twins and asked, "How badly do we really want State?"

A week ago, if I asked that question, they would have laughed me out of the cafeteria. No one spoke for a few moments. Zack shrugged his shoulders before saying, "Yeah, I still want it, I think." And Smooth added, "There's only going to be five more games. We can make it through five games." The others all nodded their heads.

"So what do we do, Joey?" Dave asked.

"The main thing is to not harass Tim like we did in practice yesterday. Make him think we're all behind him. If we keep showing him up, he's going to sulk and play badly just to get back at us. We'll hold our noses and hope we have enough talent to overcome this damn charade."

Mac gave me an incredulous look. "What the hell, Joey. Tim screwed you out of your starting spot. You sure you don't just want to strangle him."

"He's not worth the time, Mac. Just think about winning, that's what's important."

The bell rang. I hoped, while walking to class, that I'd said the right thing.

A few days later, everyone was hanging out of the windows at school cheering us as we walked to the bus for the first playoff game with Upper Moreland. I doubt that they noticed that we looked and moved like zombies, the Martin fiasco having dampened our spirits. He'd been terrible in practice, always looking for his shot, barely playing defense.

Villanova University Field House, which was built in the 1930s, seated about 5,000 people. We were the second of four games. The first, Radnor vs. Kennett Square, was already halfway through the third quarter when we arrived. After watching that game for a few minutes, we went into the visitors' locker room to get changed. Martin got dressed first and started shadow boxing before yelling, "We're gonna kill those Upper Moreland motherfuckers!" No one even looked up.

The cheerleaders began leaping when we came on the floor. Lansdowne fans arose and let out a big cheer. This was the moment we'd all been waiting for all season, and when the game started, I was going to be stuck on the bench. Instead of being jazzed, a sick, yellow feeling spread through my stomach. My only hope was that when I replaced Martin, I'd play so well he'd have to stay on the bench.

Coach told us that Upper Moreland was weak in the backcourt, with slow guards who didn't shoot very well. That did not turn out to be true. Martin's man, figuring out pretty quickly that he was playing against a patsy, started dropping one jump shot after another. This frustrated Zack, who left his man open underneath the basket to help guard Tim's man. The Upper Moreland guard noticed right away and tossed Zack's man the ball for an easy layup.

On offense, the team was completely out of synch. Martin slowed down the team's ball movement considerably. Our well-oiled machine had a misfiring piston. Zack kept getting the ball when he was out of position to shoot. He had a hard time finding Smooth or getting his own shot. Martin took four jump shots at the top of the key and missed them all. The first quarter ended with Lansdowne behind 18-12.

I thought Coach was going to put me in during the quarter break, but he didn't. Things got worse, and Coach called timeout. Zack was visibly upset and told Coach to put me in the game. The crowd picked up on this, because when the starters went back on the floor, people started chanting, "Joeee, Joeee!" I think Coach realized that he would look bad responding to the crowd's wishes, and I continued to collect splinters. But after a few minutes, he motioned to Dave and me to replace Martin and Mac. He told us to pressure the opponents on defense as soon as they brought the ball in, and to make every effort to get me open shots.

After we got on the floor, it seemed like the team had taken a magic elixir. Dan and Dave were merciless in harassing the Upper Moreland guards, who started throwing passes out of bounds, dribbling the ball off their knees, or tossing it to Zack and me for easy layups. We scored eight points in two minutes to go ahead by four. Lansdowne fans came alive, screaming and stomping their feet. This was the way it should have been from the opening tip.

When Upper Moreland did get the ball past half court, they began taking bad, off-balance shots. Smooth sucked the rebounds off the backboard like a high-powered vacuum. Zack began setting screens for me. I'd get behind him, head fake left or right, take one dribble and fire away. No thinking at all, just pure instinct. I made four in a row, and Martin came back in the game. Dan and Dave ignored him and got the ball to Zack and Smooth. Score at halftime: Lansdowne 44 Upper Moreland 32.

Coach waited until we were quiet in the locker room and began to present the strategy for the second half. Right after he said, "We're going to use the same players we started the game with," Zack jumped up and shouted, "No damn way, Coach. We played much better with Joey than Tim. If he hadn't come into the game, we'd still be behind, instead of being up by twelve."

Martin was staring intently at Coach, who was in trouble either way he turned. He repeated what he'd just said. Zack shook his head in utter disgust. Smooth and Mac stared numbly at the floor; Dan and Dave looked like they wanted to punch Coach in the jaw. It felt like *Mutiny on the Bounty* was about to take place. The buzzer sounded. We filed onto the court like convicts going to the prison yard.

Martin continued to stink. The crowd began to boo him and started to chant my name again. I got back into the game with two minutes to go in the third quarter. Lansdowne was up by two instead of twenty-two. We spent the fourth quarter keeping Upper Moreland at bay by feeding the ball to Smooth under the basket for reverse layups and dunks. Final score: Lansdowne 68, Upper Moreland 62. Coach tried to cheer us up in the locker room, telling us how great we played. We all knew that was a lie and walked onto the bus like mourners in a funeral procession, not triumphant victors.

Dan and Dave got in the seat behind Martin and began tormenting him.

"Hey, Tim, "Dave whispered.

Martin turned around. "Yeah, what?"

"You eat shit."

Instead of responding, he stared straight ahead.

Dan reached across the seat and flicked Tim's ear lobe with his finger. Martin turned around and both twins looked at him blankly.

I didn't care that the twins were ignoring my advice. Martin got up and went to the front of the bus, taking a seat right behind Coach. No one talked or made any noise. The trip back to school was interminable. Pop was waiting outside the gym. He tried to congratulate me, but I waved him off.

I just wanted to get home, get to bed and forget about this unholy mess.

After breakfast the next morning, I decided that I had to talk to Coach before class and make a last-ditch effort to salvage the season. I found him sitting at his desk, looking at an American History book.

Pulling up a chair beside him, I said, "Coach, if we can't give our best effort, like you are always telling us to do, there's almost no point in continuing the season. Dan and Dave really got on Martin during the bus ride home. You can count on it getting worse."

He sighed, and his eyes glazed over with tears. When I saw that he wasn't going to answer me, I continued. "You saw how the crowd reacted last night. You saw how poorly the team played with Tim at starting guard. When we lose, which we most certainly will if things continue as they are, people are going to have long, painful memories about this season. And they're going to be looking for someone to blame."

Coach got up and ran a hand across his balding head. He turned to the blackboard and sighed. He sat down again and began talking in a slow, mechanical tone. "I've been married for twenty-four years, Joe. I've got two wonderful children. My wife, Evelyn, whom I love very much, has a very serious drinking problem. We've managed to keep it a secret for many years. Two weeks ago, in an inebriated state, she hit an eight-year-old boy with our car. Then she fled the scene of the accident. A witness identified her.

"Mr. Martin found out what had happened and agreed not to have the police chief press charges if we agreed to pay for the boy's medical expenses, and if I put Tim back in the starting lineup. I agreed to go along with this plan. My wife is not a strong person. If she has to go to jail and endure a lot of bad publicity, I shudder to think what might happen to her."

Old man Martin must have leapt with glee when this was dumped in his lap. It made me angry. Why should the team be penalized for Mrs. Johnson's problems? Coach was in a tough spot, but it was his job to keep the team out of his family problems.

"I can appreciate this being a tough situation for you, Coach. But you'll never have a team as good as we are, no matter how long you coach. And if you continue to start Martin, you'll never be able to look any of us in the eye ever again. "

I felt the same way I did when I talked to Cindy after she seduced Zack. Sometimes there's no choice but to be ruthless. Tough on Coach. He brought this on himself.

Zack grabbed my shoulder as I walked to my first period class. He was clenching and unclenching his fists, in a state of great agitation.

We walked back to the second floor stairwell, where he gave me the bad news.

"I just talked to Cindy, and she told me her period was late. I'm going to be a father with a girl I can't stand, have no respect for and whose parents my mother hates. This is so bad, Joey."

"Girls have late periods sometimes, Zack. It doesn't mean she's pregnant. Did she see a doctor"

"I dunno."

"Maybe Martin put her up to it, just to mess with your head. I wouldn't put anything past him or her."

Zack looked glumly at the wall. He'd made a mistake that could ruin his life. "I really feel for you, Zack. This is some serious stuff. Maybe your mom could talk to Cindy's parents and get more clarity on the situation."

Zack could be a father by the end of the year. Unfathomable. There was nothing to do but sit and wait. There was an operation for ending a pregnancy, but it was illegal. And knowing how principled Zack was, he'd take responsibility for the baby and marry Cindy, even if his future was destroyed in the process.

The closer we got to the championship, the farther away it seemed. Zack and Coach were in the middle of serious crises. The biggest moron in the history of the world was starting, while I languished on the bench. Mickey Mouse and Goofy had a better chance of winning State than we did.

At lunch, I went to sit with the Mugwumps, desperately needing a respite from basketball.

"No questions about the playoffs ," I pleaded.

Fat chance of that. "Why in the hell is Tim Martin starting instead of you?" Ches asked, totally ignoring every word I'd just uttered. "When he's in the game, the offensive output declines about thirty percent. Doesn't Johnson know this?"

"Something's rotten in the state of Denmark, that's all I can say for the moment. How did it go with Traci, George?"

"Saturday night, Lansdowne Theater, to see Tab Hunter and Tuesday Weld in an epic romance. I owe you one, Joey."

Ches looked stunned and said, "You haven't had one date in three and a half years of high school, George Stevens. Why didn't you tell me?"

Steve liked to be in on anything one of the Mugwumps did. But I think what was really bothering him was that he was the only one of us who had never been involved with a girl.

"You're next, Ches," I said. "A lot of the girls in the accelerated classes hang on your every word. We all know who they are. If you don't take advantage of the situation, it's your own fault."

George and Jeff nodded in agreement. The rest of lunch was spent discussing various potential candidates for Ches' attention. Although it was obvious he was uncomfortable being put on the spot, you could see that the wheels in his mind were turning.

Coach was a bit more animated in practice. I thought Zack was going to be too worried about Cindy to be worth very much on the court, but he played harder than I ever saw him play. He dribbled past the twins, dunked over Smooth, swept rebound after rebound, and screened Martin out so hard, Tim fell to the floor in pain. We all tried unsuccessfully to keep up with him. I left practice drenched in sweat, my bones aching.

Preoccupied with the issues surrounding the team, it was easy to disregard the building mania of the upcoming Kennett Square game, but I did notice the banners pasted on the hallway walls: *Squash the Mushrooms!*, *Let's Make a Mushroom and Cheese Omelet. Kennett is a Big Fat Square.* The town, about thirty miles away, was known as *The Mushroom Capital of the World.* Bunch of farmers not usually known for their basketball prowess.

The game was in Reading, an hour-and-a-half drive, which meant we had to leave right before sixth period. Classrooms emptied out as we walked down the hallways to the yellow bus. Since Coach was going along with the status quo regarding Martin, I was feeling more numb than excited. Kennett didn't have a player over 6'1," so if we could just get the ball to Smooth and Zack, we'd probably be okay.

Two minutes after the center jump, it was obvious that we were in for a real challenge. Playing Kennett was like playing against five Dan and Daves. They were pesky, irritating and so quick to the ball, we couldn't get our offense started. And when they were on offense, it was pass, pass and more pass, like the whole team was allergic to shooting. Martin had the ball stolen every time he touched it. After five minutes of play, the score was tied 4-4. Coach called a timeout. He replaced Mac and Martin with Dave and myself. Our instructions were to get the ball past half court any way we could and set up Zack and Smooth for easy shots.

The Kennett players covered us like a bad case of acne. Every step we took was contested. They all seemed to have foul body odor, probably from rolling around in horse manure all day. Kennett was dirty in other ways as well. They pinched and spit on us, and when I hit a few shots from the corner, the player guarding me began grabbing at my balls whenever I went into the lane. Coach yelled at the refs, but it did no good. Score at halftime: Lansdowne 14, Kennett Square 12, a merciful end to the most frustrating half of basketball I'd ever experienced.

As soon as we sat down in the locker room at half-time, Martin jumped up and screamed at Coach, "If you kept me in the game, Johnson, we'd be up by way more than two."

Zack got in front of him, put his hands on Martin's shoulders and shoved him back onto the wooden bench. "Shut up," was all he said.

Putting his hands in his pockets, Coach addressed the team. "Kennett Square is the dirtiest team I've ever seen. The refs are letting them get away with murder. That's the reality, which we have to accept. What we must remember is to not let them rattle us. We'll start with the same lineup that finished the first half. We need to match their quickness and not turn the ball over. Lansdowne's a much better team than they are, so let's go out there and show it."

The game wrenched itself forward like a wounded seal. Neither team could get into an offensive rhythm. It felt like being in a prison yard pounding rocks. Our fans were pretty silent, since there wasn't much to cheer about. The insides of my thighs were bright red from being pinched. Number Eight grabbed my balls underneath the basket. I sank a layup on a great pass from Zack and called him a *fuckhead* as I ran back on defense.

With two minutes to go, Lansdowne was ahead by six. It didn't seem possible, but Kennett intensified their defensive efforts. Zack let a pass go through his hands and out of bounds. We were up by only two baskets. Finally, the refs started to call fouls on Kennett Square. We scored six points from the line while holding the Mushrooms to zero points. Final score: Lansdowne 28, Kennett Square 24. I wanted to soak myself in the shower for at least an hour. Glassy-eyed fans gathered around us, but no one was celebrating.

As has become our habit, Zack and I sat together on the bus, neither of us saying much. We had a job to do, and now it was over.

When we reached Norristown, Zack put his hand over his mouth and whispered to me, "Cindy told me this morning she'd gotten her period."

My body relaxed; what a blessed relief.

"It was like it was no big deal to her, like she was telling me what time it was or something. But it *was* a really big deal. And I have to tell you something, Joey. I don't know why I'm saying this, but I'm not sure she was telling the truth."

"Have her bring you a used Kotex wrapped in toilet paper."

"Hell, she'd probably bring in her mother's."

"Just take what she said at face value, Zack. It's the only thing you can do. Even though she's probably still pissed at you for dumping her, I don't think Cindy deep down really wanted to have your, or anyone else's, kid."

I fell asleep for the rest of the trip home. As usual, Pop was waiting for me in the Chevy; luckily, he wasn't very talkative. Looking out the windshield at the night sky, I saw a crescent moon surrounded by glimmering stars. All of those heavenly bodies oblivious to all of the world's consternation calmed me down. I felt something I hadn't felt in a while — peace.

In Problems of Democracy class a few days later, the teacher, Mr. Harold Munchak, a balding, pudgy man in his early thirties, was standing by the chalkboard, droning on about the woman's suffrage movement. Munchy, as usual, seemed to have no passion about the issue whatsoever. He's that way about everything he teaches: the Volstead Act, the Bill of Rights, McCarthy, all presented like he's reading the phone book. How can anyone live his life this way?

He wears a wedding ring, but never talks about his wife. I can see him coming home every night, pecking her on the cheek, having a dinner of bland food, grading papers, watching a bit of TV and turning in at 8:30, day after day after day.

We have the unique privilege of writing the crap he dishes out down in our notebooks and regurgitating it back to him on the weekly test. It was beyond tedious, and I was sick of it.

He noticed me waving my hand and said, "Joey, do you have a question?"

"More of a statement, Mr.Munchak."

"Go on."

"This is the most boring class I've ever had in my life. You lecture us in a monotone that hasn't changed since September. You never add any material that's not in the textbook. You're a pretty young guy. Do you want to be boring your students for the next thirty years?"

An audible gasp arose from the class, followed by a few nervous giggles. Munchak's face had turned pink, and he was gripping his pointer with both hands.

"I'm sorry you feel that way, Joey. As you know, Problems of Democracy is a required class for all seniors because the material is deemed essential knowledge for young American men and women to know. I'm sorry my presentation of the information is not to your liking, but this is important stuff."

"I don't deny that it is, Mr. Munchak, but if it doesn't excite you, how can it excite us? Do you think anyone would be sitting in this class if we had a choice?"

The room started buzzing. Munchak looked lost and flustered. I felt bad for him, but what good was it for us to have our minds put to sleep day after day?

He blundered through the next fifteen minutes, obviously upset. I went up to him after class and said, "I didn't mean to embarrass you, Mr. Munchak. But maybe you can figure out some ways to spice things up in here. Bring in stories from the newspaper or something."

Most of the class was waiting for me out in the hallway, smiling and ready to pat me on the back. Why the hell was I the only one to speak out? Just about everyone thinks P.O.D. is torture. Tomorrow it will be more of the same, and I'll knuckle under like everyone else, not wanting to jeopardize my future.

Many people's heads turned when I entered the caf; news travels fast at Lansdowne High. Ches was smiling from ear to ear as I came to the Mugwumps' table.

"Joseph," he said, beaming, "Munchak won't be able to eat his dinner tonight; he'll have nightmares. You join my pantheon of heroes, along with Albert Einstein and Galileo."

"We've been arguing about this," Jeff added. "I think you took an unnecessary risk. There could be serious repercussions."

"You're both wrong. I'm no hero, and nothing will happen to me. I probably should have kept my mouth shut. Munchy isn't going to change. I just made him feel lousy, which I feel kind of bad about, but he is *so* goddamn boring. Every one of us has handed in all of our high school assignments no matter how much we hated doing them. That big paper that's going to be worth one third of our grade in P.O.D., I'm not going to write it. This is the second semester of our senior year, who's going to care about my final grades? No way I can fail. I'll do well enough in his tests, they're so damned easy."

The Mugwumps stared at me, mouths agape. To not hand in a major assignment in any subject was unthinkable.

"You might be on to something, Joey," George said, biting into an apple, "but that's a big risk not doing the paper."

I waved my hand dismissively as my stomach did bellyflops.

McChesney looked perplexed as well as dismayed. "I've been noticing this hard core of cynicism in you lately that I've never seen before. I can't say I like it much. And has been the downfall of many men. I'd watch myself if I were you."

"I'm not being cynical, Ches, just realistic. And I don't think it's hubris not to do the paper. " My friend's words, however, did bother me, although I didn't show it.

Even though he knew everyone hated it, Martin was once again blaring his transistor radio in the back of the bus as we headed to the quarter-final game in York. He's like a puppy that can't be housebroken. "Sorry" by Brenda Lee was playing. I've always hated her Barbie Doll voice, and I wasn't the only one. Dave flew down the aisle and told Martin to turn it off. When he wouldn't, Dave grabbed the radio from his hand and threw it out the window onto the Pennsylvania Turnpike.

"You're gonna pay for that, Irwin," Martin screamed.

"I'm not paying for shit," Dave answered.

Coach was sitting right behind the bus driver and missed or ignored the whole incident. I was sure Martin was going to run up to him and rat out Dave, but he slumped down in his seat and scowled instead.

Our opponent, Mechanicsville High School, offered little opposition. They had no one who could guard Zack or Smooth, who dominated under the boards. Even Martin hit a few jump shots. I got into a rhythm and hit six shots from the corners and top of the key. It was astounding that they'd gotten so far in the tournament. Final score: Lansdowne 74, Mechanicsburg 40.

The cheerleaders, students and other Lansdowne fans gave us a big cheer as we exited the locker room. Martin was lapping it up, raising his fists in the air and whirling around like he had just won a heavyweight championship fight. He scored eight points, three field goals and two foul shots. Big deal. The man guarding him played like Minnie Mouse.

Zack had been unstoppable, scoring 32, almost half of the team's total points. He looked exhausted, immediately leaning back and falling asleep.

If anyone had told me at the start of the season how many things I'd have to deal with, I would have thought they were crazy: Martin and his family, Cindy, Coach and his wife, Superintendent Adams, finding out who my real father was, Helene and Jeff. Through all of that, I seemed to be doing okay. When I was about six years old, I was fixated on Howdy Doody, the famous little cowboy puppet. I would never miss the show, which came on every day at four in the afternoon. On one show, I thought Buffalo Bob, Howdy's human sidekick, got mad at the little guy. I immediately started crying and ran to my mother in the kitchen; she comforted me as best she could. The world had to be a certain way for me back then. I guess that's the case with most young kids, feeling that the world they've created in their minds *is* the real world. Ha ha.

The greatest basketball player in the history of Lansdowne High and my former idol, Jim Brady, aka "The Hawk," addressed the team before practice on Wednesday. Coach did not tell us, but he'd asked Hawk to scout our next opponent, Wilkes Barre, who'd just beaten Reading High by 16 points.

Hawk put his hands in his pockets and began to speak, "Wilkes Barre is better than any other team you've played, even better than McKeesport. They have two all-star players, Thaddeus Jones, a 6' 8" center, and a guard, Dominic DiFranco, who is built like a linebacker with an awesome outside shot. All their other players are solid, if unspectacular. The only weakness that I could see is that their bench is kind of thin. If you can get them in foul trouble, it will be to your advantage.

"They played vicious man-to-man defense and used a very efficient full court press for about half the game against Reading. On offense, if you concentrate on Jones, DiFranco can kill you from outside. Wilkes Barre's other players are decent shooters as well. Everybody has to help out and make it as difficult for them to score as possible."

Finally, we were going to face a tough opponent, the first one since the Harrisburg tournament. I knew deep down in my gut that this was going to be a dogfight.

Coach had Dan and Dave harass Martin and me as we tried to bring the ball upcourt. Tim lost the ball at least a dozen times, but I held my own against them. Hopefully, Coach noticed.

When practice was finished, Hawk called to me to sit beside him in the grandstand.

"Pretty nice work, Joey. Those Irwins are super-pesky."

"Thanks, Hawk."

"I've been talking to Coach Johnson about how you've become an all-around player and not just a shooter. I watched you play in the last two playoff games and was pretty impressed. You've come a long way since you used to hang around the outdoor court watching the older guys play. I know you've always been a good student, but what are your SAT scores?"

"680 verbal, 501 math."

"The verbal score is great. If you're not going to major in science or mathematics, I'm sure the Admissions Office at Princeton will be willing to overlook the lower math score. The Dryden brothers and I have all done well playing for the Tigers. They've had good experience with players from Lansdowne High."

It felt like a thunderbolt had come hurtling out of the sky and hit me right smack in the middle of my forehead. Hawk could shoot from anywhere on the court, rebound and play great defense. He was Captain of the Princeton team his senior year and made All Ivy three years in a row. He was even drafted by the Philadelphia Warriors, but decided against a pro career. I heard that when he played for the last time at Princeton, the crowd stood up and cheered for five full minutes when he came off the floor at the end of the game. The Dryden brothers were both very quick, great passers, and never seemed to take any bad shots. The fact that Hawk was willing to put me in the same league as the three of them dumbfounded me.

"No worries about majoring in either math or science, Hawk, but are you *serious*?"

"Quite serious, Joey. And if Lansdowne gets by Wilkes Barre, I'll do everything I can to get Coach Willoughby to come to the state championship game."

"You're not saying this to get me psyched up for the final two games, Hawk?"

He laughed and got up to leave. "Did you ever hear of the expression 'Don't look a gift horse in the mouth,' Joey?"

"Yes. I believe I've heard that. By all means go for it, Hawk, and thanks for the scouting report."

He shook my hand and was off. Was what just happened a dream? I wasn't going to tell *anyone* else about this, until a formal offer was made.

At dinner, I found myself unable to withhold the astonishing news. I looked at Mother and Pop and told them what had happened after practice.

Pop said, "Princeton, that's a pretty good school, ain't it?"

Mother sat stolidly, staring blankly at the dining room wall. For years and years, she had impressed upon me the importance of getting into a good college. Now that I had a chance to get into one of the most elite Ivy League universities, she showed no excitement at all.

Finally, she spoke. "I don't think you should get your hopes up, Joey. If you want to go to an Ivy League school, Penn is only a half hour away. The National Merit Scholarship could come through for you."

I guess this shouldn't have been a surprise; there seemed to be no end to Mother's ability to disappoint me. It was time to tell her the truth. "When I found out the truth about you and Pop, Mother, I tore up the application form. The deadline for applying has passed."

She looked like a person who had just witnessed a serious car wreck. "I cannot believe that you would do such a self-destructive thing. Your entire life has become dedicated to destroying me."

"Don't be so dramatic, Mother. I can go out West to Colorado or someplace and enroll in a state university. And there's nothing you can do to stop me."

The old man was getting ready to give me a lecture about being respectful to my mother. I told him to bag it and went upstairs to do homework. I've been slacking off a bit lately, second semester of senior year and all that. No more. Hawk's offer had been a wake-up call. If Princeton *was* going to take a serious look at me, mediocre grades in the last semester of my senior year simply would not do.

I started to outline Munchy's paper. I'd planned to write about Eugene Debs, a true hero in my eyes. He got the workers to overcome beatings, killings, threats until they achieved their goals. But even though, I found an interesting topic, I was tempted to keep my pledge and hand in nothing. A bad grade in P.O.D. would be hard to explain to the admissions office at Princeton, but I felt stubborn about keeping my vow and decided to put of writing the outline.

I translated three pages of Moliere and made a point to talk with Ches about how to calculate the density of cones for Solid Geometry. I reviewed my notes on *Catcher in the Rye* for the test on Friday. Mrs. Childress will give three essay questions, as she always does, and I'll have to start thinking about what they might be. One possibility was, why did Holden Caufield want to save innocent children from the corrupt world, when the only reason they were innocent was because they didn't know what the hell was going on, not because of any great moral qualities on their part? I was thinking so much, my brain started to gyrate.

That night I had a dream. A mallard duck, the one with all the beautiful multi-colored feathers, was walking through a lush jungle. There were all kinds of animal noises coming from the trees, beautiful birds flying around, streams of sparkling, iridescent water, everything was bright green. As the bird walked, things started falling away. The trees fell over, streams dried up, birds flew off. Every time the duck would move, it lost another feather. Pretty soon, a big pile of feathers was sitting beside the naked water fowl. Soaked in sweat, I woke up panting and gasping as if I'd been underwater. This was one of those dreams when you're desperately relieved to find out it wasn't real. I was pretty woozy and not really in the mood to analyze, but I did wonder if my unconscious mind was telling me that I was going to be a dead duck.

The team assembled in the gym after third period for the three-hour drive to Hershey. Just as before, kids were hanging out the windows of school, cheering and yelling. It hit me how important we'd become, the keys to agony and ecstasy in our back pockets. It was an uneasy ride; we all knew a great task awaited.

After lunch at a Howard Johnson's in Lancaster, we got to Hershey and drove down Hershey Avenue, the main drag, past the chocolate factory. It was a complex of large brick buildings with a mammoth smokestack beside a huge billboard that read: *Hershey's Chocolate: Quality Candy Since 1891*. The whole town was permeated by the smell of cacao beans. I guess if you lived here, you'd get sick of it, but I loved the glorious aroma, sucking in one deep breath after another.

Hershey Civic Auditorium, built in World War II, was another old, cavernous building. The cheers of the crowd were going to echo off the walls.

Eight boxes of Hershey bars were sitting on the locker room floor, four of solid mild chocolate, four of chocolate with almonds. I'm not sure how they got there, but there they were. Dan and Dave grabbed the cartons and started handing out candy. I scarfed down two of each kind in about thirty seconds, but stopped myself from eating more, because I didn't want to make myself sick.

About an hour later, during warm-ups, Martin looked like a seasick sailor; God only knew how much chocolate he'd eaten. When the buzzer sounded for the respective teams to head for their benches, he bolted to the locker room holding his stomach. Coach put his hand on my shoulder and told me I'd be starting. I couldn't help but wonder if he'd planned the whole thing.

Anticipation was thick in the gym, bass drums were being pounded, cheerleaders were leaping in the air, the crowd was on its feet yelling. My stomach was doing back flips as the ref tossed up the ball. Smooth tapped it to Dave, who dished it to

Zack as he headed toward the basket. We'll draw first blood, I thought, a good omen, but Thaddeus knocked the ball out of bounds just as it left Zack's hands. It came back to me. Acting on pure instinct, I threw up a high-arcing shot that dropped straight through the hoop. After the ball went in, Wilkes Barre star Tony Di Franco said to me, "Ridiculous shot, Six, your luck will run out soon."

I hoped he wasn't right as we got back on defense. Lansdowne went into a zone. DiFranco got the ball and came right at me. He was too big, too strong, too fast, knocking me down and cruising for an easy layup. Thaddeus stole my inbounds pass and jammed it through the net to the delight of the roaring crowd.

On offense, when we got the ball to Smooth, Thaddeus was all over him like a case of the measles. He was so sleek, full of rippling muscles, and moved with an economical, fluid motion, like a cheetah or panther. Di Franco was guarding Zack and giving him all kinds of trouble. Our two main scoring options were being put on ice. The player guarding me, twelve, was very strong and hard to shake. That left the offense to Dan, who seldom shot, and Mac, who usually scored following missed shots. The team was totally out of our element, playing like polar bears in the middle of a desert.

Coach called time out, with us losing by eight points. He put the team back in a man- to-man defense with Zack, not me, guarding DiFranco, a good move. "We have to be as tough as they are on defense," he said. "Start pressing them as soon as they get the ball inbounds. On offense, pass the ball until the best opportunity presents itself." We put our hands together and yelled, "Lancers!"

I didn't know if I'd ever played a harder half of basketball. The Wilkes Barre team, like Hawk said, had no weak spots.

Coming from a coal mining town, they knew the value of hard work. We had to claw and scrape for everything we got. When Dave replaced me with two minutes left in the half, sweat was dripping from me in rivulets; my head felt groggy and my thighs were so sore, I wobbled to the bench. Having the twins in the game was a good move, as they stole the ball and scored three times in a row. Score at the half: Wilkes Barre 32, Lansdowne 28.

Since Coach never made inspirational speeches, I was a bit astonished when he stood up on a wooden bench and said these words: "I'm reminded, gentlemen, of George Washington spending a brutal winter in Valley Forge, his troops in threadbare clothing, with little food, but having the patience to wait and cross the Delaware to defeat the British in a surprise attack. The first half was our Valley Forge. Wilkes Barre is sitting in their locker room feeling very confident about themselves, just as the British did in 1774. We have to gather our strength, find our second wind and come out with only one thing on our minds, (*his voice rose as I had never heard it before*) winning this game and going to the state championship game!" The team, except for Martin, who still looked pretty bilious, jumped up and shouted. Coach had given us exactly what we needed.

Coach stepped down from the bench and continued, "Since Young and DiFranco have pretty much shut down Zack and Calvin, both of them will start setting picks for Mac. When they start keying on Mac, I want Joe to get the ball, particularly in the corner, where, as we all know, he can be deadly. Now, let's get on that court and win a basketball game."

I forgot about my aching thighs and exhaustion, and we all flew out of the locker room to take some warm-up shots. Coach had given me such a shot of adrenaline, the ball started leaving my hand like it had wings; everything I shot was dropping.

The strategy worked for a while. Zack was lethal when he set a pick, blocking out the opposing player like a football lineman protecting the quarterback. Mac made two medium jump shots and drove around his man for an easy layup. I made two jumpers as well. The Wilkes Barre coach, a red-faced man named Tom Boyle, appeared like he was constantly on the edge of exploding. He started screaming at the ref that Zack was manhandling his players. The ref ignored him, which made the coach complain even more intensely. "Take off your goggles, Ref, before they put my kids in the hospital. What's Lansdowne paying you for letting them get away with murder?" Wilkes Barre's rooting section got into it, yelling and screaming derisively. Then *our* fans started booing very loudly. The atmosphere in the gym became poisonous.

The refs stopped the game and walked over in front of the scorer's table to confer. The official who was being browbeaten called a technical foul against Boyle and told him if there were any more outbursts, he was going to be thrown out of the game. Then the place really went nuts. Thaddeus and DiFranco grabbed their coach's arms and forcibly put him on the bench. Empty soda cups and other debris started pouring out of the stands.

Butterflies were tap dancing inside my stomach. It felt like a prison yard must feel right before a riot. The game might have to be forfeited. Coach told me to take the technical foul shots, which I did, dropping both, to the cheers of our fans and derisive booing from the Wilkes Barre rooters.

The game seesawed back and forth. Thaddeus and Smooth were having a battle royale. They were blocking each other's shots, contesting every rebound. Zack had to work for everything he got against DiFranco, and vice versa. This was the total opposite of most of the games we'd played all season long, where we got an early advantage and coasted to victory.

Walking back onto the court after a timeout, I felt it was time for me to step up. I dribbled past my man at the top of the key, faked a pass to Smooth and took a jump shot. Swish. Next time I got the ball, I slid between two Wilkes Barre players and threw up a shot as I fell forward, another basket and a foul shot. The Wilkes Barre coach leapt up from the bench and screamed: *That was no foul!* He was right; no one had touched me. The silver-haired ref, the one he'd been having trouble with, went over to the scorer's table and gave the sign for a technical foul. The Wilkes Barre fans got even uglier, loudly booing, shrieking, cursing. It was becoming apparent that the game was not going to end nicely. At the other end of the court, ten Pennsylvania state troopers stood, billy clubs in their clenched fists.

The older ref then made a theatrical motion in front of the Wilkes Barre coach that he'd been thrown out of the game. This guy could have been the conductor of a symphony orchestra. Boyle shook his fist at the official and began stomping his foot on the court. Each time he made a gesture, the Wilkes Barre fans screamed louder. The coach eventually did leave, and the assistant coach took over. I took the technical foul shots and made them both. There were eight minutes left in the game. We were ahead, 60-56.

For the next six minutes, I was in an impregnable bubble, rolling blissfully up and down the court. Every time I got the ball on offense, I shot it the second it touched my hand. I must have made five or six shots in a row, all from long range. Wilkes Barre was keeping up with us. Smooth had gotten tired and Thaddeus was having his way with him underneath the basket. Dave dribbled the ball off his knee; Di Franco picked it up and drove for a score. We were up by only two points. Zack drove to the basket and had his shot blocked. My man lobbed a pass into Thaddeus, who scored on a thunderous dunk. Di Franco had seen enough and hit me with a vicious pick that knocked me to the floor. No foul was called.

Coach brought Dan into the game. Mac suddenly got hot. He tapped in a missed shot, made a turn around jumper from the top of the key, stole the ball and scored on a fast break. Thaddeus was going wild; he must have scored at least 30 points.

With the score 72-71 in favor of Wilkes Barre, Coach called another timeout. There were thirty seconds left to play. He took Mac out and put me back in the game. Dan and Dave were to dribble the ball until there were ten seconds on the clock, then Zack would screen out my man, and I would take the last shot. I ran near the half court line and took a few deep breaths, hoping I could live up to the challenge.

The gym was in mayhem. I'd never felt such intensity in my entire life. Dan threw the ball to Dave and he began dribbling around the court like a whirling dervish. With the clock at twelve seconds, Zack set a pick on my man. DiFranco knew what we were trying to do and ran past Zack until he was right in my face. Zack, being Zack, knew Coach's plan was not going to work and rushed to the top of the key, where Dan hit him with a perfect pass. Thaddeus sped from beneath the basket and lunged forward to try to block Zack's shot. The trajectory of the ball looked a bit skewed as it headed toward the basket. The ball skidded off the rim into the hands of a Wilkes Barre player. There was no time left on the clock. Utter wild chaos. The basketball season had ended.

Unnoticed in the confusion, the silver-haired ref had run over to the scorer's table, blowing his whistle until his face turned bright red. Slowly, the crowd began to take notice. When the din died down, the ref shouted out, "Number twelve, Wilkes Barre, on the wrist, two shots."

Ten more troopers had gathered underneath the other basket. And when the crowd erupted, they came to the center of the court. A tall, burly man, whom I guessed was their captain, addressed the crowd. "If order is not restored in this auditorium in five minutes' time, the game will be forfeited, and the winner of the other semi-final will play Lansdowne High school for the state championship."

Zack walked over to me, looking disgusted. "Thaddeus never touched me, Joey. It wasn't even close. That ref has a vendetta against Boyle. If I sink these free throws and we win the game, it will be a complete fraud."

The only response I could think of was, "If you miss on purpose, Zack, you'll never be able to forgive yourself."

Coach brought us together and said, "No matter what the outcome is, as soon as this game is over, the state troopers will form two lines. Each one of you is to run between them and get out the exit doors to the bus. I've arranged to have someone get your clothes and valuables from the locker room. We're in a very dangerous situation here. "

I hoped my words sank in, but as I watched Zack stride toward the free throw line, I wasn't sure if missing the foul shot wasn't the morally right thing to do. I also wondered if missing the shots wasn't the safest thing to do.

Zack makes almost all of his free throws. He puts the ball in both hands, bends his knees deeply and tosses the ball up underhanded. It takes a long time to fire up a shot and it's hardly a thing of beauty, but the ball goes through the hoop ninety percent of the time. Expressionless, Zack took the ball from the ref, paused briefly and spun the ball toward the basket. The ball went right through the hoop. The game was tied. More debris started flying, paper cups mostly. Wilkes Barre fans, sounding like sledgehammers, started stomping on the wooden stands.

The refs went to the scorer's table and motioned to the Wilkes Barre assistant coach. While they were talking to him, Boyle came running out of the locker room, fists held high in the air. If the fans come onto the court, which seemed very likely, someone could get really hurt. A furious argument began between the Wilkes Barre coaches and the refs.

Finally, the Wilkes Barre assistant, waiting until Boyle left the floor, got on the microphone and said, "The referees have informed me that if order is not restored and the Lansdowne player is not allowed to take the final free throw, we will forfeit the game. If you care anything about Wilkes Barre Crusader basketball, you'll settle down right away."

Zack had never left the free throw line, where he stood with the same stoic expression on his face. After the commotion died down, he took another deep breath, squatted and released the ball. Same result; it went right through the rim.

Final score: Lansdowne 73, Wilkes Barre 72. We had gone from complete dejection to utter exhilaration. Our Dream was still alive!

Coach waved at us to move through the two rows of state troopers, which we did in a manner of seconds. The bus was waiting right outside the front entrance, doors opened wide. The team piled in and quickly found seats. We were all very quiet, listening to the thunderous roar coming from the auditorium. For some reason, the bus driver was having trouble starting the bus. Coach was standing right behind him, begging him to get the thing moving. A bunch of Wilkes Barre fans emerged from the gym. As soon as they saw us, they got on either side of the bus and began to shake it back and forth. A guy started jumping up to my window and began to scream, "Come out of that bus, chickenshit Lansdowne motherfuckers!" He started to kick the side of the bus as hard as he could. It was crazy and terrifying, and there was nothing anyone could do about it. After what seemed like a century, the bus started to move. The Wilkes Barre mob kept up the pounding until we were out of the parking lot.

Within ten minutes, we were on the Pennsylvania Turnpike, headed home. My body relaxed and I slumped down in my seat. That was the most intense basketball game I had ever played, and with all the end-of-game chaos, there was not much gas left in my tank.

Zack said, "The gray-haired ref wasn't going to be satisfied unless we won the game. Thaddeus wasn't close to blocking my shot. His hands were about a foot away from my body."

"I'm glad you made the free throws, Zack."

There was a lot more I wanted to say, but had no energy to say it. I curled up into a ball and went right to sleep, even though the bus had a weak heater and I was still in my sweaty uniform.

I woke up about 10 a.m. the next morning, exhausted and groggy. The phone rang. It was Zack asking me to meet him and the twins at Johnny and Jimmy's Diner for lunch at 1:00. Smooth was too tired to get out of bed, no surprise there. Mac was going somewhere with his father. I agreed and went downstairs to get some breakfast. Mother had my favorites, scrapple and scrambled eggs, ready. Pop was sitting in the breakfast nook reading the *Philadelphia Inquirer,* a cup of coffee and a plate of raisin bread toast in front of him.

"Your game is the top article in the sports section," he said. "Says the Wilkes Barre fans went pretty crazy, breaking car windows, throwing rocks at Lansdowne fans. State Police and the Reading police had to arrest fifteen people."

"They should have arrested five hundred, the way those people were acting."

Mother stopped cooking and looked at me. "Patricia Bolton dropped off your clothes this morning. She told me the whole story about what happened at the game. You're very lucky to come away in one piece, Joey. The state championship game could be more of the same or worse."

"Yeah," Pop chimed in, "you guys are going to be playing Chilton, the armpit of the western world."

Our old nemesis had won the other semi-final game. Not exactly a surprise. "Since it's the championship game and on television, I'm sure they'll be taking every precaution. By the way, I scored 28 points, my career high, and there were a lot of college scouts in the stands. I might be hearing from other schools besides Princeton."

Mother kept rattling on. I went upstairs and had a much-needed shower. After drying myself, I set the alarm for 12:30 and fell asleep immediately. If I dreamt, I didn't remember. The buzzer went off, I woke up, threw on a pair of dungarees, a black turtleneck and my usual Converse High-Tops.

As soon as I came through the front door of the diner, Tony Ianuccil, the co-owner, yelled, "Our high scorer, Joey 'Jump Shot' Garden. Without him, we wouldn't be going to the state championship!" The rest of the diners applauded and cheered. I smiled and joined Zack and the twins in a rear booth.

Tony brought me a huge plate of French fries, along with a cheeseburger, and said, "It's on me, kid." I wasn't that hungry, but figured I'd find the room. The other guys were all eating French fries and cheeseburgers, too.

"I want to know how you guys felt about the game," Zack said, wiping catsup from his chin. "Because I feel like shit. Wilkes Barre beat us fair and square. They're the ones who should be going to State, not us."

"Are you fucking nuts, Zack?" Dave cajoled. "The scoreboard had us ahead 73-72 when the buzzer went off."

"It does matter, Dave," Zack continued, "the refs were calling one bogus foul after another on them. Boyle and the fans had a right to be pissed. Imagine how we'd feel if we were the team that got screwed."

"How do you know what would have happened, if the fouls weren't called?" Dan added, "Maybe Joey would have hit a few more jumpers and we'd have won by more than one."

Zack, looking very irritated, answered, "That's total bullshit, Dan, and you know it. Wilkes Barre was the better team. Smooth and I were outplayed for the first time all year."

"Why didn't you just miss the foul shots if you felt that way?" Dave asked.

"I thought about it, believe me. On the second shot, I wanted to aim the ball to the left of the rim, but just couldn't do it."

Dan and Dave looked stupefied. This was not the Zack they thought they knew, the hard-driving fanatic who would stop at *nothing* to win a state championship.

It was time for me to say something. "I know you want everything to be clear-cut, Zack, but sometimes it just isn't. If Martin hadn't eaten all that chocolate and played in the game, we could have lost by 20."

Dave put his hand on my shoulder and said, "And you took advantage of it, Joey. You were pure death in the second half."

Dan joined in, "One thing we can be thankful about, after

Joey's performance last night, no way Coach can start Dipshit for the championship game."

"I don't know about that, Dan," I answered. "Martin keeps rising from the ashes. Tim becoming a starter would have destroyed a lot of teams, but it didn't destroy us. Don't worry about who's going to begin the game."

Turning to Zack, I said, "The way we won last night's game bothered me too, but what happened wasn't our fault. We played as well as we could; no one was slacking off, no one made any bonehead plays. Boyle should have realized his mouthing off was hurting his team; he didn't, and we caught a break."

Zack looked down before quickly staring at the ceiling. Powerful emotions were racing through his body. "Oh, what the hell," he said, before slumping against the back of the booth. "I just want to win the championship and be able to feel good about it. We'll play better and work harder than Chilton and win the game, with no complications."

"Fat chance," I answered him, changing the subject. "I'm still shook up about the way those Wilkes Barre bastards rushed the bus after the game. The guy who came up to my window, I'm sure he would've strangled me if he could've."

Dan laughed, "You should have seen Martin crouched down in his seat in the bus, shaking like he was pitching a fit. What a pussy. When the bus started rocking back and forth, I thought he was going to shit himself."

We all enjoyed the thought of Tim doing just that. Dave, grinning from ear to ear, said, "You know guys, I think ole Timmy ate all that chocolate so he'd have an excuse to bag out of the semi-final; he's a complete waste. He'll probably get appendicitis before the championship game."

Dan put his hand on my shoulder and said, "You'll be the starter, Joey Boy."

Zack and Dave nodded. But they didn't know what I knew. I'm not sure how it happened, but I blurted out, "Mrs. Johnson got drunk and hit a young kid with her car, before fleeing the scene. Evidently, she's done this kind of thing before. Old man Martin found out about it and agreed to keep everything quiet if Tim became a starter again. Coach told me the whole story if I promised not to tell anyone else. Swear you won't tell a *soul* what I just said."

As soon as I uttered those words, I knew I'd made a mistake. Even though Coach had betrayed the entire team, I'd promised not to reveal his secret.

All three of them had that caught-in-the-headlights look in their eyes. Zack spoke first. "What a dumb son of a bitch Coach is," he railed. "To almost ruin the team because his wife is a drunk, that's the stupidest thing I ever heard of."

"Yeah, it's hard to figure," Dan added. "Our old man gets shit-faced every night of the week. They could put it on the evening news and on the front page of the *Philadelphia Bulletin* for all Dave and me care."

"That's right," Dave went on, "the best thing our father could do for us is die. Johnson should have been glad she got caught."

I felt a need to protect Coach. "Look, guys, he's been dealing with his wife's problem for a long time. He was worried that if the town found out about his wife's accident, there'd be a big scandal, which could destroy her and his whole family. I told him he made the wrong choice; obviously, he didn't agree with me. The one thing about this mess, if we didn't know it already, is that the Martins will do *anything* to get what they want."

Zack, thoroughly disgusted, added vehemently, "Why didn't Coach divorce her? Who the hell wants to live with someone who's blotto most of the time, anyway?"

I waited for the right time to make my point as the discussion raged on. "Like I just said, don't tell anyone else about Mrs. Johnson. And, in case you've forgotten, we have a state championship basketball game to play. We don't need any more distractions. Let's shake on it and move on."

Each one of them shook my hand and promised to keep their lips firmly sealed. Zack would not break his word, I was certain of that. But Dan and Dave were something else indeed. They wouldn't maliciously break their promise, but both of them were pop-off artists. I had to cross my fingers and hope there'd be no reason for them to spill the beans.

"One good thing Coach did," Zack said, "was send Hawk to scout Chilton. He's gonna tell us at Monday's practice what he found out. Those bastards knocked us out of Regionals in '55, '57 and '59. We lost every game by at least fifteen points. They didn't just beat us; they crushed us. I was on the team two years ago. It was a very sick feeling, riding home in a dark, gloomy bus with our tails between our legs."

"They just beat McKeesport High and Curtis Wilkerson," Dave chimed in. "They'll be as tough as Wilkes Barre."

Chilton was a tough oil refinery town. I'd seen the '57 and '59 games. Both were over by the end of the first quarter. They were too fast, too strong and too talented for puny little Lansdowne High. Just about all of their team was black. A number of their former players had gotten scholarships to schools like Michigan State, Maryland and Tennessee. "I used to think that once we were rolling, no one could beat us," I said.

"After Wilkes Barre, I no longer believe that. But knowing we aren't invincible will make us work even harder."

"Joey for President," Dave said. "I'll tell you one thing; the game will be very close. If Chilton wins, they're gonna have to earn it."

"What do you mean?" Zack almost yelled. "Don't even let those thoughts enter your minds. We're gonna play the best game of our lives and kick Chilton's ass. Then we can forget about the Wilkes Barre game, Martin, and everything else. Put your hands in, guys."

Very corny, but we all did that as we yelled "State Championship," to the delight of the other patrons in the diner. The wind was whipping through us as we said our good-byes in the parking lot. Having the old Zack re-emerge had re-energized us.

Cars, multi-colored blurs, whizzed by me as I walked home down Baltimore Pike. Even a near-genius like Steve McChesney couldn't explain why things happened the way they did. We're actors in a play but don't know our lines ahead of time. Fate smiled on us when we played Wilkes Barre, for reasons beyond anyone's comprehension. Fate could kick our asses in the state championship game. We could play great, go all out and still end up on the trash heap. God, I hoped there was no more drama. But unlike Zack and the twins, I just knew Coach was going to start Martin. There was no point getting upset about it; we'd simply need to figure out a way to minimize the damage. I felt bad all over again for exposing Coach. But I couldn't afford to let it bring me down. Everything would be forgotten if we won State, anyway.

I still felt sore on Monday morning at school. People I didn't even know began coming up to me. "Great game, Joey, you shot like a real champ." "We wouldn't be going to State without you, Joey." "Whatta game, Joey!" Then there was Benjamin Coopman, the sickest, most prejudiced person in the world. "We killed the niggers from Wilkes Barre and we're gonna smash the coons from Chilton, Joey." *Thank you so much for those kinds words, Ben. Have you not noticed that one of the stars of our team, our center, is black?*

Three banners were hanging on the wall over the entrance to the auditorium. **Chilton Bulldogs - All Bark-No Bite. Neuter the Bulldogs. Lansdowne High School-State Chaaaaaamps!!!** Melanie Sinclair and Debbie Fulsen each grabbed one of my arms and began whisking me down the hallway, a pleasant but strange experience.

Somehow I was able to get my books out of my locker and get to Advanced English. Everyone's eyes were on me as I took my seat. Mrs. Childress came into the room, took roll and said, "Before we continue with our discussion of *Catcher in the Rye,* I'd like to congratulate our basketball star, Mr. Joey Garden."

The class began with a boisterous cheer. I stood up and bowed. Students started yelling, "*Speech, speech, speech.*"

"You don't really want to hear what I have to say; you just want to get out of English." Much laughter and mock protestation. "Zack and Smooth were being shut down and somebody had to pick up the slack. I decided it should be me. Every time the ball left my hand, it seemed destined to go right through the hoop. This has happened to me before, but not in such an important game. I'm thrilled that Destiny smiled on me Friday night."

Everyone clapped. Mrs. Childress thanked me and began a discussion about why Holden got so upset seeing "Fuck You" etched on a museum wall. Cool that a teacher could say that phrase in class with no hullabaloo whatsoever. She talked about how depressed Holden got, realizing that he was going to be dealing with this kind of thing for the rest of his life.

It made me wonder about Tim Martin. Next year, when I'm in college, he'll be nothing but a bad memory. How many other Tim Martins will there be in the coming years? There always seems to be some kind of rust, dirt or impurity smudging our lives. Zack wants everything to be pure. I've never seen the world as simply and idealistically as he does.

The rest of the day drifted by. It was hard to concentrate in class. At 3:15, I found myself in my gym clothes sitting in the first row of the bleachers, patiently waiting for Hawk to tell us about Chilton. After about five minutes, he came walking across the gym floor dressed in tan khakis, brown loafers and a brown jacket over a red-and-white-checked long-sleeved shirt. One thing about the Hawk, even though he almost played in the pros, he's always been a low-key guy.

He put his hands in his pockets and began to speak. "I traveled to Pittsburgh on Friday and watched Chilton beat McKeesport and Curtis Wilkerson. There's no question that they're a very good squad. But they're *definitely beatable*. You should go into the championship game knowing that Lansdowne High is fully capable of winning the big prize.

"Chilton's star player is a 6' 8" center named Othelia Briggs. He played Curtis to a standstill. Sorry, Calvin, but he's tough. Once he gets the ball close to the basket, Othelia's almost unstoppable. He doesn't have a jump shot. The key is to deny him the ball and when he does get it, make him work for his shot. He gets frustrated pretty easily, so hang all over him. Another really good player is Malcolm Jeannette. He has a devastating jump shot and can shoot from anywhere on the court. The other guard, Wesley Tynes, dribbles like a Harlem Globetrotter. He's a great passer, but hardly ever takes an outside shot. The forwards, Cleotha Gordon and Mac Winston, are both 6' 6" and built like fullbacks. Both score mostly on rebounds, but they can make a shot if necessary.

"In order to win, you're going to have to be maniacs on defense for the entire contest. And on offense, try to take a good shot every time you have the ball, because Chilton will almost certainly dominate the boards. Everybody in town will either be at the game Saturday night or watching on TV. Dig down deep and play your best game."

The team stood in unison and cheered. The Hawk had given us great information and helped boost our confidence, without minimizing how difficult the job was going to be. It was just what we needed to get focused for the rest of the week.

Hawk came up beside me. He put his hand on my shoulder and said, "Coach Johnson had Mr. Lester film the Wilkes Barre game. I sent a copy to Coach Willoughby at Princeton. He called me this morning and said he'd be at the championship game. I'll build you up every chance I get. If you play well after your 28-point performance in the semi-final, I just know he's going to offer you a scholarship."

"Coach told me today that William and Mary and Lafayette have also expressed interest. It's pretty amazing."

Hawk looked delighted and crouched down, bringing his face close to mine. "That's great, Joey; it gives Coach W even more incentive to sign you up on Saturday night."

As I walked toward Coach, who had just blown his whistle to start practice, it dawned on me that, barring some great calamity, I was going to be away at college next year on a basketball scholarship, probably at Princeton. It didn't feel real.

The scrimmage began. Dave and I in the backcourt, Mac and Zack at forwards, Smooth at center. Maybe I was going to start after all. Martin was guarding me and doing his usual inferior job. Just by making a few head fakes, I got past him easily. Dave got me the ball and I drilled three shots in a row. Coach blew his whistle and reprimanded Tim for his lackluster defense. This made Tim angry and he stormed off the court. No one seemed to care. Coach put in a sub and we continued to scrimmage, moving the ball around like pros. This felt like most of our other practices, the games in West Philly, the talents of each of the starters meshing perfectly with each other.

In school the next day, three freshman girls saw me, started to giggle and ran off. Now I knew how Elvis felt. My back must have been slapped fifteen times before I got to English class. I needed a pair of shoulder pads.

At lunch, McChesney looked ready to pounce, and he did. "Joseph, I've been thinking a lot about this matter. I think the laws of probability are bound to catch up with the team. You've been lucky to survive at all with Tim Martin as the starter. And you were clearly outplayed by Wilkes Barre. Chilton has beaten us badly the last three times we played them. They have to feel a sense of psychological dominance. I'm sorry to say this, but I feel Lansdowne is going to come home Saturday night second place in the state."

Very smug. Like some math teacher just finishing up an explanation for a quadratic equation. What the hell was Ches trying to do anyway, steel himself against disappointment?

"Following the premise of your argument, Ches," I replied. "Since Chilton has beaten us in Regionals three times, doesn't it follow that they're *probably* going to lose the fourth game? I find your logic appallingly faulty. And for the five thousandth time, no talk about basketball, please. This school is a virtual nuthouse and there are four entire days left until the big game."

I decided that this might be a good time to bring up the news about my potential scholarship offers.

"Nothing is certain, gentlemen, but three colleges have expressed interest in wanting me to play basketball for them next year: Lafayette, William and Mary and Princeton."

They were speechless. "Princeton?" Jeff asked, a tone of annoyance creeping into his voice.

"Hawk arranged it. Their head coach is coming Saturday night to check me out. Everything is hypothetical right now. A lot depends on how I play in the big game. If I do well, a few more colleges might express interest."

"Joey," George said, looking at me with what seemed like awe, "if you get into Princeton, you'll be set for life."

Jeff cut in. "I don't know why people consider Princeton to be more prestigious than Penn. They're both Ivy League schools."

"Those kind of things are never fully explicable, Jeff," Ches interjected. "Maybe some university in Podunk, Indiana, has a more outstanding faculty than an Ivy school, but no one's ever heard of it, so there's little recognition. And, by the way, it's bad form to be so gung ho, defending a school that hasn't even accepted you yet."

Couldn't have said it better myself.

Walking home from practice, I saw that every single store on Lansdowne Avenue had messages in their windows urging the team on. Even the staid old gray building that housed

Lansdowne Savings and Loan had a message that took two windows: BE THE CHAMPS — GO LANCERS!!!

Old man Sandler, smoking a nasty-smelling cigar, motioned me inside the drugstore where I held my first job.

"Can I give you a black cow or a chocolate shake, Joey?" he asked. "Totally free of charge."

Sandler, who squeezed every nickel he had until the buffalo choked, was not known for giving away anything for free. I declined his offer.

"The colored boy," he said, " has got to play a lot better if we're going to win the title. He needs to hustle more and not back down so easy."

A lot of people who knew almost nothing about basketball probably felt the same way. "Calvin goes all out on every play, Mr. Sandler," I answered. "The guy who played against him in Wilkes Barre will be in the pros in a few years."

As I left the store, everyone, almost on cue, cried "Go Lancers!" It was hard to imagine the intensity getting any stronger, but I knew it would.

I never liked pep rallies much. People always said the same kinds of inane stuff, while an enthusiastic crowd cheered its lungs out. Being on a team that was one game away from the state championship, I wanted this one to be different. Before school, I asked George, who was on the stage crew, to look and see if there were any Renaissance hats, the kind that Shakespearean actors often wore. Luckily for me, he found a big floppy purple headpiece that suited my request perfectly.

Friday finally rolled around; I'd finished writing my speech the night before. I took the hat out of my locker, stuffed it inside my jacket and headed toward the gym. When the team filed out of the locker room and onto the floor, the place erupted like

Jesus Christ and Elvis just arrived. Martin, a wannabe Rocky Marciano, did the same thing he did at the last rally, flexing his biceps and raising his arms over his head as he paraded around in front of the stage.

The rest of us quietly took our seats and waited for Coach to speak. He walked slowly to the podium, took a piece of paper from his pocket and began to read: "This year's squad has been the best team I have ever coached. We won the Harrisburg Tournament in January, we won the Deerfield Conference title, we made the finals of the State Championship, and we have remained undefeated for the entire season. Saturday night's game will not be our first loss." Thunderous applause. "Finally, I want to introduce our captain, Zack Bolton, who will be followed by Joe Garden, Dan and Dave Irwin, Jim MacWilliams, Calvin Newsome and Tim Martin."

Zack strode to the microphone and stood there for about thirty seconds as the crowd went wild. He pointed at the audience and began to speak. "Chilton High has knocked Lansdowne out of Regionals three times in the last five years. *Not this year* (loud applause)! We're the best team in the state! We've proved that over and over. Everyone in this gym is going to be part of history, because LANSDOWNE HIGH IS GOING TO WIN THE STATE CHAMPIONSHIP!"

Pandemonium. I didn't think the noise in the gym could get any louder. Once again, I was wrong. I put on the cap, which flopped over my right ear, took a few deep breaths, and strode toward the microphone. It was too late to back out. I was either going to belly flop or execute a perfect swan dive. Having no idea which one was going to occur, I began to speak. "I want to dedicate this speech to Mrs. Childress' Advanced English class. It is based on Hamlet's 'To be or not to be' soliloquy."

To lose or not to lose,
That is the question.
Whether it is better
To say we've done enough
Or take arms
Against a vicious opponent
And by facing them
End their season!!!

To be able to rest and dream
Is devoutly to be wished.
But if we do so too soon,
There will be a rub.
Lansdowne High will
Win no championship!!!

That, perchance, is not
To be our fate.
We will not become sicklied o'er
With pale doubt and fear
And lose the name of action.
LANSDOWNE HIGH WILL BE
STATE CHAMPIONS!!!

I knew the second I'd finished, I'd hit a home run. The Prince of Denmark himself would have been right proud. The gym was in complete hysteria. Shakespeare wrote that more than three hundred and fifty years ago; his words still had great power, even though I paraphrased a lot of them. My knees were shaking as I walked back to my seat. The rest of the senior players each got up and said a few words, but everything after the soliloquy was an anti-climax.

Walking out of the gym, it felt like I was getting ready to take off and fly. When the hell else in my life was I going to ever get this kind of platform?

"Joseph, you just keep topping yourself," Ches said, coming up to me while smiling ecstatically. "That speech was simply brilliant. I was almost shaking with awe."

George took the hat from me before adding, "That was so boss, Joey. You're the coolest guy in the school."

We chatted for a few more minutes before I left for home. Walking down stately Greenwood Avenue, where I usually felt dwarfed by the giant oaks, elms and sycamores that lined the street, I felt like I was their equal.

As soon as she put food on the table at dinner, Mother faced me with a morose expression on her face. "I feel kind of bad telling you this, Joey," she said, holding a napkin tightly in her hands. "But I don't think I'm going to be able to make the game Saturday evening. People, some of whom I don't even know, have been coming up to me all week, congratulating me and wishing me luck. As you know, I'm a very private person, and I find this kind of thing very disconcerting. I've never been very comfortable in large crowds, either. So I'm hoping you won't feel too angry if your stick-in-the-mud mother watches the game on television instead of in person."

Pop added, "Yeah, kid. I think it's best if I stay with your mother. So I won't be goin', either."

My parents looked like they'd just dropped an atomic bomb or something. I'd kind of assumed Mother and Pop would go to the championship game. I understood her concerns, but I still couldn't help but think she continued to have some kind of grudge about my success at basketball. The *Disappointed in Mother* station had come on the air once again. But there was too much at stake to fret about this.

"I understand completely," I said, digging into a piece of fried chicken. Mother had tears in her eyes. Pop was smiling ear to ear.

"It's such a relief to hear you say that, Joey," Mother exclaimed. "And I want to tell you right now, that I'm as proud of you as I've ever been. Gladys Martin made a special trip into the bank today to tell me how much the Martin family appreciated you not making a stink over losing the starting spot to Tim."

Oh my God, this again. The Martins might not be so complimentary when they see me walk on the floor for the center jump instead of Timmy Boy. I nodded and smiled. After dinner, on TV, my namesake, Joey Giardello, from the East Passyunk neighborhood in South Philly and Pop's favorite fighter, was going against another Italian, Frank DiNucci, in the Boston Garden. It was a good fight. DiNucci injured his left hand in the last round, but hung on for a draw. I'm glad there are no ties in basketball. It's strange when there's no winner, like the contest didn't even take place. The old man acted pissed, but I could tell he admired Di Nucci, another courageous paisan. We chatted for a while. He reminded me to give it everything I had tomorrow night, and to never give up, no matter what the score might be. Good words of advice, not that I particularly needed them.

When I went to sleep, I dreamt that I was in a very dark location, a cave, a cavern, a forbidden place. Things started popping out of the dark stone walls: huge brightly colored flowers, clown faces with different kinds of make-up, exotic animal heads like gazelles and cheetahs. When I tried to concentrate and examine each one, they disappeared back into the darkness. I woke up at 2 a.m. sweaty, frustrated and feeling tantalized. My first reaction was that the dream was a premonition that the state championship was going to be in our grasp, only to elude us at the last second. Such an unpleasant thought. I put it out of my mind immediately and went back to sleep.

When I woke up, I thought about the dream again and wondered if it might be a reminder that beauty, magic and other transcendent moments never last very long in our lives.

It was 10 a.m. when I got downstairs. The phone was ringing off the hook, one call after the other. I could hear Mother's voice, but not well enough to understand what she was saying. Pop was sitting on the sofa reading the morning paper.

"They got a whole page on the game in the *Inquirer* sports section, Joey," he said. "The writer says you are 'a very plucky guard with a picture-perfect jump shot.' Pretty nice description."

I nodded, but didn't say anything. Coach had warned us not to get caught up in all the pre-game publicity; I'd made it a point not to read the papers or watch TV reports about the game.

"You know, son," the old man said, letting the paper drop into his lap and taking a very serious tone, "When I was in South Philly High, nobody knew who I was. The only class I did well in was auto shop. Who in the hell cared about that? I got no idea what you're goin' through right now, not a damn clue."

"So what do you want me to do, Pop, apologize?"

He waved his hand across his face. "Nah, just sayin', that's all."

I ate breakfast, then went back to my room and turned on the radio. Chuck Berry, Little Richard and the Everly Brothers,

Buddy Holly and various doo-wop groups helped me get through the next three hours.

Pop offered to drive me up to the high school. I accepted his offer. He had to park as soon as he turned onto Essex Avenue, as there were cars and people everywhere. It occurred to me that there probably hadn't been this much excitement in Lansdowne since World War II ended. I pushed through the adoring throng, taking about ten minutes to reach the team bus, which was parked, as usual, right in front of the gym. Coach and the rest of the team were waiting on the sidewalk. After a huge cheer from the crowd, we boarded. Zack and I sat where we usually did, in one of the middle rows.

Martin came stumbling in last, waving to the crowd and yelling, "Isn't this the greatest thing in the world!" before flopping down on a rear seat.

Coach told us that we were going to be stopping at Johnny and Jimmy's Diner for a pre-game meal. He said that the Ianucci brothers had offered to feed us; they're such generous people. He added that having only Hershey bars before the Wilkes Barre game had affected our performance. And since tip-off was at 7:30, we had plenty of time to digest our food.

Both brothers greeted us as we entered the diner. Jimmy's a big, broad-shouldered guy with a personality to match. Johnny is much smaller and very quiet. There was a sign in the front window that read: *Diner Closed For State Champions*.

I got into a booth with Calvin, Dan and Dave. Johnny announced that we were all having T-bone steaks and lobster tails, but that we could order dessert and drinks from the menu. That was superb news; I loved their Boston cream pie.

"As we waited for the food, Dan asked Smooth, "Are

you worried about covering Othelia? His elbows are as big as sledgehammers."

"I'd be worried if I didn't have the three of you to pester him. When Othelia gets the ball in the pivot with his back to the basket, you're all going to have to drop back and knock it out of his hands."

I doubted that I had the strength to do that, but hoped I could at least bother the huge center. The meal was filling and delicious. I could manage only one piece of pie. Everyone on the team thanked the Ianuccis, the waitresses and the cook. We were off to West Philly and the Palestra.

Zack, staring out the window as we drove off, was in a pensive mood. "You know, Joey," he said, "a lot of people are going to be disappointed if we lose this game. I feel a great weight on my shoulders. You and I were born here; we've never lived anywhere else. Think of how great it will be if we're state champions, the best high school basketball team in the state of Pennsylvania for 1961."

He and I are very different in this regard. I want to win for the other guys on the team and, frankly, for myself. I like Lansdowne, but don't particularly think I owe my hometown anything.

Penn's gym, the Palestra, was built in 1927 and reeked of history. Many great players from Philly and elsewhere have played there, including: Wilt the Stilt Chamberlain of Kansas, Tom Gola of LaSalle, Paul Arizin of Villanova and my personal favorite, Hal Lear of Temple, one of the greatest shooters of all time. Zack and I saw the Hawk and Andy Dryden play for Princeton against Penn here a couple of years ago. Chills ran up and down my spine as I wandered around the empty gym, which seated about 9,000 people, who watched the game from long wooden benches. Huge banners hung on the walls saying: **Pennsylvania State Championship Game.**

The team sat down behind the press row, which was right at the half court line. People started drifting in, filling up the bench. I looked up and saw Thaddeus Jones and Dominic DiFranco, the two Wilkes Barre stars, standing over me. Jumping up, I immediately shook both of their hands. What a great gesture, to come see us before the game they should be playing in, not watching.

"Hey, Dead Eye," Dominic said to me, "You're gonna need that killer jump shot tonight. We played Chilton at a Christmas tournament in Scranton and beat them by two points in overtime."

"They a bunch of punks," Thaddeus added, a look of pure disgust passing through his face. "They play dirty, cuss and whine to the refs the whole game. Othelia the worst of all of them, crying like a spoiled baby when he don't get his way."

"Wow," Zack answered, "the way you guys got jobbed in the semi-final, I thought there'd be no way you'd be rooting for us."

"Wasn't your fault our coach is an Irish hothead," Dominic answered. "That ref was his ex-brother-in-law. You guys played us tough the entire game."

"I hate those Chilton motherfuckers," Thaddeus interjected, not able to help himself. "They don't deserve to win nothin'. You guys need to kick some Chilton ass."

With that, the two departed, smiling and wishing us good luck.

"Ex-brother-in-law?" Dan chortled. "Are we swimming in shit, or what?"

Having to wait for so long had made us all jittery. Coach shouldn't have gotten us here so early.

After about ten minutes of staring blankly at the court, I turned and saw Coach's wife wobbling down the stairs like a quivering mass of Jello. Mrs. Johnson went to take her normal seat, right behind our bench. She looked very confused, shaking and staring vacantly into space. A man took her arm and helped her sit down.

"Holy shit," Dave exclaimed, "Mrs. Johnson's a goddam potted plant."

"Three sheets to the wind," Dan said, "we've seen it hundreds of times."

Well, I hadn't. Seeing Mrs. Johnson so obviously soused was very disturbing to me. Zack, Smooth and Mac looked totally disgusted. Why didn't Coach have more control over his wife?

It was time to go to the dressing room and get set for the biggest game of our lives. When we were ready, Coach got up on a bench and began to speak. "We've come a long way to be here tonight, gentlemen. Our team reminds me of Charles Lindbergh ready to descend to LeBourget airport in Paris, the final destination on his incredible journey across the Atlantic.

"What we have to fear most tonight is losing because someone didn't chase after a loose ball, got a technical foul for verbally abusing the ref, carelessly threw the ball out of bounds, didn't follow their shot, or didn't communicate on defense. These kinds of mental errors need to be kept to an absolute minimum.

"If Chilton proves to be a better team tonight and honestly defeats us, which I don't think is going to happen, that will be no reason to hang our heads. You know in your hearts that you deserve to be state champions; now go out and prove it to the rest of the world!"

Coach had gotten the team jazzed. We were chomping at the bit to get on the floor. "One more thing," he said. "Tonight's starting lineup will be Bolton and MacWilliams at forwards, Newsome at center and Dan Irwin and Martin at guards."

A powerful bomb had just gone off. Dan and Dave rushed up to Coach and poked him in the chest with their index fingers. "You can't do this to the team," Dan screamed. "Joey had 28 against Wilkes Barre while Martin was puking his guts out on the bench. Just because your wife is a goddam lush is no reason to wreck our chance at the championship."

Holy Christ, this was so bad. No one had ever talked to Coach like that.

Dave continued, "And by the way, Coach Johnson, your darling wife is sitting behind our bench right now, drunk as a skunk."

Coach looked ashen. He had completely lost control of the team and the situation. I hoped that in the hullabaloo, he hadn't noticed that I had broken my promise to keep my mouth shut.

Martin stood up on a bench and shouted, "Give Coach Johnson a break. I'm a better all-round player than Joey, and every one knows it."

That brought utter chaos. Every single player, even the scrubs, were screaming at the top of their lungs. An official knocked on the door and told us it was time to get on the court. How could we beat a team as good as Chilton in such emotional chaos? Somehow we were able to get a layup drill started. When we finished and began shooting jump shots, I went to the twins and said, "Hey, guys, we have to forget all this bullshit and figure out a way to win."

"How the fuck are we supposed to do that, playing with Asshole, Joey?" Dan snapped. "Rummies, they're everywhere."

There was deep despair in both brothers' eyes. Coach's astonishing cowardice had been a knife through their hearts. "I don't know, but we have to think of something," I answered without much conviction.

Zack walked over, put his hand on my shoulder and said, "I'm really sorry, Joey. You didn't deserve this."

Microphones were brought out to the middle of the court and various officials from the Pennsylvania Interscholastic Athletic Association began making speeches about what a great event the state championship was, the importance of high school athletics in molding young people's characters, the great history of the title game. Do people all get more boring as they get older? They droned on for at least fifteen minutes, making me groggy and agitated at the same time.

Dave Zinkoff, the announcer for the Philadelphia Warriors, began to introduce the starting players. "For the Lansdowne Lancers, at one forward, Jiiimm Mc Willlllliams!!!, the other forward, Zaaaaack Boooolton!!!, at Center, Callllvin Newwwwwsooome!!!, at one guard, Daaaaaannn Irwiiiinnn!!!, and the other guard, Tiiiiimmmm Maaarrttiiiin!!!"

There was an audible gasp from the Lansdowne rooting section, when Martin's name was announced, followed by very loud chants of "We want Joeee!!! We want Joeee!!!"

Halfway through Zinkoff's introduction of the Chilton players, there was some kind of commotion behind our bench. Mrs. Johnson had fallen down into the aisle, dead drunk, her dress up over her waist. It was impossible not to notice she was wearing polka dot panties underneath her garter belt. What a great image, right before the most important game of our lives.

Some PIAA officials rushed over to her. When Coach finally saw what was going on, he blew past me, screaming, "Oh my God, oh my God!"

One thing I'd discovered these past few months was that as bad as things got, they could always get worse.

A doctor arrived, propped Mrs. Johnson up, and began to administer smelling salts. He needed to get her the hell out of the gym.

Mrs. Johnson quickly regained consciousness and began shaking her head vehemently back and forth, upset about something the doctor had said. Three attendants arrived. With Coach holding her hand, Mrs. Johnson, protesting very loudly, was put on a stretcher and carried down the length of the court in full view of the entire crowd, as her husband walked beside her.

A team can't take the floor unless a certified coach was on the bench with them. The officials had no choice but to delay the game until Coach returned to the floor.

"Coach's secret is out," Dave said to me. "Maybe he'll put you back in the starting lineup."

The thought had not occurred to me, but 9,000 people had just seen what Coach had tried, at great cost, to hide from the rest of the world.

"Let's hope he comes back soon," I answered.

We waited fifteen minutes, milling aimlessly around the court. Marco Lear, Chilton's great ball handler, ambled over to me.

"Hey, Six, you the one with the great eye?" He asked.

I nodded.

"I seen yo momma in the tenth row. Surprised she made it, we was out so late last night."

Othelia walked up beside him and they both laughed. It

was easy to see why Dominic and Thaddeus had called them punks.

"My mother doesn't like basketball. She's not here. You must have mistaken her for your sister."

Marco did not like that remark at all and probably would have taken a swing at me if there weren't so many people around.

Othelia bent down and put his huge face an inch away from mine. "Smart-ass little white boy, you get near the bucket, I'll take yo' head off. Wouldn't be surprised if you didn't score one point."

The twins noticed what was going on and stood on either side of me.

Zack came over, then Mac and Smooth. The other Chilton starters got behind Marco and Othelia. Both groups glared at each other.

Dave shouted, "Make the first move, Chilton motherfuckers." Was there anything he wasn't afraid of? A melee seemed seconds away, when Coach ambled back onto the court, looking lost. He called the team over and said, "Play a good game, team." His mind was a thousand miles away.

Looking into the crowd, I saw Hawk with the Princeton coach, probably trying to explain why I wasn't starting. I went to the far end of the bench, not wanting to be anywhere near the man who was destroying my life. If Coach remembered, through all this chaos, that I had ratted him and his lovely wife out, I might not play at all. My stomach sank down to my feet. At the very least, I could try to cheer the team on.

The whistle sounded for the center jump. Smooth out leapt Othelia; the ball flew toward the sideline. Dan grabbed it and dribbled to our end of the court. At the top of the key, Marco reached down and knocked the ball out of Dan's hand, the first time I'd ever seen that happen. Zack picked it up and sped down the floor, making an acrobatic leap beneath the basket and made a reverse layup. Our Captain, despite all the distractions, had come to play.

Chilton got back on offense quickly. Othelia got the ball a few feet from the basket, and turned around for an easy hook shot, which Smooth smashed back into his face. The game was less than a minute old and we had made two great plays. Dan stole the ball and took it in for an easy layup. Zack blocked Malcolm Jeanette's jumper. Mac got the ball and passed to Dan, who scored another basket.

The Chilton coach called a timeout as the Lansdowne rooting section exploded with cheers. Instead of feeling elated, I came to the grim realization that I might have to witness Lansdowne winning the state championship spending the entire game gathering splinters on the bench. Walking over to the timeout huddle, I heard Coach saying, "Just keep with what we're doing, boys." Nothing about making any adjustments. Nothing about things to anticipate.

Since Zack was guarding Malcolm Jeanette, Martin was on one of Chilton's forwards, a bigger, stronger guy than him, but one who didn't seem to shoot much. That changed after the timeout. The ball started going to Tim's man every time Chilton was on offense. Martin looked like a mannequin as his man drove around him for easy baskets and backed him into the lane for turnaround jump shots. Our lead was quickly erased. Zack started missing shots. Othelia began to dominate Smooth.

Lansdowne rooters began to chant "*Joee, Joeee!*" I heard the radio announcer behind me say, "It's very puzzling why Coach Johnson will not put guard Joey Garden into the game,

He had 28 points against Wilkes Barre in the semi-final." Indeed.

Coach called for a timeout. Martin looked like he would rather be on the bottom of the ocean than on the court. Coach motioned for Dave to replace him; Tim sat down beside me on the bench.

"Toughest team I ever played against," he moaned, wiping his face with a towel.

"Wilkes Barre's better," I answered. "You'd have known that if you hadn't gotten sick eating all that chocolate on purpose."

"Nothing you can say is gonna bother me, Joey. Because you are never going to get off this bench."

The twins started to play like maniacs, stealing the ball, never giving Chilton's guards a moment's peace. Mac began to assert himself, dribbling past his man for short jump shots. Smooth was steadily gaining confidence playing against Othelia, knocking the ball out of his hands in the pivot and dunking three of our missed shots for six points. But Malcolm Jeanette began hitting from the outside like he was out of his mind.

With Zack being double-teamed, and the twins no offensive threat, we needed an outside shooter. Deciding to take matters into my own hands, I got up and sat down beside Coach.

Putting my hand on his forearm, I asked, "Why are you keeping me off the floor? If I can start hitting, it'll take some pressure off Zack."

He stared vacantly at the court and said nothing. I wasn't even sure he heard me. His mind was on Saturn. Then I did something that might have changed the course of my life. Taking off my warm-up jacket, I threw it on the floor, walked up to the scorer's table and said, "Garden in for MacWilliams." If Coach wanted to stop me, he could've. I'm not sure he even noticed that I had come into the game.

"Jesus Christ," Dave said, "I never thought he'd put you in, Joey."

"He's completely out of it. I put myself in."

Waving the guys over, I got down on one knee and told them, "Forget about Coach. We're going to have to win this game by ourselves. Get me the ball any way you can. If I miss, Smooth and Zack, hit the boards like maniacs. Dan and Dave, get ready to catch their outlet passes for easy layups. C'mon, we can do this."

The other players looked energized and let out a small whoop. I waited to be yanked off the court, but nothing happened. Marco Lear came over to guard me.

"You ain't scoring a point, Six. In two minutes, you gonna be back on the bench where you belong, you teeny-ass white motherfucker."

He wasn't counting on Zack coming up behind him and setting a savage pick. I moved to my right, where Dan hit me with a bounce pass. Sometimes shots look like perfect works of art; other times they look like ugly stepsisters. This was one of the latter, hitting the backboard at a weird angle, rolling around the rim a few times before thudding through the basket. It was ugly, but it was two points.

It felt glorious to be back on the court. I made another basket from the corner, but the Chilton forward I was guarding was too big and strong for me and got free for two layups. We were going to have to figure out another defense.

Othelia was giving Smooth a very hard time again, backing him close to the basket with his very sharp elbows and an iron-hard butt. Zack had begun to shut down Malcolm Jeanette, but Dave had his hands full with Marco Lear. Dan was in the same position I was, guarding a much bigger, stronger man. Even though the first half had been excruciating, when the buzzer sounded, Lansdowne led 42-40.

Coach walked behind the team like a ghost. I half expected him to remain on the bench. As we sat down in the locker room, Tim's face was bright red with rage.

Coach began to speak, but before he was able to utter two words, Martin stood up and fumed, "In case you didn't notice, Johnson, Joey put Mac on the bench and went in without you saying anything. The deal was that he was going to sit for the entire game."

Martin's rage seemed to ignite something in Coach. With what had happened to his wife, there was no need to keep to whatever pact the Martins had dreamed up. He looked at Tim very calmly, then turned and spoke to the rest of the team.

"I have an apology to make to you players," he said, voice filled with contrition. "I let my personal life interfere with the team I've loved more than any other I've coached. Something I will regret for the rest of my life. Find some strength inside yourselves, gentlemen, exhausted as you might be, and go out on that Palestra floor and play the best half of basketball you've ever played in your lives."

Finished, he bent over and began to cry, huge, wracking sobs that resonated off the locker room walls. Coach was such a cerebral, low-key man, which made the scene all the more shocking. I think we all hoped he'd pull himself together pretty quickly, but even though it was kind of scary and embarrassing to watch him weep, it was kind of a relief to see him let go of all the emotion that he'd been trying to clamp down inside himself.

Three minutes passed before Coach wiped his eyes with his sleeve and looked up at our expectant eyes. Martin seemed to take that as a cue and screamed as loudly as he could, "Like I said before, Johnson, *a deal is a deal*. I'm starting the second half."

Zack leapt up, grabbed Martin by the shoulders and slammed him so hard against the lockers, it felt like an earthquake had occurred. Tim fell to the floor, moaning, while Zack hovered over him.

"You're such a total asshole, Martin," he sneered, "a complete disgrace. Everybody in the world hates you, except your parents. You've done nothing for this team except try to destroy it. If Coach puts you back in the game, the rest of us are going to walk off the court. You can go running to your parents. You can throw a tantrum in the middle of the Palestra. You can cry and sulk like you usually do, but we are done with you."

A great cheer erupted. Coach raised his hand and got everyone to quiet down before speaking, "The same lineup that was on the floor at the end of the second quarter will start the second half. Zack, I want you to set some picks for Joe, so he can get some open shots. He has to score right away and the rest of the offense will open up. If he isn't able to do that, Mac will come back in to give us defense and rebounding. Our points will have to come from somewhere else. I don't mean to be harsh, but Chilton is too big and strong to allow us to have three guards on the floor for very long.

"On defense, we are going to switch to a 2-1-2 zone. Zack will play in the middle to cut off any drives to the basket. Dan and Dave will be out front. Calvin and Joe will play underneath the hoop."

We poured onto the court minus Martin, who stayed behind, stewing in his own juices. It was such a relief having Coach back. I knew I must do what he wanted and hit some quick buckets. I *had* to do this; there was no way I was going to go back to the bench.

Taking a deep breath, I waited for the center jump. Smooth won it for the second time, tapping the ball to Dave. I streaked down the court, where he hit me with a pass right at the top of the key. Shooting in rhythm, the ball went effortlessly through the hoop, making the net wrap around the rim. The crowd roared and a bolt of energy shot through me.

Marco telegraphed a pass to Malcolm, which I intercepted, racing down court for an easy two. Even though I made two more outside shots, it did not feel like it had against Wilkes Barre, where I was in my own zone, impervious to harm. Chilton called a timeout and as they walked off the court, I could hear Othelia yelling at the other players, "Y'all playin' like a buncha pussies, lettin' that scrawny lil' white boy score like that." As predicted, the big center was starting to unravel and we were ahead, 50-40.

I guess I should have expected it, but didn't. Dogs that they were, instead of devising a defense to shut me down, Chilton decided to maim me instead. I got the ball in the corner and looked for an open man. Seeing no one, I dribbled right and went up for a jump shot. Marco was able to block the shot and pound my arm at the same time. I fell to the floor, writhing in pain. Coach shot up from the bench and screamed at the ref, "That Chilton player just about dismembered him. Call the foul!" I motioned to Coach to take me out of the game.

Someone had to continue scoring, and that person was Zack. He took it upon himself to show that he was one of the best high school basketball players in Pennsylvania sports history. He began to fake out his man and dribble toward the hoop, drawing Othelia from underneath the basket. He would make an acrobatic shot or shovel the ball to Smooth for an easy dunk or a layup.

Chilton was forced to triple-team him, which left the twins open, where they did something they hadn't done all year, hit open jump shots. Then they started leaving Mac alone, and he banked a couple of fifteen-footers off the backboard.

The only Chilton player up to the challenge of playing against us was Malcolm Jeanette. Zack couldn't continue to keep shutting him down. Malcolm was truly in the Zone. Thirty-footers from the top of the key, jumpers from the corners, drives to the hoop, the balls floating over Smooth's outstretched hands. This was a truly great player. If it weren't for Malcolm, Chilton was finished. Score at the end of the third quarter: Lansdowne 68, Chilton 60.

My arm was quite red and still throbbing, but the pain had died down. I felt good enough to play, but wasn't sure how well I'd be able to shoot. Martin finally made it back to the bench where he sat down beside me. "Lansdowne's gonna lose," he sneered, "because you're all a bunch of pussies. You're a pussy because you got hurt. Zack's a pussy because he can't guard Malcolm. Coach is a pussy because he went back on his word. And when the final score has Chilton beating us for the fourth time in six years, I'm gonna be smiling from ear to fucking ear."

I had no time for this. "I thought you enjoyed pussy, Tim," I said.

His face flushed as Coach motioned to me to sit down beside him. "How are you doing, Joe?" he asked.

"My arm still hurts, Coach, but I think I can still help the team."

He nodded and turned his attention back to the game.

Chilton began contesting the ball the second Zack passed it in bounds. The twins had no problem when they got their hands on the ball, but Mac got flustered by the pressure and lost it three times in a row. With Lansdowne holding a four-point lead, Zack shot from the corner and missed. Othelia and Smooth both went up for the rebound. Othelia got the ball and when he came down, swung an elbow right at the Smooth's temple. A huge sigh arose from the crowd as he crumpled to the floor and lay motionless. Coach ran out onto the court. The Palestra's doctor was right behind him, and began to administer smelling salts. After about five minutes of no movement at all, Smooth rose slowly from the floor, to loud applause. Zack and Mac helped him to the bench. No foul had been called. Coach was yelling vociferously at the refs, to no avail. He came up to me and said, "Go in for Calvin, Joe. Zack's at center, you and Mac at forward."

When I got back onto the floor, Marco smirked at me. That was all I needed.

I said to him, "Obviously, you don't think Chilton can win this game fair and square."

Marco got in my face and barked, "Whyn't y'all go tell that to Othelia? He standin' right over there. That man never take a cheap shot in his whole life."

"Bullshit!" I exclaimed, walking away from him in disgust. Marco ran and pushed me in the back with both hands. I turned around and pushed him back. One of the refs came over and got between us. As I walked away, I said to the official, "*Finally*, you've started doing your job." Stupid bastard, a blind man would have been more competent.

Amazingly, without our great center, we were able to maintain the lead. Even though using my arm was excruciatingly painful, I managed to make two short jumpers. Zack drove to the hoop for a few layups. But Mac and the twins couldn't make a basket. Chilton began getting the ball to Othelia on every possession. Neither Zack nor anyone else could stop his devastating hook shots and dunks. With fifty-eight seconds left, Lansdowne led Chilton 82-81.

After a timeout, Chilton stopped pressuring the ball. Dan and Dave dribbled easily upcourt, hitting Zack with a perfect bounce pass. He turned his back toward Malcolm and began to back him toward the foul line. Hoping to catch Chilton off guard, he slid the ball to Mac, who was alone under the basket. Not expecting the pass, Mac let it hit off his fingers and out of bounds.

Malcolm and Marco dribbled the ball up the court past the twins like a pair of magicians. Chilton passed the ball from man to man, trying to run down the clock. With fifteen seconds left, Malcolm faked a jump shot and fired the ball to Othelia. He turned around and leapt, holding the ball in both hands before smashing it through the rim as the crowd's screams resounded off the rafters of the Palestra.

Coach called time and set up a play to get the ball to Zack. The twins were brilliant with their dribbling, getting me the ball by the right sideline. I saw Zack out of the corner of my eye, moving toward the basket. I hit him with a bounce pass about five feet from the hoop. I'd seen him make this shot a thousand times. The ball hit right in the center of the backboard, dropped into the basket, spun and came right back out.

Othelia got the rebound, but Zack, following his shot, knocked the ball out of the big center's hands. It was rolling out of bounds when I reached down and grabbed it. With no time to aim or think about what I was doing, I threw up a shot as I was falling backwards. A primal roar rose from the crowd. My first thought was that it was the Chilton fans celebrating. When the entire Lansdowne team mobbed me and knocked me back on the floor, I knew the shot had gone in.

I felt like a cork spinning in a whirlpool. Zack scooped me up in his arms and began to dance around in circles until the crush of the crowd knocked him down. Smooth hugged me as the twins leapt up and whooped. Mac put his head on my shoulder and began to weep. Coach, trying to maintain his balance, had tears in his eyes. There was no time to think or feel, just to ride the wave of exaltation.

After about five minutes of sheer mayhem, I managed to look over at the Chilton bench, where players sat looking stunned and bewildered. A microphone was shoved into my face; a reporter standing in front of a TV camera began asking questions.

"This is John Duncan of WFIL Sports. We have the hero of the state championship game, Joey Garden," he announced. "How does it feel to have made that improbable winning shot in the most important game in the history of Lansdowne High, Joey?"

"I haven't had time to figure out how I feel. Everything happened so fast."

"How were you able to get the shot off, falling away from the basket with Malcolm Jeanette's hand in your face and almost no time left on the clock?"

"Pure desperation. I knew it was our last hope, so I just threw up the ball and prayed."

"Obviously someone was listening, Joey, because Lansdowne High has won the Pennsylvania State Championship!"

Right after he said that, a bunch of rooters mobbed me and shoved me to the center of the court, where I saw the most astonishing sight: Steve McChesney, the most emotionally composed person the world has ever known, jumping up and down and crying out: "You defied the laws of probability and physics, Joseph. We're the champs!!!" He whirled me around and when I came down, Jeff and George were alongside me. Three cheerleaders started hugging me; right behind them, to my extreme disbelief, were Gully, the Mole, and Kit Lambert in their customary dirty Levis and black motorcycle jackets. Even the Mole was grinning ear to ear.

When the hullabaloo died down, the team returned to the bench to wait for the awards ceremony. The head of the PIAA made a brief statement about the great game that had just been played. He handed out silver medals to the Chilton players. I hoped they were made out of cheap tin; that's all those guys deserved, except for Malcolm.

Then he announced: "And now for the 1961 State Champions of the great state of Pennsylvania, the Lansdowne High Lancers!" A gargantuan roar arose, followed by frenetic applause and thousands of feet pounding on the grandstands. The team lined up to receive their medals. I followed Smooth, Zack and Mac and when my name was announced, the volume went to max level. The championship trophy was presented to Coach. We crowded around him and posed for a group picture.

We ran off the floor to more cheers. I took my uniform off as quickly as I could once inside the locker room, and when I got into the shower, I began to weep as water cascaded over me.

All the intensity of the season: Martin, Coach's wife, Coach, Zack and Cindy, the riot after the Wilkes Barre game, all the practices, the bastards from Chilton, came pouring out of me, going down the drain with soap, shower water and sweat.

Standing right outside the locker room door were Thaddeus Stevens, Dominic DiFranco and the great Curtis Wilkerson.

Dominic and Thaddeus pounded me on the shoulder, while Curtis wrapped me up in a big bear hug. "Acrobatic fall-away jump shot with one second left on the clock," he exclaimed. "You became a legend tonight, Joey, a Pennsylvania high school legend!"

"Man," Thaddeus said, "I thought Lansdowne was done after Othelia hit Calvin with that cheap shot."

"It felt so good to see those Chilton bastards go down," Dominic added.

Zack and Smooth walked over and we talked for about five more minutes. Great guys and great basketball players, treating me like their equal. My exhilaration knew no bounds.

When we finished talking, Hawk and Princeton's head basketball coach, Tom Willoughby, approached me.

The coach shook my hand and said with a big smile of approval, "That's one of the most exciting endings to a basketball game that I've ever seen in my life, Joey. Congratulations!"

"Thank you, sir."

"I'm sure you know that Hawk has approached me about your possibly attending Princeton. He said that your grades and SAT scores were excellent. And after what I saw tonight, I can definitely say that we're extremely interested in you becoming a Tiger next year."

"I didn't do that much until the final score, Coach. I had a much better game in the semi-final against Wilkes Barre."

"Although I just saw a film of that game, I have to respectfully disagree with you, Joey. Tonight, you took good shots, played solid defense against a much bigger player. You didn't let Chilton's pressure bother you and you played within yourself, never forcing the issue on either offense or defense in a pressure-packed game. I should add that it took a lot of guts to return from that punch on the arm from the Chilton guard."

"I appreciate those comments, Coach."

"Make an appointment with my secretary, Hawk will give you the number, and come to campus for a visit with your mother and father. Bring your transcript and last year's tax returns, because we do base financial aid on the parents' ability to pay."

Before they walked away, Hawk gave me a big, ecstatic hug and shouted, "We're the state champions, Joey. The state champs!"

How much better could it get? As we filed out of the Palestra into the chill night air, the Chilton team came up behind us, heads down, gym bags in their hands.

Malcolm Jeanette saw me and extended his hand. "One of the best clutch shots I've ever seen, Six. You guys deserved to win." We hugged while the rest of the team walked past us, sullen expressions on their faces, saying nothing. Othelia with his huge Adonis-like torso was last, lagging behind the rest of the team. When he saw me, he stopped, put his gym bag on the ground and said, "You pulled that shot out yo' ass, Six. Lansdowne a bunch of lucky motherfuckers."

Zack and Smooth had sidled up behind me. Emboldened by their presence, I answered, "Without your cheap shot elbow on the side of Calvin's head, Othelia, Chilton would have lost by at least ten. You're too good a player to do that kind of stuff."

The center's body tightened. After looking at the three of us for a few seconds, he shook his head, picked up his gym bag and walked off without saying another word. Seconds later, the Lansdowne fans found us. A huge throng, between two and three hundred rooters, started jumping up and down, screaming their lungs out as they charged the team. A few men whom I didn't know lifted me up on their shoulders and carried me around the parking lot like I was King Tut. Once I got down, Helene, in her cheerleader garb, grabbed me in the tightest hug and kissed me, her tongue dancing across my tonsils. The crowd cheered. Barbara Turley came up and did the same thing. It was time to start thinking about girls again.

As we rode the bus on the short ride home, I basked in the glorious moment. Tonight there were no disappointments, compromises, wait-until-next-year thoughts — just sheer joy. I put my head on the metal headrest behind the seat in front of me and let another jolt of emotion pass through me.

A second mob had gathered at Lansdowne High and when the bus pulled in, they started to yell and scream. A mad crush of people began shoving me this way and that; I felt like an hors d'oeuvre being passed around a party. I noticed a giant beehive hairdo bobbing in the air above the crush of people. Before I could hightail it out of there, Mrs. Gladys Martin had her alligator paws on my cheeks, saying, "You're our hero tonight, Joey. We always knew you could do it." I thought she was getting ready to kiss me, so I put my head down and bulled my way through the rest of the crowd. I should have spit in her face. Right before I escaped the mob, a large middle-aged man, who I didn't know, jumped in front of me and began to dance around and scream. He looked and acted like an ape. The team worked and struggled for this?

I spied Pop's bald head about ten feet away and moved toward him as quickly as I could. "Let's get the hell out of here," I said.

He'd parked three blocks away, at Greenwood and Wycombe. When people saw us, they screamed "Way to go, Joey," "You're the man, Joey." Inside the car, Pop's hands were shaking as he tried to put the key in the ignition. Then he stopped, looked at me and tried again. Finally, he put his head on the steering wheel and began to weep. Sentimental Italian! I just wanted to get home.

"Your mother's a nervous wreck," he said, pulling the Chevy away from the curb. "If I hadn't made her sit down, she would have missed seeing you take that last shot. After it went in and you won the game, she couldn't talk and just stared at the TV for a long time. 'Our Joey just did that?' she kept sayin' over and over, when she started talkin'. Don't be disappointed if she went to bed, Joey. That game took a lot out of her."

"Frankly, Pop, the only thing I want to do right now is get something to eat and hit the sack for the rest of the weekend."

"I thought you might be real hungry, so I went and got a pizza from DeLuca's, some Frank's black cherry wishniak soda and a coupla Tastykakes."

I could have leaned over and kissed him.

After eating, I walked quietly upstairs to my room, took off my clothes, dumped them in the hamper and put on a pair of striped pajamas. I lay on my bed and pictured the shot leaving my hand, destination unknown. It was a plea, some kind of desperate prayer that got answered. A religious person could say that God smiled on us because we were better people and deserved to win. That's not something I could go along with. Horrible people win all the time. Look at the illustrious Martin family. If there were any justice in the world, they'd be living in a sewer somewhere being overrun by rats. How about mobsters, killing, torturing, shaking people down, bribing cops and judges and getting millions of dollars for their troubles.

One could speculate about this kind of stuff forever and not come up with one tiny little answer. The only certain truth was that, *I*, Joey Garden, not Zack, not Smooth, not Mac or the twins or Wilt the Stilt or the Hawk made that shot.

I stared at my small right hand and muttered: *You did this, you actually did this, hand. Eyes, you saw that ball before anyone else saw that it was rolling on the floor. Feet, you helped me leap into the air to launch the winning shot. My feet. My eyes. My arms. My soul. All had driven me to redeem a certain lost cause.*

Not able to help myself, I began to weep all over again. Pop rushed into my bedroom and asked if everything was okay. When he saw my face, he figured out what was going on. Leaning over, he clumsily put his arms across my shoulders, pulling me close to him. I don't know how much longer I continued to cry, but it seemed like a long time.

So many people came over to the house on Sunday, it was a relief to get back to school. Every single neighbor in Gladstone Manor arrived and many more from other parts of town. Mother greeted them all, trying hard not to look uncomfortable. After about an hour, Pop went out to the garage to work on the Chevy. I'm not sure exactly what they all wanted, to get my autograph, touch my clothes, or what? Even old lady, Brinkerhoff came by, she must have screamed at me a hundred times when I was younger for walking on her lawn or tramping on her flower beds. I smiled at everyone and said very little, remaining in the state of wonder I'd experienced last night when I went to bed.

Because of the shot, the course of my life had changed, I was sure of it. What exactly those changes might be, I didn't know.

Back at school on Monday, I wanted the bubble to burst. People ran up to me and yelled my name. It wasn't frantic or overwhelming. The feeling in school was one of lightness, muted happiness. First period was a pep rally in the gym. When my name was announced, I stepped forward with my arms raised in the air, absorbing the tumultuous cheers. I'd told myself: *no more tears*. Taking the mic from Coach, I said these simple words: "It's been a great honor to represent our school and play with my teammates, whom I'll remember for the rest of my life. Zack could have easily made the winning shot, or Smooth or one of the twins, or Mac, but the ball rolled right in front of me, and I was able to seize the opportunity. Everyone in this gym was in some way responsible for our school's first state championship." Huge applause. They would have cheered their hearts out for me if I started barking like a seal. Walking back to my seat, all the responsibility, tension and anxiety I had taken on for the team lifted from me like a cloud.

The Mugwumps were my obvious choice for lunch companions. Most of the school hated them; I was pretty certain to be left alone. But, when I entered the caf, my fellow classmates all began cheering: *Joeee, Joeee, Joeee!*

My three supercilious friends looked up at me and said nothing. As I cut into my Salisbury steak, McChesney reached his hand across the table and shook my hand. The silence continued for a few more minutes before George offered, "I guess you're pretty happy you didn't join the Hi-Q team, huh, Joey?"

"Yeah, I am, Georgie Boy. My whole world changed because of that decision."

"C'mon, Joey," Jeff asked, in an exasperated tone. "Tell us how it feels being such a huge hero?"

I couldn't resist answering, "Not so bad for an ape running around in his underwear, huh, Jeff? When I stop levitating, I'll let you know."

"How in the name of Jehosephat did you have the presence of mind to take that shot, Joseph?" Ches asked. "From where we were sitting, it looked you like emerged magically from a group of Cyclops like Hermes in his winged shoes."

"Probably the worst shot I ever took in my life. I just threw the ball in the general direction of the basket, Ches. That moment will be with me for the rest of my life."

The bell rang for fifth period and finally I was back on the ground. Joey Garden, big hero, senior in high school, was going to French III class.

A little freshman girl with glasses and pigtails was waiting for me in the alcove between the second and third floors. She handed me a notebook and pen and asked for my autograph. Enough was enough. I brushed by her and snapped, "I'm not Elvis." She ran off crying.

Coach had notified all the senior players to meet in his classroom right after school. When I saw Zack, Smooth, Dan, Dave and Mac, sitting very subdued in front of Coach's desk, I realized that over the course of this deranged, magical season, I'd acquired four brothers.

He reached into a cardboard box and took out a bunch of envelopes. Zack got a huge pack, held together with a thick rubber band. Smooth also got a very fat package. I got a few envelopes. Dan, Dave and Mac did not receive any, which made me feel bad.

"I have to say," Coach said, "this is only the third day after the championship game. There'll be many more offers and inquiries from colleges in the weeks to come. Be patient."

Zack dumped his pile on the floor, put his hand over his eyes, bent down and said, "Whatever one I pick, that's the school I'm going to." His hand settled on a bright red envelope. "University of New Mexico! I'm going to be a Lobo, whatever the hell that is."

Everyone laughed, including Coach. I tore into my envelopes: Rider College, University of Delaware, Penn, and Temple. Along with William and Mary, and Princeton, six schools had expressed interest in me. One month ago, languishing on the bench, just fantasizing about something like this happening would have been preposterous.

We sat around for about half an hour talking. Smooth, Zack and I all assured Mac and the twins they'd be getting theirs. It was easy to see the disappointment in Mac's eyes, but the twins could have cared less. "Me and my brother," Dave chortled, "are going to start our own toilet cleaning business. That's about all we're good for."

We all shouted "No" at the brothers as they doubled over with laughter. Maybe they were hurting deep down, but you couldn't have proven it by me.

As the other players got up to leave, Coach asked me to remain. He walked over and put his hand on my shoulder. "I believe I owe you a special apology, Joe. I never should have relegated you to the bench. Even so, you scored 28 in the semi-final and made the winning shot in the championship game. I don't think I've ever admired a young man as much as I've admired you."

His words had little impact. "You shouldn't hold me in

such high esteem," I said. "I told the other guys about your secret deal with the Martins and the police chief when I promised I wouldn't, Coach. I hope I never feel the need to protect my wife the way you tried to protect yours. We almost lost the championship because of you. Maybe I'll forgive you for that someday, but right now I can't."

On the way out of school, my emotions churning, I took the letter from Penn, Mother's favorite school, and threw it into a trash can. Even though it would have been great to play basketball every day in the Palestra, unless something unforeseen happened, I was going to be at school in Princeton, New Jersey, in the fall and that was that.

On Saturday morning, the entire team rode down Lansdowne Avenue from Borough Hall to the high school football field in 1957 Chevy convertibles. A stage was erected in front of the north goalpost, with 200 folding chairs set up on the football field. The rest of the crowd was sitting in the grandstand, with red, white and blue bunting hanging in front of the first row. Before the presentation of the team was about to begin, something magical occurred. A gate at the far end of the field opened, and a man dressed in knight's armor, sitting atop a white horse and holding a long steel lance, came bounding onto the track. The knight and his steed galloped in front of the bleachers three times before walking onto the field and stopping in front of the stage. The horse reared up on its hind legs and stayed in that position for a few moments before the rider got it under control. They departed through another gate, right by Essex Avenue. The crowd screamed: Go Lancers!!!

Transcendence was short-lived, as Superintendent Adams came to the podium. I was utterly sick of speeches, and I knew his was going to be a huge pile of manure. It was a definite struggle to stay awake listening to how great a community Lansdowne was, how the team had brought everyone in town together, and how our success mirrored the excellence of our wonderful school system. Blah blah and blah. How do people like him get to represent the rest of us?

When Adams finished speaking, he turned around to us before saying, "To speak for the best basketball team in the state of Pennsylvania is senior guard Tim Martin." After the shock wore off, the starters were so convulsed, we just about fell out of our chairs. The crowd saw our reaction and began laughing as well. Martin stumbled through some inarticulate gibberish and quickly sat down. The entire town knew Tim Martin was a complete sham. But his parents and their stooge, the superintendent, had to trot out their sweet darling one more time, not realizing that he had become a figure of ridicule.

A beautiful medal engraved with a basketball going through the hoop and *State Champions* emblazoned across the top attached to a garnet-and-gray cloth was hung around each player's neck. We all were also handed a gold trophy with our name and *Pennsylvania State Title* engraved beneath a gold basketball player ready to launch a shot. Pretty damn nice. It didn't take long to see that Smooth hadn't gotten his. As everyone slapped each other on the back, he sat alone, crestfallen.

Zack walked furiously toward the podium and grabbed the microphone. "Someone has made a mistake," he barked. "There was no trophy or medal for our center, Calvin Newsome. We would have never made the tournament without him. In the last two games, he had to guard two of the best centers in the country, Thaddeus Jones of Wilkes Barre and Othelia Briggs of Chilton, and did a tremendous job on both of them. He also had to endure a serious concussion in the championship game from an elbow to his temple. Let's hear a round of applause for our great center. "

A loud cheer rang out. After a few minutes of searching through some cardboard boxes, no trophy or medal were found. Adams went to the microphone and apologized, saying, "This terrible mistake will be rectified. I assure you this magnificent player will get his awards."

We stood on the stage for a few more minutes, acknowledging the applause from the crowd, who were all on their feet. *This is it*, I thought, *the last accolade*. Life was now officially going back to its normal, boring routines, a sad and comforting thought. We got back into the Chevy convertibles and headed back to Borough Hall and a free lunch at Horn and Hardart's.

When the team entered the restaurant, all the patrons got up and cheered. The manager took us to a large table right in the middle of the place. After everyone got settled, Tim Martin came marching in, with Cindy Devers on his arm.

"Great day, huh, gents?" he said, motioning to Cindy to sit down beside him.

No one looked up from their menus. After the waitress took our orders, Dan asked Martin, "What in the hell were you doing making a speech, Tim? Was it because you are such a great speaker? Or because you did so much to help us win? Maybe it was because you showed everyone you were a world-class puker before the Wilkes Barre game, when you ate too much chocolate like a three-year-old kid? Or was it because the Superintendent had his tongue up your father's ass?"

Squirming like there were worms in his underpants, Tim answered. "My old man talked to Adams. He was still pissed off that I hadn't played much. I tried to get out of it, I swear."

Dave stood up and raised a glass of iced tea. "I want to

offer a toast to the great hero of the Lansdowne High state championship basketball team."

Dan added, "Without him, we would not be here today."

"His winning shot will be remembered for a hundred years," Dave rejoined.

"He learned to play solid defense," Zack said.

"He's been a great teammate, who was able to get us through a number of difficult situations," Smooth chimed in.

Mac lifted his glass of 7 Up to the sky and exclaimed, "Joey Garden is God!" After the laughter died down, I looked at the group and said, "One thing I want you never to forget, gentlemen: *Basketball is just a game.*" More raucous laughter.

Zack took a big gulp of Coke and asked, "How could that jackass of a superintendent forget Smooth's trophy? I wanted to break that skinny prick's neck."

"I couldn't believe how you stormed the microphone; way cool, Zack," Mac said.

"He apologized to me afterwards," Calvin said. "People make mistakes."

"That was no goddamn mistake," Zack snorted. "One of the stars of the team, who happens to be the only black player, was the only one who'd been forgotten. That was no goddamn accident, Smooth."

I stood up, lifted my glass over my head, and said, "To a great player and an even better person: here's to Calvin Newsome."

We cheered as loud as we could. Calvin grinned and said, "I'm never going to forget you guys."

It was Dave's turn to get up. "I just want to add, that I'll never forget my twin brother, Dan, either. How can I, when he farts all night in his sleep."

"The same to you, fuck face," Dan answered, giving his brother the finger.

When it seemed that our good times couldn't get any better, the food arrived. As Tim looked at the waitress putting his hot roast beef sandwich in front of him, the twins unscrewed the salt and pepper shakers that were beside him. When Martin went to season the sandwich, the sandwich got buried in the condiments. He tried to pretend he was in on the joke, but when he saw that Cindy was laughing along with everyone else, he stared at the twins with a look of pure venom.

My parents had decided to give me a party, the first one since my tenth birthday. It was set to begin in two hours, so I thought this might be a good time to take care of some unfinished business. As I stood in front of Marilyn's house at Albemarle and Windermere, I remembered when I stood in the same spot on Christmas Day, alone and missing her really badly.

Mr. Thompson was in the front yard weeding some flowerbeds. He stood up when he saw me and extended his hand. If he was upset, he wasn't showing it. He directed me into the house, where Mrs. Thompson was in the kitchen icing a cake.

Surprised to see me, she put her knife down and said, "What did we do to deserve this honor, Joey? All anyone can talk about is that shot you made. Take a chair, please."

Marilyn came in and sat down, turning her chair around and putting her arm across the top rung, where she rested her head. Her green eyes were wide open. Dressed in dungarees and a green tee shirt, she looked stunning. Her long black hair was shining, her skin soft and creamy.

Getting right to the point, I said, "I guess it must be a little bit shocking, me being in your kitchen after I avoided you for so long, Mrs. Thompson. Maybe it's too late, but I really want to apologize. First, by breaking your trust by being alone in your house with Marilyn against your wishes. Second, for being such a coward and not talking to you right away about what had happened."

There it was, quick and to the point. Why had I avoided this for so long? I took a quick glance at Marilyn; her face was stone-cold. Mrs. Thompson picked up the cake and put it on the sideboard. "I accept your apology, Joey," she said, "although I do wish you had come to me sooner. It was very difficult for my daughter to share in the success of the team with this hanging in the air. You did a good deed today."

There really wasn't much more to say. We exchanged pleasantries for a few moments. I thanked her for seeing me and left. Walking toward Ardmore Avenue Field, I could feel someone walking behind me. It was Marilyn.

"I really appreciate you doing that, Joey." She said, arms folded across her chest. "Now I can stop putting myself down for letting you be my boyfriend." I knew by her clipped, businesslike tone that there was no hope for a reconciliation.

Watching her walk back to her house, a sharp pain spread throughout my body. I should have never waited so long, but that's who I was back then. Some things are beyond fixing.

When I got home, I thought I might have some time to go to my room for a while and think about what had just happened. No such luck. Mother made me put a bunch of cold cut trays together and take cases of soda and Hawaiian Punch down to the basement. Pop had put a big piece of linoleum on the floor; balloons and multi-colored crepe paper were hanging from the rafters. The phone began to ring nonstop, all calls for me. McChesney wanted my opinion about the Smooth incident.

Grandpa and Nan called from Florida with their congratulations. I couldn't get them off the line. The coach from William and Mary was the next caller, a guy named Bill Freeman. He wanted to set up a visit. I said I'd get back to him.

About five o' clock, our little home began to buzz with activity. The Petersons, the Millers, Coach and his wife, Mac and his family arrived, one after the other. I shook hands with the men and hugged the women, taking their coats and putting them upstairs on my parents' bed.

Zack arrived with his mother and Barbara Turley. We went to a corner of the living room where I asked him, "What is this, Zack? You only go out with girls with big ones?"

He laughed, "Winning State has had its benefits, Joey. After Cindy, I'm not Mr. Shy Guy anymore. I guess she did me a favor. Hey, did you hear about Dan and Dave? Donna Drummond's parents went down the shore last night. Our dynamic duo spent the night with her. Don't think they'll be here, probably haven't come up for air yet. Take advantage of the situation. I know you want to."

Smooth and his parents arrived. Zack and I went over and greeted them. I wasn't sure they would feel comfortable enough to come. Pop took their drink orders and had them sit at the dining room table. I was proud of him. Some black people were guests in our home, and he was treating them with respect.

One of his buddies, a plumber named Stan Wozciak, was sitting in the living room with his back toward the Newsomes. I never liked him very much, a real loud-mouthed jerk. When Pop walked over to him, Wozciak said in a bullhorn voice, "All kinds of people were complainin' about about how rude it was for Adams to forget the black kid. You ask me, it was no big deal. He shoulda been happy he was even sittin' on the stage. Goddam Ubangis are startin' to think they're just as good as everyone else."

Pop snorted and said nothing. Had he learned nothing? Mr. and Mrs. Newsome were sitting frozen to their chairs, like people who'd just gotten some catastrophically bad news. I looked at Pop and motioned for him to meet me in the kitchen, where I laid it right on the line. "You go to Calvin and his parents and apologize to them for your friend's comments, or make Wozciak apologize himself."

"What the hell, Joey. Making a big shot doesn't make you Mr. Big Shot, talkin' to me this way."

"Ubangis? With Smooth's family six feet away? You have to take care of this *right now*."

Grimacing, he went back in the living room and said something to the plumber. Wozciak shook his head vehemently and took a long slurp of beer. Pop walked over to the Newsomes and said, "Since Stan didn't want to apologize for his comments, I'm going to have to do it for him, Mr. and Mrs. Newsome. I'm real sorry both of you had to listen to that stuff. You have a great son in Calvin. My wife and I are honored to have you in our home. Now, if you would, let me get you a couple plates of food."

I could have kissed the old man. It'd have been better if he had taken the initiative on his own, but I couldn't complain about this minor miracle.

Calvin got a chair and sat down beside Zack and me.

"Sorry about those comments, Smooth," I said. "The guy lives around the corner. He's a dumbass plumber who's spent too much time with his head in toilet bowls."

Smooth shrugged before answering. "My parents are still pretty upset about the trophy. My mom wanted to get up and leave after she heard that guy. My father and I convinced her that we belonged here just as much as everyone else."

The three of us watched as the entire cheerleading squad entered, led by Helene, followed by Lansdowne's favorite couple, Tim and Gladys Martin, along with their wonderful son, Tim Jr. Wouldn't be a party without this stellar group.

I got up and wandered into the kitchen, where Mother and Mrs. Bolton were having an animated discussion.

"Where do you think you'll be going to college, Joey?" she asked. "Zack's decided on Michigan State. They have a great Physical Education department and play in the Big Ten, one of the toughest conferences in the country. "

"Leaning toward Princeton, Mrs. Bolton," I answered. "If that doesn't work out, I've heard from Delaware, Temple and William and Mary, as well a few others, so I'll be going somewhere."

"You're such a good student, Joey. Princeton is a great choice for you. Plus, you'll keep the tradition alive of Lansdowne basketball players going there and playing on the team."

"Could you excuse us for a few moments, Patricia" Mother asked, whisking me to the cellar stairs and closing the door.

"Zack's mother finds out about these offers at the same time as *I do*, Joey? What's gotten into you?"

"So much going on, Mother. I just forgot."

"We're going to sit down tomorrow and go over each one of those colleges and decide which one is the best choice."

"No need. Princeton's coach invited us up for a visit. There's about a 95% chance of a scholarship. Hawk set up an appointment for next Saturday. I see no reason to even consider other schools."

"You're still living under *my* roof, Joey Garden. This will be a joint decision, and that's final."

"Listen to yourself, Mother! Years and years of me having to finish my homework before I went out to play. Lecture after lecture about keeping up my grades so I can go to a prestigious college. Princeton, the last time I looked, is one of the most elite universities in the world. Most parents would be overwhelmed with pride. When we go up there, you'll need to bring last year's tax returns, so they can figure out how much aid they're going to give me. If I don't get a full ride, I can get a campus job to help pay the difference."

"We'll just have to see about young man."

I thought as I watched Mother disappear back into the kitchen that I'd have to go to see Mr. Munchak, apologize and ask for an extension on his paper. Not writing it was a stupid thing to do. What was I thinking?

There was a loud knock . Helene, standing in front of a bunch of other kids, opened the door and shouted, "Hey, Joey. It's time to dance!"

In the basement, she opened my metal box filled with 45s and picked out "Bony Maroney" by Larry Williams, and a bunch of other songs. In a matter of seconds, the entire group was gyrating and bouncing around on the linoleum.

Jeff and I dragged McChesney onto the dance floor. Sally Humphreys, always the good sport, agreed to be his partner. Ches looked lost as "Twilight Time" by the Platters came on, but as the song continued, it seemed like he might even be enjoying himself a little bit. People cheered when the song was over, and, to everyone's astonishment, Lansdowne's resident genius began to jitterbug to the strains of "Long Tall Sally" by Little Richard. Ecstasy was in the air. I danced with every girl I could get my hands on. There were a few cases of Ballantine beer in a corner of the cellar. The cans were warm, but that didn't seem to bother anyone as my fellow students assaulted the cardboard boxes.

Kids started filing out of the basement at about ten o'clock. The beer was finished, but there was a whole lot of Pepsi left over. My parents were going to find the empty cans. I'd have to deal with the consequences. Stepping out of the front door, Helene gave me a huge hug and whispered in my ear, "C'mon up to my house, Joey. We can meet in the backyard." Sounded good to me.

I went upstairs to the kitchen, where Mother was brewing a pot of coffee. I asked if I could go to the diner. She nodded her head.

As I was leaving, the old man jumped out of his chair and gave me a big bear hug. "You're the greatest son any father could have, Joey," he shouted, three sheets to the wind. The remaining adults all laughed. Sparks were going to fly when they left. Mother hates it when Pop gets looped, which is why it doesn't happen very often.

"Going to Johnny and Jimmy's," I said, waving to everyone.

Outside, the Mugwumps were waiting for me, leaning on Jeff's father's silver Buick.

"Was I a veritable Fred Astaire or what, Joseph?" Ches asked, with a wide, beaming grin. "Sally and I talked and she said she's always admired my 'intellectual prowess.' What a gas!"

"Maybe, Ches," I answered, "she can admire some other things about you if you give her the chance."

Inside the car, McChesney continued, "I've never experienced anything like this before. Athena and Zeus have beamed down on our little backwater of a town. This should never end."

George added, "My aunt's a Catholic. She says that God has given the whole town sanctifying grace. It's something that is bestowed on people because God is in a good mood or something."

"It's as good an explanation for what's happened as anything else," I said, as the car pulled out from the curb.

Jeff dropped me off at the diner. Luckily, the three of them were partied out and wanted to go home. I hadn't uttered a word about Helene. It was none of their business. There was a *Trojans* dispenser in the men's room of the diner, which was the real reason I was there. Johnny Ianucci insisted on feeding me. I begged off dessert, which doesn't go too well with beer and settled on a plate of French fries and gravy.

After going to the men's room, I bought a pack of rubbers and said goodbye. It was a one-block walk down Rigby Avenue to Helene's house. She was sitting on the front steps, smoking a cigarette. Smiling and taking my arm, we walked into the backyard. I thought I was going to be scared shitless, but that was not the case.

She opened the door of her father's '57 Pontiac, removed the back seat and took it underneath a big tree that sat beside the garage. Sitting down, I took her in my arms and we kissed for a very long time.

"D'ja bring something, Joey?" she asked.

I took the pack of Trojans out of my back pocket. We began to laugh. What a great girl she was. Standing in a shaft of moonlight, she eyed me coolly and took off her blouse and bra. Looking at those perfect full breasts with large round nipples shining in the soft silver light made me swoon. No longer able to restrain myself, I began sucking on them while removing her skirt and panties. We lay down on the car seat and in a few moments, Joey Garden was a virgin no more.

Even though it was the first time I'd done this, it wasn't hard to figure out that I had been too quick on the trigger. When I apologized to Helene, she put her finger on my lips, and we lay on the seat, naked, staring at the stars. Maybe half an hour later, we started making out again. I realized I had bought only one pack of Trojans.

"Don't worry about it, Joey," she said, stroking my hair. "I just had my period."

Making an effort to do everything as slowly as I could, I tried to savor every moment of this glorious experience. As we began doing it for the second time, I realized how utterly beautiful Helene was as she lay beneath me, so soft, so vulnerable, so giving. All that tough chick Helene the Machine stuff had nothing to do with the person she really was.

After we finished, I took her face in my hands, kissed her eyes and all over the rest of her face.

"You learn fast, Joey," she said as she began to dress.

"I had a great teacher, Helene. You are one special girl."

She turned away from me and began to cry.

"What in the world is wrong?" I asked.

"You *are* different than other guys, Joey. Even if you hardly knew what the hell you were doin', you paid attention to how I was feeling. In the fall, you'll be away at some fancy college, and I'll be workin' at Pruscilla's Beauty Salon, givin' old ladies perms. I'll marry some bum and have a bunch of bratty kids."

"There's no reason you have to settle for a life like that."

I hugged her, and she cried a while longer. We watched the stars some more. I had no idea what time it was, but knew I'd better be getting back home.

Helene and I held hands as we walked to Baltimore Pike.

When we finished kissing goodbye she asked, "When will I see you again, Joey?"

"Soon," I answered, "very, very soon."

Cars kept honking their horns at me as I made my way home. A few people pulled over and offered me a ride. I turned them down. A feeling of humility came over me, thankfulness. Tonight I entered a new world, one that I was going to be trying to understand for the rest of my life. The cool April air, the gleaming moon, the branches of the trees filling up with buds, all of this was pouring into me. Walking felt too restraining. I began to skip, to leap, to run at full speed, crying out, loud joyous sounds that echoed through the night.

Acknowledgements

Every novel is a work of collaboration involving many more people than the person whose name is on the cover. I would first like to thank my good friend and fellow writer, Janet Constantino for seeing *The Education of Joey G.* through years of changes, always being very positive and always making good suggestions for improvement.

Also to be recognized for making major contributions toward the publication of this book: Linda Jay for her excellent copy editing, Elizabeth DiPalma for her creative and striking page and cover design and Judy Baker for her marketing, Internet and self-publishing expertise. Also to be mentioned is BAIPA, Bay Area Independent Publishers Association, a wonderful resource filled with many brilliant people.

Not to be forgotten for helping *The Education of Joey G.* come to fruition are: Joan Aikens, Karla Clark, Guy Cottle, Frank Dineen, Mike Gilger, Janice Lehne, Judy Moyer, Rose Murphy, Morgan Ray, Ad Ross, Susan Salenger, Wayne Schake, Matt Schultz, Bill Snyder, Donna Staples, Diane Swan, Naneene Van Gelder and Major Woolard.

33018593R00172

Made in the USA
San Bernardino, CA
21 April 2016